"You do not belong here."

The shaman turned her head to stare, the solid-white orbs of blind eyes pinpointing Doc. "Nature has been violated by your passage. The balance is disturbed, all things tremble."

"They took me," Doc said firmly. "This is not my doing. I only want to go back home!"

"To your family," the women said in unison.

"Yes!"

The drums beat faster, and the fumes from the fire rose darker, thicker, sweeter, until the air in the lodge was murky with swirling fog. Doc blinked hard. No, the air was clear. His mind was filled with a mist. Was he being drugged? Or was this it, was he finally going insane?

JAMES AXLER

DEATH LANDS®

Perdition Valley

THE
COLDFIRE
PROJECT
BOOK I-I

A GOLD EAGLE BOOK FROM

WORLDWIDE®

TORONTO • NEW YORK • LONDON
AMSTERDAM • PARIS • SYDNEY • HAMBURG
STOCKHOLM • ATHENS • TOKYO • MILAN
MADRID • WARSAW • BUDAPEST • AUCKLAND

For Melissa, as always

First edition December 2006

ISBN-13: 978-0-373-62586-4
ISBN-10:   0-373-62586-3

PERDITION VALLEY

Our worst enemies here are not the ignorant and the simple, however cruel; our worst enemies are the intelligent and the corrupt.
—Graham Greene,
The Human Factor, 1978

THE DEATHLANDS SAGA

This world is their legacy, a world born in the violent nuclear spasm of 2001 that was the bitter outcome of a struggle for global dominance.

There is no real escape from this shockscape where life always hangs in the balance, vulnerable to newly demonic nature, barbarism, lawlessness.

But they are the warrior survivalists, and they endure—in the way of the lion, the hawk and the tiger, true to nature's heart despite its ruination.

Ryan Cawdor: The privileged son of an East Coast baron. Acquainted with betrayal from a tender age, he is a master of the hard realities.

Krysty Wroth: Harmony ville's own Titian-haired beauty, a woman with the strength of tempered steel. Her premonitions and Gaia powers have been fostered by her Mother Sonja.

J. B. Dix, the Armorer: Weapons master and Ryan's close ally, he, too, honed his skills traversing the Deathlands with the legendary Trader.

Doctor Theophilus Tanner: Torn from his family and a gentler life in 1896, Doc has been thrown into a future he couldn't have imagined.

Dr. Mildred Wyeth: Her father was killed by the Ku Klux Klan, but her fate is not much lighter. Restored from predark cryogenic suspension, she brings twentieth-century healing skills to a nightmare.

Jak Lauren: A true child of the wastelands, reared on adversity, loss and danger, the albino teenager is a fierce fighter and loyal friend.

Dean Cawdor: Ryan's young son by Sharona accepts the only world he knows, and yet he is the seedling bearing the promise of tomorrow.

In a world where all was lost, they are humanity's last hope....

Chapter One

Moaning softly, the child baron hugged himself tightly and began to rock in the wooden chair. The motion made it creak slightly and he shuddered at the noise.

Tightening the grips on their longblasters, the two sec men in the throne room of Broke Neck ville exchanged nervous glances.

"Baron?" the corporal ventured, advancing a step. "Is there anything we can do to help?"

Drooling slightly, the youth looked at the guard with unseeing eyes. "He has the secret," Baron Harmond whispered, the words slurred slightly. "But he doesn't know it. Not yet!"

"Secret, sir?" a sec man dared to ask, tilting his head. "Who has what secret?"

"Vermont!" Harmond screamed, grabbing his temples as blood began to trickle from his nose. "He's here, but also back there! I can see him in a hundred places! A hundred times! But Tanner has stayed too long! There is a new future! A different casement! The universe is ripping apart! Time is healing itself!"

Worried, the corporal looked at the window, but

could see nothing wrong with either the sill or the concrete casement. What was the doomie baron talking about? Harmond had accurately predicted future events a dozen times before, and saved countless lives, both civie and sec men. But had the young baron finally crossed the line of sanity?

"Should I fetch a healer, Baron?" the sec man asked, starting for the doorway.

"Too late!" Harmond screamed, both of his hands clawing at the empty air. "He is the disease and the cure!"

"Sir?" a sec man asked, puzzled, starting to sweat. An insane baron. He knew of villes with those, and it was never good.

"Cold, so cold," Harmond whispered, hugging himself tightly.

"Would you like a blanket, Baron?" the corporal asked. "Or we could make a fire."

"Yes, cold…fire," the baron wheezed, fighting for air. "The cold…is a fire…consume us all…" Lurching to his feet, he stared at the open window and pointed a shaking finger at the empty air of the north.

"Coldfire is here!" the baron shrieked, then shook all over and collapsed to the floor.

Rushing to his side, the guards turned the child over and pressed fingers to his throat to see if their baron still lived. Or if this was the long-ago prophesized day of death and the second end of the world had finally begun.

"Y-YOU HEARD ME, outlander," growled the young sec man standing in front of the ville gate. With a double click, the guard cocked both hammers of the homie shotgun. "All of you, j-just move along now, and there won't be no t-trouble."

Masked by the night, the six people on horseback gave no reply to the warning. There was only the low moan of the desert breeze mixing with the sound of the panting horses and the jingling of the metal rings in the reins and stirrups.

Looking down at the nervous teenager from the back of his stallion, Ryan Cawdor tried to control his growing temper. Dark clouds covered the moon, so the only light came from the sputtering torches set on either side of the wooden gate. However, Ryan could still see that the huge wep held by the sec man was obviously not scavenged from predark days, but a homie, built from iron pipes reinforced with layers of steel wiring wrapped around each barrel. The wooden stock was hand-carved and the firing mechanism seemed to be taken from another blaster, perhaps a handblaster. Yet the double barrels of the scattergun were worn from constant use, plainly stating the wep was in good working condition and had seen plenty of action.

Even if the guard hadn't, Ryan decided. There was dried blood on the sec man's clothing, but none of it was his, and his face lacked the hard expression of a person who had taken the life of another. There was determination, and even bravery, but not the slightest sign of combat experience. For all Ryan knew, this was the teenager's first shift of standing guard at the ville gate.

"Now, look, friend…" Ryan began impatiently.

"I said, keep moving!" the teenager ordered, grimly leveling the deadly blaster. "We don't want your kind around here!"

"And what kind is that?" Ryan asked gruffly, leaning over slightly in his saddle to pat the neck of his horse.

The sweaty chestnut stallion nickered at the touch and shuffled its unshod hooves in the dry sand. Heavy saddlebags were draped across the muscular animal's withers, and on its flanks was the brand of Two-Son ville, a lightning bolt set inside a circle. Even though covered with dust from the long ride, Ryan was well-dressed, wore good boots, pants without any patches and a heavy coat trimmed with fur. A shiny longblaster was hung across his shoulders and a slim handblaster rested in the holster of a predark gunbelt. A bandolier of ammo clips crossed his chest, and at his side was a large knife of unknown design.

Licking dry lips, the guard gave no reply. But he kept stealing glances at the left side of Ryan's face.

Touching his leather eye patch, Ryan grunted in understanding. Yeah, he thought so.

It had been a week since the companions had left Two-Son ville in the south and charged across the Zone, going from ville to ville, chasing down the rumors of the chillings of one-eyed men. But they were always one day behind the ruthless coldhearts who jacked everybody with silver hair like Doc's, and chilled any man with only one eye like Ryan's. Left or right eye, it made no dif.

It had been three long days of finding nothing but death and dust, until now. So Ryan as sure as nuking hell wasn't going to be turned away from a ville where the chillings were so fresh that a green sec man still had dried blood on his clothing.

"Move along, rist," the guard said, tightening his grip on the scattergun. Behind the teen, two small hatches in the thick wooden gate swung open and dark metal glistened in the dim torchlight.

In spite of the poor lighting, Ryan caught the subtle motion with his good eye and shifted his position to get a clear shot with his handblaster at whoever was standing at the hatch. If trouble came, it would be from the snipes hiding behind the gate, and not this nervous kid.

"And how do you know we're not the ones doing all of the chilling?" J. B. Dix asked, adjusting his wire-rimmed glasses.

Sitting astride a chestnut stallion, the short, wiry man was dressed in loose denim blue jeans, a T-shirt and a heavy leather jacket. A pump-action scattergun was strapped across his back, a 9 mm Uzi rapid-fire rested on his thigh and at his side hung a large canvas bag bulging with lumpy objects.

"W-we don't want no more trouble," the teenager stated roughly, stepping away from the gate to give a clearer field of fire for the folks at the blaster hatches. "So just git. And I m-mean now!"

This boy was terrified, Krysty Wroth realized. But not of us.

"Go fetch your sec chief," the redhead demanded, her long hair moving gently around her shoulders as if stirred by secret winds.

There was a bloody bandage on her left cheek and another on her wrist from the recent fighting down in Two-Son. The woman was riding a roan-colored mare. A bearskin coat hung across the saddlebags. A predark MP-5 rapidfire was draped across the pommel of the saddle, and a weird-looking wheelgun rode in a leather holster at her shapely hip. The cowboy boots in the stirrups were decorated with the silver embroidery of falcons, and the toes were steel, although at the present the metal was caked with gray dust.

The guard frowned at the sight. The redhead was better armed than any sec man. The loops of her gunbelt were filled with live brass, more than the teen had seen in his entire life.

"Ain't got a chief. He's..." The teen shut his mouth tightly and hunched his shoulders.

"He was one of the people killed—excuse me—chilled, by the strangers," Doc Tanner rumbled. "Thank you, that explains everything."

Dressed as if from another century, Doc was in frilly white shirt, with a frock coat that spread behind him across the horse like an opera cape. A mixed pair of big-bore handblasters rode in a gunbelt made of closed ammo pouches, and an ebony walking stick with a silver lion's-head handle jutted from his backpack like a tribal totem.

"By the Three Kennedys, sir," Doc said, turning to address Ryan, "we must be hot on the trail of the coldhearts if the locals haven't even replaced their sec chief yet!"

"That's an ace on the line," Ryan drawled, rubbing his unshaven chin. Surreptitiously, he shifted the reins from his left hand to his right. The one-eyed man was naturally right-handed, but he'd been hurt in a fight a short while ago and his shooting arm wasn't completely healed yet.

Just then, the blaster hatches closed and there came the sound of heavy bolts being slid aside. With creaking hinges, the thick gate was pushed open and five armed sec men walked out of the ville, the ground crunching under their boots. As the portal closed again, Ryan and the others saw a dozen more men inside the ville, positioned behind a sandbag wall, working the bolts on longblasters and notching arrows into homie crossbows. These people were ready for a war.

"Guess I'm the new chief sec man," the oldest man stated gruffly, hitching up a gunbelt. He was dressed in ragged clothing, his predark motorcycle boots patched with duct tape, but his blasters shone with fresh oil. "And yeah, Baron Harrison was aced, along with Chief Rajavur."

"You guess?" Mildred Wyeth asked, brushing a

plait of beaded hair back off her dusty face. Riding an appaloosa mare, the physician was armed with an MP-5 rapidfire and a wheelgun rested in her belt. At her side hung a predark canvas bag.

Touching a freshly stitched scar on his chest, the sec chief shrugged. "Ain't nobody alive to tell me no," he stated honestly.

"Who aced baron?" Jak Lauren asked, leaning forward in his saddle. The palomino mare under the albino teen obediently altered her stance to accommodate his new position, and snorted softly with impatience.

The albino teenager riding the beast had a huge handblaster in his gunbelt and an MP-5 rapidfire in the longblaster holster set alongside the saddle.

The chief sec man shrugged. "Damned if we know who aced him."

"Where are the bodies, then?" Ryan demanded, glancing up at the clouds overhead. He carefully noted that none of the stars was being eclipsed by anybody walking along the top of the wall around the ville. Good. The locals weren't friendly, but neither were they trying to jack the companions.

"Hell's bells, just follow the birds, you can't miss them," a sec man growled. A couple the armed men standing behind him nodded in agreement.

"Nuking hell, it was awful, like something from a nightmare!" the young guard muttered, shaking his head as if trying to dislodge the memories of the sight.

"Shut up," the sec chief barked at the lad. Then he turned to face the companions. "All right, rist, you asked some questions and got some answers. Normally, we're always interested in trading, even better is getting news from across the Zone, but not tonight. Now get moving, or we start blasting."

In the flickering light of the torches, Ryan saw more blaster hatches swing open, and realized the new sec chief meant every word. There was nothing more to learn here. The answers they sought were back in the desert. Follow the birds, eh?

"Let's go," Ryan ordered, shaking the reins and starting his mount into a slow walk. The rest of the companions were close behind.

"Friendly folks," J.B. commented as the companions rode away. Judiciously, the Armorer eased off the safety of the 9 mm Uzi in his lap. "Never seen people so rattled before. So their sec chief got himself aced. Big deal. That's no reason for the whole ville to go triple red."

Squinting into the distance, Ryan saw a flock of birds circling a distant hill. Smoke was rising from a small campfire, but that was all he could see from this angle.

"Let's go see if there was a reason," he growled, kicking his mount into a full gallop.

Chapter Two

A couple hundred miles away, a pale man walked slowly through the cold rubble of the burned-down building. He was tall and slim, almost skeletal, his face so smooth that it seemed as if the man had never needed to shave. His blond hair was slicked back tightly to his head and a tiny silver stud twinkled in his left earlobe. His pants and vest, more practical than the robe he usually wore, were cream-colored, spotless and perfect. Not even the dust raised by his walking through the ash seemed able to adhere to the odd fabric. Instead of boots, he wore sliver slippers, the woven material strangely luminescent. But even more bizarre was the fact that the man carried no visible wep of any kind. No blaster, ax, crossbow, knife or even a simple club.

In utter horror, Delphi stared at the decomposing bodies of the men and the muties mingling together on the ground, bits of white bone and golden brass glittering from the gray ashes like broken promises.

"Dead, they're all dead," Delphi whispered,

gently kicking aside the distorted skull of a stickie. The operative of Department Coldfire couldn't believe his eyes. This was impossible!

Moving listlessly among the wreckage, Delphi found more and more of the bodies everywhere, the death toll incredible, and every one of the muties had been shot through the head, even when there was only a head remaining with no torso attached. The surviving sec men had shot the dead stickies, just to make sure the muties really were deceased. That was ruthless efficiency he could appreciate. In spite of all his arduous work, and endless planning, slaving over every little detail, the hidden nest of stickies in Two-Son had been utterly destroyed in a single night. One night! Then the locals had done everything but sow salt into the land to make sure the stickies would never return.

"My precious little ones," Delphi moaned, bending to pick up the blackened skull of a stickie. A cooked eye fell out as Delphi raised the skull high in his palm, wondering if he had known this particular mutant. Then Delphi had a sudden flash in his mind of Hamlet doing the exact same thing, and he cast the grisly remnant aside. It sailed across the smoky destruction to crash against the side of a marble staircase that rose high into the empty air and abruptly ended at nothing. The smashed bones went flying everywhere.

Bowing his head, Delphi tightened his fists, attempting to control his growling rage over the slaughter. How long he held that position, Delphi had no idea, but his somber reverie was disrupted at sound of hooves beating on sand.

Quickly looking up, Delphi scanned the nearby predark city until locating a man on a horse coming this way through the crumbling ruins.

"Hey, rist!" the rider called, tightening his grip on the reins and bringing the stallion to a halt on the cracked sidewalk. "Get the nuking hell out of there! The foundation is weak and could collapse at any second!"

His face an inert mask, Delphi walked across the debris and onto the sandy street. A soft breeze was blowing, mixing sand with the ashes of the obliterated stickie nest.

"Rist?" Delphi said curiously, tucking his hands into his sleeves.

The sec man grinned in embarrassment. "Sorry, Baron O'Connor told us to stop using that word. It means outlander or stranger."

"Does it now? Well, I am a stranger," Delphi muttered, his eyes narrowing. "And from those black-powder weapons, you must be a sec man from Two-Son ville. That's only a klick away, correct?"

His instincts flaring at the tone of the question, the rider let an arm drop so that his fingers rested on the checkered grip of the handblaster resting in the holster at his side.

"Ain't no other ville for a hundred klicks in any

direction," the sec man stated, tightening the reins as the horse shifted its hooves in the hot sand. "Now what's your biz here?"

"My biz?"

"What do ya want?" The sec man leaned over the pommel of his saddle and scowled. "Are you a lost pilgrim, or a trader?"

"Ah, an intelligent question at last," Delphi said, slowly smiling. "Most astute. What I want at the moment is your prompt death."

Recoiling at that statement, the sec man drew his blaster and fired. But in spite of the fact that the pale outlander was only a few yards away, he somehow missed. Quickly, the sec man fired twice more. The black-powder charges threw out great volumes of dark smoke, and he had to wait for the desert wind to clear the air so that he could see the chilled body.

But the outlander was still standing, unfazed and untouched, without a single wound to be seen.

Snarling obscenities, the sec man fired again and this time actually saw the soft lead ball slam into the man's face. No, wait. The lead had stopped in mid-air, flattened into a misshapen lump as if it impacted a sheet of predark mil armor. But there was only air between the two of them! How was this possible?

Throwing back his head, Delphi began to laugh as the cooling sphere of lead fell impotently to the sandy street.

Fear swept over the sec man and he briefly debated galloping away. But the very idea of retreat made him snarl in suppressed fury, and the sec man quickly fired the last two rounds in the handblaster. This time, he saw the billowing clouds of gunsmoke form a halo around the rist, revealing a sort of ball, or sphere, as if the man were a bug in a jar. An invisible glass ball that could stop blasters?

As the sweating sec man hastily went for the knife in his boot, Delphi extracted a crystalline rod from within his left sleeve, and pointed it at the horse. With a snort, the animal went absolutely still, then toppled to the street like so much cooked meat. Wisps of steam rose from the nostrils and ears.

Unable to leap from the saddle fast enough, the sec man hit the asphalt hard, the impact making him drop the knife. Then he heard the bones in his leg snap loudly under the deadweight of the horse. Son of a bitch! A split second later, the pain arrived, and he screamed curses. But then he stopped abruptly as thick blood began to flow from the slack mouth of the deceased horse, as if its internal organs had been liquefied. The sight galvanized the sec man into action, and he desperately clawed for the scattergun hidden in the saddlebags.

As Delphi approached, the sec man yanked the wep clear.

"Eat this, mutie lover!" the sec man snarled,

swinging up the scattergun to fire both barrels at point-blank range.

Flame and thunder filled the street as the hell-storm of lead ricocheted off the defensive forcefield that surrounded Delphi. The mix of buckshot and bent nails sprayed randomly to strike the nearby buildings. Predark glass shattered and a rusted wag shook from the barrage, but that was all that happened.

No longer chuckling, Delphi approached the trapped man and stopped just out of reach as the sec man swung the smoking scattergun at his leg, trying to smash a kneecap.

"Do you know how long it took me to make those stickies smart? To raise their baseline intelligence above that of a slavering beast?" Delphi whispered, his hand ever-so-slowly lowering the crystal rod. "To teach them how to sharpen sticks into spears. How to hide and ambush an enemy? Do you? Do you have any idea of the effort I invested into this project?" His hand began to shake slightly, as his voice took on a hysterical tone.

"Now I have to start from scratch again somewhere else!" Delphi bellowed. "More of my precious time wasted! More inefficiency!"

"What are you, a feeb? The muties were chilling us!" the sec man panted, his shaking fingers fumbling to shove a fresh load of black powder and nails into the chamber of the weapon. "The triple-damn stickies were eating our kids! They would have wiped out the whole ville in another few months! We had to ace them. We had to!"

"Cretinous fool, that was the idea!" Delphi yelled, waving the wand.

There was a flash of blue sparks, and a powerful hum filled the air. The partially loaded blaster suddenly turned red-hot, then white-hot, and the sec man threw it away just as it detonated. The blast ripped the scattergun apart, and blew off both of the sec man's hands. Now shrieking in pain, the mortally wounded man raised his arms to stare at the ragged stumps spurting bright coppery blood.

Delphi gestured again, and the tattered strips of flesh dangling off the ruptured arms glowed with a terrible cold fire, and the gaping wounds closed, as if the limbs had been thrust into a raging furnace and cauterized. The sobbing sec man couldn't believe it. The bleeding had stopped, but there had been no pain. No pain at all!

"Fool. You're not going to die that quickly," Delphi said in a flat monotone. "First, you must pay for your crimes. Only then can I leave to find Ryan and his crew."

Ryan?

"Wait! I can help! I know Cawdor!" the sec man whimpered, trying to hide behind his half arms. "He trusts me! I can find him for you!"

"Oh, my hunters already know where he is," Delphi said, his merciless eyes starting to twinkle.

"Besides, I never deal with traitors. Tsk, tsk, turning on the man who saved your ville. How sad. Now your death will be much more…unpleasant."

The crystal wand flashed again.

RIDING UP THE SIDE of the hill, Ryan and the companions spread out slightly so that they didn't offer a group target to anybody hidden in the thick cactus growing on the sandy dune. There was no sign of anybody, but only a feeb took chances.

Cresting the top, the companions stopped as they saw the row of bloody crosses sticking out of the damp soil. There were the tattered remains of people nailed onto the wood, the bodies hanging limply with their stomachs slit open, the distended bowels hanging down into bowls on the ground. The prisoners had been opened wide, and their intestines removed, but left connected. Alive, but disassembled. There was a growing smell in the air of blood and nightsoil, a foulness so thick that the companions could almost taste the hellish reek.

Leaning over sideways in her saddle, Mildred began to noisily lose her breakfast, and Krysty closed her eyes to mutter a prayer of forgiveness to the Earth Mother Gaia.

Leveling their blasters, Ryan and J.B. checked for traps as they started toward the horribly mangled bodies. Neither of the warriors had ever seen anything quite like this before, which disturbed them greatly. Bits and pieces of the prisoners were tossed around, the ground alive with insects and green lizards. Scorpions battled over a split tongue, while a swarm of beetles hurriedly consumed something too obscene to be closely identified.

"Remember the craz eunuch from Nova ville?" J.B. asked out of the corner of his mouth.

"Eugene," Ryan replied. "Yeah, I would have sworn this was his work, if Shard hadn't aced the bastard right in front of us."

"There were students, folks he was teaching his techniques at the ville. Mebbe..." J.B. left the sentence unfinished.

Ryan clicked off the safety on his 9 mm SIG-Sauer blaster. "Yeah, mebbe."

Just then a soft moan sounded from among the sagging figures on the crosses, and Ryan inhaled in shock as a woman opened her eyelids to expose raw empty sockets.

"Ace...me..." she hoarsely whispered, the words almost lost on the dessert breeze. "Whoever ya are...please..."

Without hesitation, Ryan swung his blaster up and fired. The woman jerked back as a black hole appeared on her temple and the back of her head exploded in a grisly pinkish spray across the filthy wood beams.

As the body went limp, Ryan started to ride along the row of crosses, putting a slug into the face of every prisoner, Usually they wouldn't waste the ammo, but mercy was demanded here. Soon, the other companions followed suit until the dark hilltop rang with the sweet release of death.

"Triple-crazy shit," Jak said. "Like predark cold-hearts Mildred told about. Natzies?"

"Nazis," Mildred stated, wiping her mouth clean on a handkerchief. "They were called Nazis, and yes, this is exactly the sort of torture they did to enemies of the state." Then she added, "Not exactly my time, I wasn't born yet when the Allies took down Adolph Hitler and his mad followers."

"That's the baron who tried to take over the world?" Krysty asked, tucking away her S&W Model 640 revolver.

Glumly, Mildred nodded. "Close enough, yes."

Muttering something in Latin, Doc closed the cylinder of his Ruger .44. The predark revolver was a recent acquisition from Blaster Base One, a redoubt the companions had discovered filled with military supplies. The old man still carried the LeMat at his side, but the black-powder weapon from the Civil War took a long time to reload, while the Ruger took bullets and could be reloaded in a matter of only moments.

Whinnying softly, the horses were clearly nervous among all the carnage, and even Doc had to admit to a certain queasiness in his stomach. This hadn't been the work of sane minds.

"Well, I'll be nuked," J.B. said, walking his mount around in a circle. "Anybody notice something odd about the placement of these crosses?"

"They're not facing each other," Krysty said, brushing back her hair. The copper-colored lengths caressed her fingers for a moment before letting go and moving back into place. "The logical thing would be to arrange them in a circle so that all of your prisoners could watch the others being taken apart."

"But these aren't."

"No."

"They're all facing north," Ryan observed, shifting in his saddle. His horse whinnied nervously, and the one-eyed man gently stroked its neck to try to calm the animal. Even though these horses had been trained for war, this much death and bloodshed was making them apprehensive. Shitfire, it was making him apprehensive. He had witnessed cannies cut up their victims to make them sing "death songs", the screams supposed to make the flesh taste sweeter. But that had been a clean chill compared to this form of butchery.

"This done for us," Jak stated, as if there was no question in the matter. "Catch attention, make mad."

"I am mad, sir!" Doc thundered, brandishing a fist. "I am absolutely acrimonious!"

"That not good," the teen responded, scratching his mare behind an ear. "They want angry, you be calm. Not do expected."

Breathing through clenched teeth, Doc radiated a fine fury for a few minutes, then relaxed his shoulders. "You are correct, of course," the old man stated. "That is wisdom, indeed, my young friend. I shall endeavor to comply."

Raising a hand to shield his face from the crackling campfire, J.B. studied the moon behind the clouds. The Armorer wore a sextant on a chain around his neck, which could pinpoint their exact position anywhere on the planet to within a few miles.

"Yeah, looks like the bodies are all facing north-by-northwest," he reported, tucking the compass into a pocket. "In the direction of the Mohawk Mountains."

"Isn't there supposed to be another redoubt hidden among the peaks?" Krysty asked, brushing away flies. The cloud of buzzing insects was getting bigger with every passing minute. Soon the campsite wouldn't be habitable by anybody with exposed skin.

"Somewhere, yeah," Ryan answered, sliding the Steyr SSG-70 longblaster off his shoulder and checking the internal clip. The bolt-action held five rounds in a transparent clip, and Ryan wanted to make sure it was carrying predark brass taken from Blaster Base One, and not some of their hand loads. When he faced down the coldhearts who did this kind of chilling, he sure as hell didn't want to chance a misfire. "Come on, let's go find the bastards."

As the companions began moving off the hilltop, Krysty slowed her mount until she was the last one remaining. Reaching into the saddlebags, she pulled out a mil canister, pulled the ring, flipped off the handle, then tossed the charge into the middle of the blood-soaked ground

Kicking her mount hard in the rump, Krysty started to gallop down the side of the dune. She had travelled only a few yards when the predark gren detonated. A sizzling white light shattered the night as the "willie peter" gren cut loose, the charge of white phosphorous washing over the hellish scene in a searing chem inferno.

As she rejoined the others, the top of the hill was alive with writhing flames, thick smoke rising into the starry sky.

"Why do?" Jak asked with a scowl, his white hair streaming out behind. "Waste gren."

"They left a message for us," Krysty said. "So I'm sending one right back!"

"Blood for blood," Jak said with a nod. "Good think. Mebbe make them mad, eh?"

Stoically, Doc grunted in reply.

"We're gonna chill these coldhearts on sight, then burn the bodies and piss on the ashes!" Ryan said in a low growl.

"Damn straight we will!" Mildred added savagely. Deep within the woman there was growing the heated rush to kill, an unusual sensation for the peaceful healer. But experience had taught her that some people had to be treated like cancer cells. You killed them to save the rest of the body. So be it. If these fools wanted a fight, then cry havoc and let slip the dogs of war!

"Blood for blood," J.B. agreed, his eyes glinting hard.

As the companions reached level ground, Ryan kicked the big stallion into a full gallop, and the companions urged their mounts to greater speeds across the sandy plain.

In the far distance, the Mohawk Mountains stood immutable on the darkling horizon, the jagged peaks rising like the teeth of some great slumbering beast waiting for its next kill.

Chapter Three

"Faster, you bitches. Faster!" Rolph Gunter cried, leaning dangerously forward in the wooden seat of the cargo wagon.

Holding the reins tight in one hand, the slaver lashed out with the whip in his other, forcing the team of horses on to greater speed. *Run from me, will you?*

In the rear of the heavy wagon, a dozen chained slaves desperately held on to the iron bars of their cage, as the wag bounced madly across the rough ground. The floor of their prison was covered with straw and windblown sand. The water bowls were empty, and the few insects stupid enough to wander into the cage were eagerly consumed by its starving occupants.

Behind the speeding wag rose a spreading cloud of dust from the wooden wheels crushing the loose soil. The cart was made of scrap lumber, but the cage itself had an iron floor and roof, with steel bars for walls. The only way inside was through a trapdoor in the ceiling, but the hatch was too high to reach, and firmly bolted closed. With iron on their ankles, and inside a steel cage, escape was considered impossible, although many tried. Tried and paid a terrible price under the brutal whip of the slaver.

"Crash, please crash and chill us all," a woman whispered as the wag shook along the rocky path, the wheels leaving the soil as it hit a bump.

For a moment, the cart went airborne, then it crashed onto the ground again with Rolph nearly leaving his seat from the impact. The captives cried out as they tumbled in the cage, smashing into one another so that their chains became hopelessly entangled.

"Shut up, back there!" Rolph snarled, letting go of the reins with one hand to brandish the hated bullwhip. "Keep quiet, or I'll skin you alive!"

"Do it!" a man spat back, pressing his face against the shaking bars. "Chill us, ya fat fool!"

Furious at the open sign of rebellion, Rolph lashed out with the whip, but the knotted length only smacked onto the bars and failed to reach the living cargo within.

"Mutie fucker!" the man screamed. "Drek-eating prick!"

The whip flew again, this time hitting the man across the face. But as he fell backward with a cry, another slave made a desperate grab for the whip, his fingers missing by only inches.

Flicking the whip forward to urge the horses on to greater speed, Rolph started to pepper the cage with short strokes from the whip, driving the slaves back to the rear of the cart. Stupid meat! Would they never learn to obey?

Suddenly alert, Rolph spotted a motion out of the corner of his eye in the dark desert sand. There they were! The pilgrims he had discovered walking along the Mohawk River! They had dropped their backpacks for better speed, but then left the hard dirt road to struggle across the loose sand of the dunes. That made no sense. Then he saw the reason why, as large murky shapes rose from the desert like square-cut mountains. Ruins!

Black dust, if the pilgrims get in there, I'll never find them again! Rolph thought. And there was no way he would let all of those potential slaves escape, especially the two females. A fortune in brass was getting away from him. Okay, then, he had no choice.

Tying the reins to a wooden peg set in the middle of the seat, Rolph pulled out a heavy crossbow and worked the lever to pull back the drawstring, then notched in an arrow. Rocking to the motion of the bucking wag, the slaver targeted the three running people, adjusted for the wind and bucking cart, then pressed the release lever. The wooden shaft lanced through the darkness and slammed into the back of the child running between the two adults. She threw her arms wide and tumbled to the ground.

"NO!" SHARON SHOUTED, dropping the canteen to dart back to the sprawling girl.

Kneeling alongside the still form, the woman gently turned the child over and burst into tears of relief at the sight of the small chest rising and falling regularly. Alive, Manda was still alive!

"How bad is it?" David demanded, stepping breathless out of the darkness. Fumbling inside his clothing, he produced a rusty revolver and struggled to open the corroded cylinder. It was empty.

"She's not too hurt," Sharon replied, lifting the still form. "Look!"

Searching for any live brass in his pockets, David cursed at the sight of the blunt arrow. Filthy stinking slaver wanted them alive. "Can she run?" he snapped.

"I don't think so," Sharon muttered, nervously looking into the night. She could hear the rattle of the slave cart, but the desert wind made the noise seem to move about until she wasn't sure which direction it was coming from. "The arrow broke some ribs."

"Nuking hell," David growled, sliding a single live brass round into the old revolver. Out of food, no water, and down to their last three rounds for the blaster, a piece of drek he won in a dice game the previous month. The cylinder wouldn't rotate anymore, but the former owner swore that blaster could still shoot, as long as you took out the spent brass and inserted a new one into the same hole.

"Here, take this," David ordered, yanking a bandanna from around his neck and tossing it to his wife. "Stuff this into her mouth and start running. I'll try to ambush the slaver when he goes after you. Fems are always more valuable than men."

No matter the age, he added grimly. Three rounds was all he had, one predark, and two hand loads of questionable reliability, but it was better than nothing. The slaver had chosen his targets well. Sharon and Manda knew enough to keep going if he fell, and he would have done the same if Sharon was taken, but neither of them could leave their only child behind alive.

"David, if...if he takes us," Sharon started, and touched the knife on her hip, asking a silent question.

Forcing back the hammer on the patched blaster, the man gave a quick nod. It would be better to ace the girl rather than doom her to a life in a gaudy house to be the toy of drunken sec men and jolt addicts.

The clatter of the wooden cart was getting louder, and another arrow shot out of the gloom to hum between the two adults. Instantly, Sharon grabbed the little girl in both arms and took off into the dunes.

As the dry breeze blew across his face, David brushed away a tear, watching them disappear. Then he slipped into the scraggly weeds, the ancient revolver cradled to his chest for protection.

Another arrow shot through the night, and the rattling cart came into view. Blind norad, the back was full of people in an iron cage! The bastard had a full cargo, but he wanted more. With his heart pounding, David stayed low in the weeds and waited for a chance to strike back.

LOADING THE CROSSBOW again, Rolph cried out at the unexpected sight of a man rising from the weeds with a blaster in his hands. With no chance to aim properly, the slaver released the blunt arrow just as the revolver went off, throwing out a bright orange tongue of flame.

Something hot and hard slammed into Rolph's hands and he was thrown backward from the cart. Falling to the ground, the slaver hit the sand hard and had the wind knocked out of him for a moment. Forcing himself to roll out of sight, Rolph moved among the weeds on the other side of the road. The lead had hit the crossbow! He was still alive and unharmed.

The slaves in the cage started cheering as the runaway cart vanished in the gloom, and from out of the swirling dust cloud filling the road came the man, the blaster swinging back and forth as he searched for a target.

Taking advantage of the masking dust, Rolph slipped along a rocky gully to pull a small hand-blaster out of his shirt. His grandie had called the thing a derringer, but nobody used that predark word anymore. The wep had two barrels, one trigger, and he had to rotate the barrels to use the second round. Bitch of a thing to reload, but it worked like a charm, and should do the job of finishing off this feeb once and for all. Then Rolph would get back on the cart, find the females and make them pay for losing a brass. Oh yes, they'd pay.

High in the sky, the moving clouds briefly parted to admit a wealth of silvery-blue moonlight. The two men jerked at the sight of each other only yards away. Moving fast, Rolph and David aimed their blasters and fired in unison, the double report filling the area with thick acrid smoke from the combined black-powder discharges.

"MORE," John Rogan ordered, giving a soft burp.

Taking the big man's dirty plate, Lily bent over the campfire and filled the hubcap with rabbit stew. The elder Rogan took the food without comment, and started eating again with a homemade wooden spoon.

The glen was quiet this night, the only sounds coming from the cook fire and the small waterfall that splashed from the side of a large boulder near a blockhouse. Tall trees and bushes completely encircled the field of green grass, the only break in the thick foliage sealed off with a crude gate of wood, broken glass and barbed wire.

Soon, the other Rogan brothers demanded refills. Lily hastily complied. Aside from being easily twice her size, the brothers were monstrously strong, and utterly ruthless. They gave her little food and beat her from time to time. The combination left the young woman too weak to protest their treatment, much less think about escape. Although she dreamed of it in her sleep. Freedom, sweet freedom, and of course, bloody revenge.

All of the Rogan brothers were dressed in predark combat boots and loose green mil fatigues, with blasters and ammo belts covering their bodies like primitive armor. At the moment, only three of the giants were sitting around the campfire. There was a fourth seat at the fire, but the wooden box was empty. Alan Rogan was off doing a recce for an outlander called Ryan. Lily's brothers desperately wanted the man, but only because he traveled with some whitehair called Tanner. That was their real goal, and they needed Tanner alive for some reason. Lily could only assume it was for torture.

Oddly, in spite of their endless torments, the brothers had recently given their sister some predark clothing, much better than anything Lily had ever worn before. She had dark-green leather boots with good solid soles. The denim pants were without any patches, as was the camou-colored T-shirt. The thin material was no protection from the cold. She was fine during the day, but at night Lily had to stay close to the campfire or risk freezing.

The fact that Lily had to wash fresh blood from the clothing when it was offered was just something accepted as a hard fact of life. The brothers didn't barter for goods. The coldhearts took whatever they wanted at the end of a blaster, and anybody who got in the way regretted it for the rest of their lives. Which usually lasted only a couple minutes. She could almost forgive them the mindless brutality. It was their unclean fascination with predark tech that repulsed the woman to the core of her being. Science had destroyed the world, slaughtering untold billions. How anybody could want electric lights or libraries again was beyond her understanding. It made her skin crawl to merely look at the electric motorcycles with their headlights and radios. The machines somehow drew power from the sun. Power from sunlight. What could possibly be more unnatural than that?

In the distance, there was a sharp noise audible above the crackle of the cook fire, closely followed by two more reports.

Lowering his spoon, John looked up from his plate of stew. "That's blasterfire," he said, scowling.

"Way out here?" Robert rasped in his horrible mockery of a human voice. Unconsciously he touched the bandanna that covered a wide puckered scar around his neck. "Somebody must be getting jacked out in the dunes. Mebbe a nice, juicy caravan, eh?"

"That means wounded to loot," John said, almost smiling.

"Always are," Edward added with a gruff laugh, working on his third plate of stew.

The barrel-chested man was huge, almost a giant, yet he had challenged his younger brother John for control of the group only once. That was a mistake he would never make again. Edward was the biggest, but not the meanest, or the most deadly. That honor went to John. It was the elder Rogan who had created the nightmare tortures they inflicted upon the people they captured, and he always had some new idea to try, each one worse than the last. There didn't seem to be a limit to his brutality.

"Could be Ryan and his crew," Robert warned, dropping his plate into the fire and licking his fingers clean. "Mebbe they're trying to lure us out of the glen. Jack the jackers, so to speak."

"A nightcreep?" Edward said, chewing the idea over.

"Sure. Why not?"

Tossing aside his own plate, John reached behind the box he was sitting on and lifted a gleaming M-16/M-203 rapidfire. The sleek combo wep was one of the many perks the brothers had gotten from the mysterious being who called himself Delphi. The double-barrel predark mil wep was in perfect condition, without a speck of rust or corrosion. The M-16 rapidfire on top had ammo clips that held thirty live rounds of shiny brass. It could vomit a hellstorm of lead that mowed down a roomful of people like wind bending the prairie grass. But underneath that barrel was the gaping maw of the M-203 gren launcher. The portable cannon fired only a single shell at a time, but the huge 40 mm gren could blow down a house or chill a dozen muties in a thundering blast of steel fléchettes.

Working the arming bolts, the three brothers

stood and started across the glen. A few yards away, three black bikes rested on the cool green grass. Strapped across the rear fender of each were cargo pods, molded to the frame as if installed when the bikes were new. Inside the pods was a wealth of canned food, meds, clothing, grens and piles of ammo clips for the combo rapidfires. Advance payment for chilling Ryan and capturing the white-hair called Tanner. John flinched at the memory of Delphi forcibly reminding them not to hurt the wrinklie in any way. If they did, the punishment would be worse than anything the Rogans had done to their own victims. John was stubborn, but not feeb enough to doubt that the strange outlander meant every word of the dire threat.

"We take the bikes, but leave in pairs," John commanded, checking the handblaster at his side, "each covering the other as we go. Ace anybody you see who doesn't have white hair."

"Sounds good, bro," Robert stated, dropping the clip from his rapidfire to check the load. Satisfied, he shoved it back into the wep. "Let's ride."

Tucking the rapidfires into the cushioned holster sets along the front yoke of the sleek bikes, the two men climbed onto their two-wheelers and twisted the handgrips to bring the electric engines softly purring into life. The dashboard came alive with glowing green lights. But there was no sound from the vibrating engine between his legs, only a soft hum. The usual gear chain had been replaced with an enclosed transmission that connected the engine to the rear wheel. The effect was that the two-wheeler was as silent as a grave.

As the bikes came alive, Lily tried not to shudder in revulsion. Bastard tech-lovers, she thought hatefully.

While Robert and Edward opened the gate that closed off the gap in the bushes that surrounded the hidden glen, John rolled his bike over to Lily.

"Gimme," he said bluntly, extending a hand.

With great reluctance, Lily removed her clothing and passed over the garments. Taking the bundle, John rode to the blockhouse and locked them behind the iron door. He thought his sister was a feeb slut, but not crazy enough to try running without a stitch to cover her ass.

Moving like ghosts, the three Rogan brothers drove through the bushes that surrounded the hidden glen, but paused to swing the gate shut and arm the explos boobies hidden in the greenery.

Sighing in resignation, the naked girl went back to her cooking, building up the fire to stave off the evening chill. Stirring the dented steel pot full of rabbit stew, Lily shivered involuntarily at the memory of the people who hadn't been given the boon of a swift death. The men with only one eye, and the wrinklies who proved not to be the sought-after Tanner. Sometimes, Lily could still hear the screaming in her dreams at night. The poor bastards had been taken apart like a blaster, and left that way to slowly die, while bugs and muties gnawed on their guts. It was horrible beyond words. It seemed impossible that the same blood ran in her veins as in those chilling freaks. But they had all come from the same mother, even if each of them had a different father.

Kin was supposed to care for kin, but the Rogan brothers never obeyed anybody, and they seemed to take special delight in torturing their little sister. Someday, it would be her turn to taste the sharp steel of their horrible knives.

Unless she did something about it.

CRAWLING ON the ground, Rolph tried to ignore the burning sensation along his cheek where the pilgrim's blaster had just missed removing his head. Rad-sucking mutie fucker! The slaver didn't know if he had hit the bastard, but he did know for certain that blasters in the night would always attract the attention of any muties in the area. Time was against him now. Rolph had to find the crossbow, ace the man, capture the two women and get back to his cart as fast as possible.

Pausing in the darkness, the slaver listened for any sounds of folks moaning on the ground, but there was nothing. Only deep silence. There wasn't even the chirping of the bugs in the weeds to be heard.

Starting onward again, Rolph froze as something moved on the sandy slope of a nearby dune, the shadows disguising the figure. Then the clouds broke and the cold moonlight revealed only foot-prints in the shifting sand. Damn! Was the pilgrim trying to get behind him, or was he running away?

Increasing the speed of his search, Rolph bite back a cry of joy as his hand closed around the wooden stock of the crossbow. Yes! Quickly, he pulled an arrow from the quiver on his back only to discover the shaft was broken in two from his fall off the cart. Cursing, he went through the arrows until finding one intact, and hurriedly notched the deadly shaft into place. Two brass, two arrows. He had to make every shot count.

Leaving the thick weeds, Rolph proceeded along the dirt road after the escaping family. The sandy ground rose to a small crest, then dropped away into a dark plain, jagged rocks rising around the area in a circular pattern. A blast crater!

Holding his breath, Rolph saw nothing glowing in the darkness and forced himself to relax. If it didn't glow, the rads were gone and it was safe to go through. Well, most of the time, anyway, he thought unhappily.

Proceeding swiftly, the slaver found the ground softening and there was definitely the smell of water in the air. An oasis in a nuke crater? Mebbe this was what the pilgrims had been running toward, not the ruins. A hideyhole where they could get fresh water. Curling a lip in disgust, Rolph started toward the sound of water gently lapping onto a muddy bank. Bad move, pilgrim.

Staying low and moving quickly, Rolph found

only a scrawny gopher licking at the wet shoreline. Angrily leveling his crossbow at the animal, Rolph raised it again, knowing its life had been his to take. That had been fun, but he had bigger prizes this night.

Just then, bright white lights split the night and big creatures came charging over the hill in the dirt road as if they owned the world. Already keyed for action, Rolph instinctually aimed the crossbow and fired. Anything new presented a threat, and it was always best to ace odd things on sight rather than to risk being attacked for something really dangerous.

The arrow vanished into the night. Somebody cried out from behind the lights, and the desert was filled with the sound of blasters. Hundreds of them!

As the slaver dived to the moist ground, Rolph heard another scream from the water of the crater oasis, and knew that the escaping pilgrim had just gotten onto the last train west. Excellent! One down, two to go.

But the chattering blasterfire went on and on, until Rolph thought he had to be hallucinating. Nuking hell, how many sec men were there? The blasters never seemed to stop! A burst raked the ground in front of the cringing slaver, the sand flying up in tiny puffs from the impact of each round.

Impossible! Rolph thought in growing terror. Nobody could shoot that close together in unison.

These had to be—what was the word?—rapidfires!
Working predark rapidfires, with more ammo than
a dozen barons!

Capturing the mother and child no longer
seemed important, and Rolph felt a rush of raw
greed at the thought of the deadly barkers in his possession. Rapidfires! Just one of those and he could
become a baron himself! Checking the knife in his
belt, Rolph reloaded the handblaster with his last
two rounds, and notched a fresh arrow into the
crossbow. After that he was down to a knife, but
there was nobody better than him at blade chilling
in the Deathlands. Especially in a nightcreep.

Let them come! I'll slit every throat before they
even knew I'm here. Those fancy blasters are
already mine!

Forcing himself to breathe slowly and calmly,
Rolph dared to risk a look above the tall grass
edging the road. Less than a stone's throw away
three machines were parked in a group, their headlights throwing blinding cones of white light. The
figures sitting on the back of the two-wheelers each
held a weird double-barreled longblaster of some
kind. The machines didn't seem to be working; they
shook slightly, and he could see the waves of heat
radiating from the compact engines.

Muttering something low and guttural, one of the
men slid off his machine and fell to the ground. Instantly, the other climbed off their machine and went
to aid their fallen comrade. For a second, their

features were lit by the reflected shine of the lamps. Rolph saw they were big men with all sorts of mil stuff dripping off them, as if they were a group of sec men.

The man on the ground had an arrow sticking out of his chest, and he snarled as a barrel-chested man took hold of the shaft and slowly pulled it out. The wounded man grunted as it came free, then went limp. The big man tossed the shaft away, as another one opened the back of a black two-wheeler and pulled out some items. Kneeling on the ground, the tall man started to bandage the wound, while the barrel-chested man stood guard. Occasionally, he would trigger a burst from the rapidfire randomly into the darkness of the crater, the muzzle-flash resembling a fiery flower.

Med supplies, bikes and blasters? Who were these sec men? Wisdom said it was time for Rolph to leave, but lust for the blasters filled his heart, and the slaver stood to fire the handblaster at the two closer strangers.

Even before the smoke of the discharge cleared, the night was filled with chattering fire and something red-hot punched Rolph in the shoulder, belly and hip. He staggered from the multiple impacts and tried to run. But then the two rapidfires rang out in staccato destruction, and white hot knives stabbed him across the back, red blood blowing out from his shirt.

The world became chaos then, the pain blurring consciousness. Rolph tripped on a rock and went flying. He hit the ground hard, and the raw wounds flared with pain until he blacked out.

AN ETERNITY LATER Rolph sluggishly came awake. A pair of boots stood near his face, shiny new boots without patches. Worth a fortune! Then one of the boots kicked him hard in the side. Rolph wanted to play dead, but he couldn't stop himself from grunting at the blow.

"Still sucking air, eh?" a voice snarled.

A knee dropped into view and somebody roughly grabbed his hair to painfully haul his face upward. Rolph found himself looking into a furious face. This was one of the bikers. Thick bandoliers criss-crossed his chest, full of little metal boxes stuffed with live brass. Clips. He had dozens of ammo clips. The wealth of an entire ville was on display only inches away. If only he could snatch one of those....

Angrily, Edward slapped away the bloody hand of the dying man. "Ya got balls, I'll grant ya that," he said grudgingly. "But it was a triple-stupe move to shoot at us. Ya hit my bro."

"I th-thought…you were s-stickies…" Rolph panted, forcing out the words.

"Shut up," Edward ordered, backhanding the wounded slaver. "You're just lucky that Robert is gonna live, it was only a flesh wound. If you had aced him…"

Edward backhanded the slaver again, harder this

time. "If he had been chilled, John and I would have done things to you that'd make a cannie vomit." A knife came into view, the moonlight reflected off the razor-sharp edge. "But as it is, we've got friends coming. So we have to leave."

Not sure that he wanted to know what was going to happen, Rolph tried to think of a bribe to offer for his life, when the big man reached out and slashed the laces of his boots. Then he yanked them off, leaving Rolph barefoot.

What the frag? Rolph tried to summon the strength to ask a question, when there came a terrible pain at his ankles, and warm trickle sensation could be felt. Bleeding, he was bleeding!

"I just cut your tendons," Edward said with a chuckle, displaying the crimson-smeared blade. "Now ya can't walk."

"Please…" Rolph whispered, holding on to his aching chest. "I…have many…"

But the slaver was interrupted by a distant hoot. Everybody froze motionless. The cry was answered by another hoot, closely followed by several more.

"And here comes the welcoming committee," Edward said with a chuckle, slowly standing. Wiping the blade clean, he tucked it away in a sheath on his belt. "My brother lived, so you live. Say hi to the muties for me, feeb."

"No! Please…chill me…" Rolph begged, his throat constricted from the racking pain in his chest.

Weakly, he tried to rise, but his feet merely flopped at the end of his legs like dead things.

Edward only laughed in reply.

"Don't leave me like this," the slaver whined, tears on his dirty face. "Please, I'll be your slave! I'll do anything you want. Anything!"

Sneering in disgust, Edward kicked the slaver in the ribs again, doubling him up with the pain. Then the big man pulled something from a pocket.

"Hurry along," an inhuman voice called from the bikes. "The stickies are coming. We must get moving."

"No prob." Edward chuckled, twisting off the cap of a cylinder to scrape it across the nubbin that had been underneath.

With a sputtering rush, a reddish flame extended from the fat cylinder, and Edward stabbed it into the muddy ground. The bank of the little pond was now clearly revealed in the crimson glow as if painted in blood.

"Just so the stickies can find their meal," Edward said, turning to leave. Then he stopped and looked over a broad shoulder. "Our name is Rogan," he said clearly. "Remember that as they tear you apart, feeb. We're the Rogan brothers!"

As the biker joined the others on their machines, Rolph felt a surge of blind panic. Flipping himself over, the slaver started to madly crawl for the pond, using his fingers and knees.

I can hide under water, he thought. Yes, that

would work! The road flare was throwing out a lot of stinking smoke that should mask the smell of my blood from the mutie. I'm not aced yet! Get going, keep moving, crawl...

But Rolph made it only a few feet when the inhuman face of a stickie rose above the swaying weeds, and the mutie looked directly into his eyes. Starting to scream, Rolph clawed for the knife on his belt and drew it across his own throat. But he was too weak and only managed a shallow gash. There was no telltale spurting of a major artery being cut, followed by a quick and merciful ride on the last train west.

That was when the stickie grabbed Rolph's stomach with its sucker-covered hands and started to pull open the wounds.

Shrieking, Rolph slashed at the mutie with the knife, but the blade went flying into the weeds and landed out of sight. More stickies arrived, and they converged on the struggling man, tearing off gobbets of living flesh and yanking out pulsating organs. As the orgy of feeding began, the pitiful shrieks of the dying slaver seemed to last forever.

AS THE THREE MOTORCYCLES disappeared into the distance, David rose from the far side of the pond, his old blaster dripping muddy water. Black dust, it had worked! When the outlanders started shooting, he screamed and hit the water, and they assumed he was chilled.

For a moment the drenched man watched in satisfaction as the stickies enjoyed their gory meal across the pond, then he turned and started to run into the desert. The sooner he got away from the muties the better. David still had his wife and child to find. If they were yet alive.

Chapter Four

Standing on the top of the sweeping hill, Sec Chief Steven Stirling of Two-Son ville scowled deeply at the grassy vista spreading to the horizon.

In every direction there was nothing but endless fields of waving grass. To the west, purple mountains rose into the cloudy sky. To the north were several copses, and that was everything. In spite of the lush green plants, the landscape was as barren as the Great Salt. There were no ruins, or villes, or blaster craters or anything. If Ryan and his people had ridden this way, there was no way of knowing.

"Nuke-blasting hell, we lost them," Stirling muttered angrily, massaging the back of his neck. "I thought you were supposed to be the best tracker in the whole ville."

"I am, sir," Alton answered, pouring some water from a canteen into his palm.

Holding the hand out to his horse, Alton let the animal slurp the water, being careful that his fingers didn't get in the way. Many a green rider offered a carrot to their horse, only to start screaming as they drew back a bloody stump.

When the stallion was done, Alton poured in some more. The ride had been long and dusty, and the animal was thirsty. So was he, but a good rider took care of his mount first.

Inside the ville, it was blaster and brass, but outside the walls, a horse saved your ass, Alton mentally recited the ancient poem. Learning that had been his first lesson as a sec man and never forgotten. His second lesson had been to not turn his back on a wounded enemy, even if his guts were on the ground alongside him. Alton flinched from the memory. He still walked with a slight limp in the winter, caused by the lead miniball lodged near his hip, fired from the hidden blaster of a dying mercie.

The horse nickered, so Alton gave the animal one more palmful. A short, wiry man with thinning hair, Alton had a lopsided grin that never went away, even when he was chilling a coldheart, or slaver. A remade Remington 30.06 bolt-action rode in a leather holster along the side of the animal, and the saddlebags bulged with supplies, most of them being homie pipe bombs.

"Well, then, which way did they go?" Stirling demanded, scowling. His own horse was similarly equipped with blasters and bombs. The Zone was a dangerous place and with only four sec men; Stirling wanted all the edge he could get. The pipe bombs were a very recent addition to the Two-Son ville armory. J. B. Dix had taught them the secret of making something called guncotton, which turned out to be ten times more powerful than plas.

"There isn't much that I can do on solid rock," Alton replied, continuing to water his horse. "We lost Ryan back on that stony plain near the desert, and no amount of yelling is going to make their hoofprints appear."

Distant thunder rumbled in the cloudy sky, and the sec men sniffed hard for any trace of chems in the air. But the wind remained clear and crisp, without any trace of acid rain.

"What do we try next, Chief?" Renée Machtig asked, tying back her long hair with a strip of rawhide. The sec woman was dressed in loose tan clothing suitable for travel in the desert. A bandolier of ammo pouches was draped across her chest, and a big-bore longblaster hung off a slim shoulder. A crossbow jutted from one of the saddlebags on her horse, along with tufts of straw used as cushioning to protect the delicate glass bottles of a half dozen Molotovs.

Stirling knew that Renée had only come along to stay with Alton, but that was okay with him. She was one of the best shots in Two-Son ville with the BAR longblaster, and this part of the Zone in New Mex had way too many muties in his opinion. Must have been hit double-hard during skydark to yield such a bumper crop of the cursed things, he added sourly. After all, it's not like somebody is making more of them!

"We could go back and try to find their trail

again," Nathan Machtig offered from atop his horse. Tall and lean, the bearded teenager was carrying an old M-16 rapidfire equipped with a wooden handle to operate the bolt action. The black-powder brass didn't have the power to operate the rapidfire, but the mil wep still served just fine as a single shot. Nathan was the son of Renée, and in spite of his parent, the teen was without a doubt the worst shot in the ville, including the blind man who carved wooden bowls for the baron. On the other hand, the kid could throw a pipe bomb farther and straighter than anybody Stirling had ever seen. A hell of an arm. The clumsy longblaster was there just to give the teenager some measure of protection in case something attacked closer than the bombs could be used.

"That's a lot of ground to cover," Gill McGillian replied, biting off a piece of jerky. He chewed the resilient material for a few minutes before adding, "But I suppose we gotta. So, what the frag, eh?"

Gill was the former driver of the *Metro,* the flame wag Two-Son ville used to burn the streets of the predark ruins around the ville clean of muties. But the sec man had relinquished that vaunted position of honor to come along with Stirling. Gill was carrying a double-barreled scattergun, his shirt lined with cloth loops stuffed with 12-gauge cartridges for the wep. They were reloads, packed with rocks, glass and nails, but still deadly.

Sitting slumped on his horse, Taw Porter didn't join the conversation, but merely watched the others through half-closed eyes. The man looked like he was falling asleep, but that was just his way of keeping folks from seeing exactly what he was paying close attention to at any moment. During the fight with the stickies, Porter had been slow to respond. Baron O'Connor had publicly ridiculed Taw for the matter, but then incredibly offered the sec man a chance to clear his rep by going along on this journey. That seemed fair enough. But as a further punishment, the baron had decreed that Porter was to be armed with only a crossbow.

"Well, no sign of any campfires that I can see," Stirling declared unhappily. "Sure would have been nice of Ryan to light us a beacon."

"Mebbe there are too many muties around," Alton suggested, taking a swig from his canteen. "Stickies love fire."

"Ain't that the nuking truth," Stirling growled. "But, no, I think he's far away from here. Hell, we could be out of the Zone for all I know!"

Fine by me, Porter thought petulantly, brushing a fly off his neck. Let's go back home. How can anybody feel safe without a stone wall around their ass?

"Chief, if Ryan is a good day ahead of us," Gill said slowly, "then we may never find them."

"Yeah, I know," Stirling admitted. "That just means we have to ride faster."

"Ride faster in which direction?"

"Give me a second," the sec chief muttered. "I'm working on it."

"Does anybody else think that there is something wrong here," Renée asked, squinting at the horizon. "I mean, this field. This place feels odd. I can sense something wrong with it in my bones."

"Odd place, I have to agree," Alton grunted in reply. "Although I can't tell you why. Mebbe we're just used to having sand under our boot."

"Rather than grass under our ass?" Gill added.

The sec men all chuckled at that, but Stirling felt his frown deepen. He had been thinking the same thing about this grassy knoll. Something wrong here, something unnatural. Then it hit him. No insects. With all this green, there wasn't a single insect making noise in the field. That wasn't a good sign. Hurriedly glancing around, Stirling saw a clump of tall grass and headed that way. Please let it be empty...

Although it couldn't be seen from the top of the hillock, there was a body hidden among the grass. Or rather, what was left of one. The skeleton had been picked clean, the white bones still covered with straps of tattered clothing. With a sense of growing unease, Stirling studied the cloth until spotting numerous tiny holes in the material. Glancing at the boots, he saw the same thing. Holes neatly punched through the leather, including the wooden soles. Aw, hell.

"Drinker!" Stirling shouted in warning, pulling

his handblaster and firing randomly at the ground. There was no point in being quiet now. If this was a drinker territory, the underground mutie already knew they were there.

Rallying at the cry, the other sec men started peppering the soil with blasterfire, while Nathan pulled out a pipe bomb and a cherished butane lighter. Holding them tight, he nervously looked around, watching the soil for any suspicious movements.

"Get on the horses!" Stirling ordered, backing away from the skeleton. "We ride north until reaching solid rock, and then—"

That was as far as he got when a section of grassland exploded into a wiggling pile of pale green tentacles that shot into the air and lashed about, searching for food. Human food.

"Nuke me!" Gill spit, firing both barrels of the scattergun.

The double charge blew off one of the thrashing limbs. But as the tentacle hit the ground it continued to flop wildly, and there was no sign of blood on the ragged end, only a thin greenish fluid resembling watery sap.

Flicking a butane lighter alive, Renée lit an oily rag fuse and threw a Molotov at the underground creature. The bottle hit with a crash, and flames erupted at that spot. As the fire grew, the plant quickly withdrew, but reappeared a few yards farther away.

"Frag me, there's two of them!" Stirling cursed, spotting another set of waving tentacles.

Dodging around the thick grass, he tried to stay in the open field. The lush areas of growth were caused by the rotting corpses of the drinker's victims. The greenery marked the lair of the mutie plant, even as it served to hide the old bones from casual sight. A mixed blessing then, and the sec chief cursed himself as the son of a feeb for not spotting it sooner. That's why there were no tracks in the field. No animal or mutie would come this way. Even war wags avoid drinkers!

By now, the rest of the sec men were firing blasters at the ground or tossing bombs. The night shook with the explosions, and the two drinkers attacked the empty air around each strike, but not the blast hole itself. It was almost as if the drinkers understood that the bombs were being thrown.

Were the plants getting smarter, too? Stirling raged as he zigzagged across the ground. First the stickies of Two Son ville, and now this drek!

Holding on to the sec chief's horse, Gill was waving around the scattergun, with two spare shells sticking out of his mouth for faster loading. The others were spreading out, trying to confuse the mutie, firing blasters at anything that moved. The light from the Molotovs helped them to see the deadly tentacles tunneling below the surface, and Renée cried out once as a failing limb whipped across her face, leaving a score of deep scratches from the thorny tip.

That was too damn close, Stirling realized, trying to catch his breath while perched on top of a rock. Then he scowled darkly at Porter. The coward was just sitting on his horse and doing nothing. Not a fragging thing to help. To hell with the baron's orders, he was going to personally ace the yellow bastard as soon as they got out of this field alive.

But then the sec chief saw the problem. The horse had too many legs, there were six, not just four. Not legs, tentacles going straight up from the ground and into the belly of the beast! Sitting astride the animal, Taw Porter was sitting absolutely still and was even more pale than usual. Then Stirling saw the man's clothing start to move as hundreds of tiny vines crawled out of the sec man's body. One came out of his mouth to test the air, only to retreat again.

Shooting from the hip, Stirling blew off the back of the sec man's head just to make sure the man was actually deceased. Pink and greenish fluids exploded out of smashed skull, then his hair came alive as tiny vines writhed from the ghastly wound and exited from his mouth, nose and ears. Only the dead eyes stayed intact to stare calmly into the starry heavens.

Suddenly, Renée's horse screamed as a tentacle attacked, the curved thorns sinking deep into its legs. Then the vine began to pulsate as it started pumping out the rich red blood.

Waving her Browning longblaster, Renée could only curse and try to stay in the saddle. The angle

made it impossible for her to get a shot at the subterranean monster.

"Cross fire!" Stirling shouted from the rock.

Working the bolt on his M-16, Nathan cham-
bered a round and fired. The tentacle jerked from
the arrival of the 5.56 mm hardball round, blood and
sap gushing from the hole. Instantly, the tentacle released the horse's leg and slid underground.

But as Nathan worked the bolt to chamber a fresh
round, the used brass popped out and hit the soil. A
split second later several tentacles exploded upward
from that point, lashing madly with their deadly
thorn-tipped vines.

Gill put both barrels of the scattergun into the
monstrous thing, the wide spray of pellets doing the
job proper, but also catching Nathan's horse in the
rump. The startled animal reared onto its hind legs,
and Nathan had to drop the M-16 to grab the reins
and stay in the saddle.

Deciding this was his best chance, Stirling
bolted from the rock and raced across the flat
ground, expecting to be aced at every step. The sec
chief tightened his grip on the blaster as he
crossed one yard, two, three… As his horse came
into range, Stirling bodily threw himself across
the saddle.

"Yee-ha!" Gill cried, kicking his own mount
into motion, and dragging Stirling's horse along
by the reins.

Struggling clumsily, the sec chief grabbed the

pommel with both hands and hauled himself upright to sit astride the saddle and take back the reins.

"Mother nuker!" he yelled in triumph. "Gotta move faster than that, you mutie bastard, to ace a Two-Son man!"

But a split second later, the ground around their former location started to move with vines and tentacles. As the questing limbs found nothing, a deep inhuman moan sounded from below the grass, the horrible noise echoing across the lush tundra and seeming to rattle the leaves on every bush.

"If you're mad at us now, try this!" Renée snarled, flipping a pipe bomb at the thing.

"Scatter!" Stirling ordered, kicking his horse into a full gallop. The animal responded with adrenaline-fueled speed.

The sec men did as ordered and broke ranks to take off in different directions. A few heartbeats later, the bomb thunderously detonated, blowing a geyser of flame and vines into the air.

But then from the charred pit arose a...something. Only half seen in the cloudy night, it was huge with a lumpy skin that was constantly twitching. Looking around, the misshapen creation gave a low moan.

"Black dust, Buddha and drek, we got a drinker out of its burrow!" Gill cursed, looking over a shoulder. "We're in for it now, amigos!"

"Shut up and move!" Stirling ordered, pulling a blaster from his holster. The sec chief fired two fast shots, and the others obeyed the signal to converge upon Stirling while still moving at a gallop.

Dimly lit by the dying flames of the Molotovs, the drinker was starting to crawl after the fleeing sec force. As it advanced, more and more of the animal-like plant came out of the smoking hole in the ground, oddly resembling a worm pulled out of its moist burrow. As it exited, the other drinker retreated. Then the end came out of the ground, looking exactly like the front.

"Son of a bitch, there isn't two of them, just one biggun!" Nathan stormed, a fresh bomb tight in his hand. "How large do these fragging bastards get?"

"I say we keep running and don't find out!" Alton added gruffly, frantically reloading the Remington.

Hunched low in the saddle, Stirling wanted to agree, but he could see white foam on the mouth of Renée's animal. The wounded horse was doing its best, but would soon collapse and leave the woman behind to feed the giant mutie.

"Bomb count!" the sec chief shouted, moving to the rhythm of the horse as he reached into the rear saddlebags.

"Ten!"

"Six!"

"Nine!"

"Four!"

"Use one each—no, two!" Stirling barked, casting a quick glance behind. The drinker was completely out of its hole, and still coming. It was as if the inside of a dark tunnel had come to life. Triple-damn thing was larger than the Metro, he thought. "Okay, we'll take this thing the way we did that pack of wolves at Dead Man's Gulch! Now, follow me!"

The others spread out behind the chief like a flock of birds racing from an aerial predator.

Retracing their route, Stirling slowed his mount as they reached a shallow ravine. Easing his horse over the edge and down the clay bank, Stirling sprinted across the small stream to hastily scramble up the other side again.

Reaching the top, the sec chief forced his panting animal to halt, and pulled out a pipe bomb and a knife. Cutting the fuse to a short length, Stirling impatiently waited for the others to join him just as the drinker arrived. Black dust, it was big! As the other sec men galloped across the ravine, the drinker was close behind, and almost stretched itself over the gully like some monstrous bridge, then down it went, the tentacles and vines lashing and whipping madly about in every direction.

"Light it up!" Stirling bellowed, dropping the knife to grab his butane lighter to start the fuse.

The moment it caught, he flipped the bomb over the edge into the ravine. The lead pipe hit the water with a splash, closely followed by four more bombs. Slowly rising upward, the drinker lifted its inhuman face above the rim and looked directly at the tiny norms with a face crawling with vines and roots. The eyes were strangely human, full of rage and hatred.

With their hearts pounding, the sec men threw another salvo of bombs and Molotovs just as the first charges detonated. The whole landscape seemed to shake from the force of the multiple explosions in the ravine. As writhing flames rose along its side, the drinker raised both eyes to the stars and keened in pain, the cry lost in the triphammer blasts of the other pipe bombs. A volcano of muddy water and tentacles flew into the air, shrapnel zinging everywhere, and the drinker bulged oddly, then seemed to come apart from the inside, gushing viscous fluids from every orifice.

Knowing what to expect, the sec men raced for cover as the grisly debris rained down, pulsating organs impacting the ground with wet smacks strangely reminiscent of a passionate kiss. As the reverberations died away, the drinker gave an eerily humanlike sigh and collapsed onto the clay bank of the shallow ravine, its split head only inches from the grass.

Sliding off his horse, Stirling passed the reins to Renée. Drawing his revolver, the sec chief warily proceeded to the crumbling edge of the smoke-filled ravine. There was only churning water below, mixed with bloody debris. A thorny tentacle lay twitching on a small boulder, and a single great eye rested in the shallow creek, staring up at eternity in soulful reproach.

"Everybody okay?" Stirling demanded, warily watching flesh and organs in the ravine for any unnatural motion. Only a feeb trusted a mutie, even a chilled one.

"No, Gill got hit!" Alton answered loudly.

Turning from the ravine, Stirling saw Gill holding a knife in his hand and poking at the piece of tentacle across his left arm.

"Can't cut it off," the sec man grunted as a trickle of blood appeared from the end of the plat. "Fragging thorns are in deep!"

"Put that blade away," Stirling said, sliding the strap of his longblaster over a shoulder. "We gotta burn it off."

"I…was hoping if I moved fast enough…" Gill panted, stabbing the knife under the throbbing length of plant once more. Then he sighed and dropped his shoulders. "But that was a stupe's wish, eh, Chief?"

"Would have tried the same thing myself, Gill," Stirling said soothingly. "Burning is no fun. Nathan!"

"Sir?" the teenager replied spinning about with a pipe bomb at the ready.

"You and Porter—" The chief stopped and started again. "You and Alton check the horses for damage. Renée, watch their backs. I'll do Gill."

"Shouldn't we move away from here first?" Nathan asked, casting a glance at the body parts strewed about. "All this blood and meat is going to attract every pred for klicks."

"Preds, rists and muties, ya mean," Renée corrected grimly, reloading the BAR with sure fingers.

"No time," Stirling growled, helping Gill off his horse and onto a nearby mound of dirt. "We do this fast, or Gill joins the sky choir."

Sitting, the sweaty man watched as Stirling wrapped a cloth around the upper part of the wounded arm, then tied the rag into a tight tourniquet. The trickle of blood from the gaping end of the vine slowed, but not by much.

"Better find something to bite on," Stirling warned as he pulled a bag of black powder from a pouch on his gunbelt.

"I got some shine in my bags," Alton offered from among the horses. "That'll help kill the pain."

"And make me useless for the rest of the night," Gill replied, pulling off his gunbelt. "Just do it, and be fast."

Pouring the black powder along the spiky piece of vine, the sec chief said nothing, concentrating on the work. When the ammo bag was empty, Stirling passed it to Gill, who stuffed the leather into his mouth. Thumbing a butane lighter alive, the sec chief glanced at his friend. Gill gave a nod, and Stirling lit the powder.

There was a blinding flare and Gill gave a muffled scream, every muscle going rigid. He became lost in the searing glare, but as the harsh light died away, Stirling saw that the smoldering vine lay twitching on the ground. A neat line of holes went across the sec man's arm, but the bleeding had already slowed to a trickle, then stopped completely.

"Bet you could use that drink now." Stirling snorted, angrily stomping his boot to grind the charred vine into the ground. The smoking length crumbled apart with a crunchy noise, and finally ceased to move.

"Gill?" Stirling asked, raising his head.

But the sec man lay slumped over on the mound of earth.

Worried, Stirling checked the man's pulse, but found it strong and steady. The sec man had just fallen unconscious from the pain. Gently rubbing the old wound on his shoulder, Stirling really couldn't fault the man. He'd done the same thing himself once.

"Should we let him sleep?" Nathan asked, stepping closer to offer one of the new med kits. "We could build a fire, and there are plenty of blankets." The kit was just a lumpy canvas bag with the letters M*A*S*H carefully stitched into the fabric. Mildred had showed the ville healers a lot of tricks for keeping people alive, shine to wash wounds, boiled white cloth for bandages, and such. These crude duplicates of her predark med kit were the result. With one of these, a sec man had a hundred times better chance of surviving a wound than ever before. Just another of the countless debts for which they could never completely repay the outlanders.

"Hell, no. We get moving," Stirling declared, opening the canvas bag. "The smell of blood is in the wind, and soon this place is going to be overrun with animals and muties fighting over the scraps of the drinker."

From high above there came a screamwing cry, and in the distance a stickie hooted.

"Mebbe even a second drinker," Alton stated, checking the load in the scattergun. He closed the breech with a snap and set the lock. "We got enough bombs to stop another one, but not while we're also fighting screamwings!"

A blaster shot sounded, then another, and Renée appeared, reloading her revolver.

"Okay, vines fell on two of the horses and I had to ace them," the sec woman stated without emotion. "So we'll have to double up, or drop supplies."

"We drop nothing," Stirling barked, pouring shine over the sec man's arm. The raw alcohol washed the open wounds and became tinted with red. Gill gave no response. Satisfied, the sec chief put away the bottle of shine and started to wrap the forearm.

The cloth strips had been immersed in boiling water for as long as a man could hold his breath. Something about killing stuff called gems, or germs. Whatever. Mildred had taught them this. Tying off the bandage, Stirling packed the med supplies into the canvas bag. Everybody Mildred treated got better ten times faster than seemed possible, so mebbe she was right about germs.

Chilling was his job, not putting folks back together afterward.

"Okay, we're short on rides," Stirling said, slinging the canvas bag over the pommel of his horse. The animal whinnied nervously at its master, and he tenderly scratched it behind the ears. "Divvy up the food, keep all of the ammo, and we'll travel in pairs. Renée rides with me, Nathan with Gill, Alton gets all of the extra bombs and water."

The hooting sounded again, closer this time, and down in the ravine something started savaging the tattered chunks of the dead mutie.

Without comment, the Two-Son ville sec men rushed to their assigned tasks and were soon galloping away from the ravine. Taking the lead, Stirling realized that he had lost all sense of direction fleeing from the drinker. Arbitrarily, he chose the largest object in sight to guide them through the night, and headed the group straight for the jagged peaks of the Mohawk Mountains.

There was a thick copse a few klicks away that they could bed down in for the night. The sec men should be safe enough there. Hopefully.

Chapter Five

The roiling clouds filled the sky as the companions raced across the New Mex desert. A dull glow emanated from above, but whether it was the full moon or airborne rads rich with hot isotopes was impossible to say. Then the moon broke through for a scant moment, bathing the world in cool silvery light before vanishing behind the curtain of polluted clouds once more.

Hours passed as the miles flew beneath the pounding hooves of their horses. Soon, the ground turned into a mix of sand and soil, then came irregularly spaced tufts of weeds and grass. Finally the companions galloped across a flat grassland. There was no reeking taint of acid rain on the wind, only the sweet smell of living plants, so the companions gave the animals their heads, and let them run free, stretching their muscles as the group moved swiftly across one of the small sections of the Zone that was still alive.

"Lovely," Doc said, inhaling the clean breeze. "Just lovely."

Scowling darkly, Ryan grunted at the pronouncement.

"Yeah, fragging swell," J.B. added sarcastically, pulling an anti-pers gren from his munitions bag and checking the tape on the arming handle. "As long as we don't run into any drinkers. Grass and sand are a bad mix."

"Especially on the fairway near the sixth hole," Mildred said in wry amusement to herself.

Her red hair streaming in the wind, Krysty shot the physician a strange look. Mildred could only shrug, unable to explain the golfing allusion. Then she gave a start. Just a minute, there was a water hole here, and copse of trees standing in the middle of nowhere, long stretches of flat grassland... They were riding across a golf course! Okay, one overrun with weeds and bushes, now mixing with the real desert, and slightly nuked a hundred years ago, but still easily identifiable as a golf course.

"You spotted the design, too, eh, madam?" Doc asked.

"Kind of hard to miss when you know what to look for," Mildred answered, hunkering lower in her saddle. Surrounded by a slice of the past, the fairway only incurred uncomfortable memories for the woman, and she concentrated on riding. The game of golf was as far in the past to her now as a New Year's Eve party. Long gone, and only dimly remembered.

Ryan's rad counter suddenly started to click wildly, and he abruptly veered to the left, starting a long curving sweep across the flat landscape. The others had seen this sort of thing many times before, and stayed close. The one-eyed man couldn't see any indications of a blast crater, there were no glowing pits or glass lakes. But he knew that could simply mean the area had been hit with one of those air-burst atomic bombs he'd read about. Mebbe one of those neutron things that killed folks, but didn't harm the buildings or plants.

"Golf?" Jak asked, arching a snowy eyebrow. "Not see sign of ocean."

"No, not a gulf, golf. It's a game, you see, and…" Mildred started, then bit her tongue. "Never mind. Just old talk."

Bent low over his mare, the teen accepted the answer with a shrug. He knew the physician had been born long before skydark and sometimes talked about things almost impossible to translate clearly. He never would have understood the notion of an elevator until taking a ride in one in the redoubts.

Keeping careful track of the rise and fall of the clicks of the rad counter, Ryan and J.B. directed the companions past the lingering death of the invisible rad zone. Once the clicks returned to the normal level of background rad, Ryan called a halt on the crest of a low sweeping hillock. The elevation gave them a commanding view of the landscape. Even in the dappled light from the moving clouds, they could see there was nobody around for miles in every direction.

With the butt of the Steyr resting on an outthrust hip, Ryan stood guard while the companions watered their tired horses. Rummaging in a pocket, J.B. pulled out his recently acquired compass and waited for the needle to settle down. But it kept spinning about madly, occasionally pausing to then start rotating in the reverse direction.

"Aw, to hell with it," J.B. said in frustration, tucking the device away. "There's just too much crap in the air from the clouds to get a clean mag reading."

Spooning some spaghetti from a MRE pack, Mildred caught the motion, but said nothing. J.B. had been able to trade one off a baron's brother in exchange for a gren. At the time, it seemed like a bargain, but now she could see in the Armorer's face how much he wanted that gren back.

"Those really work?" Jak asked.

"Absolutely," Mildred said, shoveling in another mouthful of pasta and sauce. "Oh, a Boy Scout compass, or something from the military would be a lot better," she admitted, "but then, half the world was explored with a magnetic needle resting on a piece of cork that floated in a bowl of water."

Rubbing the muscular neck of his beast, the teen made a face of total disbelief.

"It is true, Jak," Doc added, lowering his canteen and wiping his mouth clean with a linen handkerchief that had seen better days. "In the Hung Dynasty of ancient China, a magnetic needle was worth the owner's weight in gold. That would roughly translated today into, say, twice your body-weight of live brass."

"That much?" Krysty asked, watching something flying through the distant clouds to the west. Mother Gaia, that looked like a flock of screamwings! Thankfully, the deadly winged muties were heading in another direction. Had to be a fresh chill because they were moving even faster than usual.

"Trader always said that the only thing constant was change," Ryan said, biting off a chunk of jerky from their Two-Son ville supplies. "Nowadays, a hammer is more valuable than one of those microscopes I read about."

Noticing Krysty's posture, J.B. pulled out his longeye. He had found the old Navy telescope in a pawn shop in the place they called Zero City, and it was in perfect condition. About the size of your fist, it extended to over a full yard in length, and was much better than even binocs. Pushing back his fedora, J.B. began to sweep the horizon, but all he could see was blackness. Wait a sec, what the frag was that? he thought.

"The center is chaos, the circle cannot hold," Doc spoke softly in an odd singsong manner that meant he was quoting something. Using both hands, the time traveler unwrapped a package of cheese and crackers from the open MRE in the pocket of his frock coat. The cheese was a dull gray in color, but since that was its natural color he paid it no special attention. The predark military machine wanted the food for its troops to be nourishing, and long-lasting, but apparently nobody gave a damn if it was appetizing.

"Stop misquoting William Blake," Mildred retorted, licking the spoon clean and then stuffing it into the empty pouch. "Besides, we have miles to go before we sleep."

"And who is quoting whom now, madam?"

"Stuff it, ya old coot."

"Heads up," J.B. announced, collapsing the antique telescope down to its compact size. "We're not alone. There's a ville to the northwest of here, about forty miles away."

Ripping off one last chew, Ryan stuffed the rest of the jerky into a shirt pocket. "Let's go see if we can barter for a night under a roof. We have enough black powder to trade."

Moving off the hillock, the companions started for the distant town, staying in a loose formation so that anything that attacked they would be able to strike all together.

THE CLOUDS WERE THINNING and the moon was starting to dip behind the curve of the world by the time the companions galloped over a swell in the ground and got a direct bead of the ville. It was a big place, with a yellowish glow of torches coming from behind a high wall built of huge rectangular blocks. The gate was small, but several guard towers were spaced evenly along the perimeter.

Easing on the reins, Ryan scowled. They had to have a lot of enemies to erect such a strong defense. Or else mebbe there were drinkers in the area. Either way, not very good news.

As the companions got closer, they found signs of crude farming in the surrounding land. But the crops were stunted and scraggly, clearly showing there was something wrong with the soil in spite of the lush grass spreading out in every direction.

"Lots of plants grow in places where food can't," Krysty said, riding with one hand on the reins. The other hand rested on the rapidfire lying across her lap. "Could be a mutie form of grass."

"Also means this part of the Zone is a prime location for drinkers to hide under," J.B. added, adjusting his wire-rimmed glasses. "Stay razor for any large clumps of grass."

"And if we encounter the infamous subterranean mutie?" Doc asked. "Or another of those triple cursed jellies?"

With a rude snort, Ryan answered. "Start throwing grens," he said, "and run for your bastard life."

As the companions approached the ville, they could see that cutting through the fields was the remains of a predark road that led directly to the front gate. The surface was cracked in spots, with a lot of potholes filled with loose stones as a makeshift repair. However, it was serviceable, and easy walking for the horses.

Staying alert, the companions kept off the road

and rode their beasts along the berm. The uneven ground slowed them considerably, but bitter experience had taught them that anything that seemed too good to be true usually was. A repaired road often meant boobies hidden under the predark asphalt, dead falls, landmines or worse.

Reaching blaster range, the companions broke the canter of their horses into a trot, then proceeded along in a slow walk. But they always kept moving. A sitting target was just as bad as rushing headlong into the unknown.

Craning his neck, Ryan could see that the wall around the ville wasn't made of stone blocks, but was a line of predark trucks. Or rather, just the trailers. The cabs that pulled the trailers were gone, but the huge metal boxes sat end-to-end to form an angular barrier. The metal sides were streaked with layers of old rust, the open area under the trailers packed solid with predark debris, broken sidewalk slabs, bricks, wag engines and similar trash. It was an imposing tonnage of debris that would be impossible to move without some major explos charges and an army of men with shovels.

As the companions got closer, there were unmistakable signs of old battles on the trailers: blaster holes, scorch marks from Molotovs, gray streaks from ricochets and such. Loose sand was trickling from a few of the small cracks in the trailers, while the larger rents had been patched with sheets of old iron.

Ryan and J.B. glanced at each other and nodded

in appreciation. It was triple-smart for the locals to pack the trailers with sand from the nearby desert. The stuff was easy to obtain, there was a limitless supply, and the more the trailers weighed, the harder it would be for an invader to get through them.

"Good design," Jak said in grudging admiration.

Checking the draw on his SIG-Sauer, Ryan was forced to agree. This wasn't a ville, it was a fort, as big and well-protected as Front Royal, his home back in the east. Then the startling similarities of the towers behind the wall hit him hard. Fireblast, he thought, they were positioned in almost exactly the same formation as those back in Front Royal. How could that be?

"Ah, lover…?" Krysty said softly, putting a wealth of questions into the single word.

"Yeah, I noticed," Ryan replied. "Might just be a coincidence. Most people made crossbows after skydark for the same reasons—they were easy to build, and you can use the arrows over and over again."

"Great minds think alike, and all that," J.B. added in agreement.

"Make that great mind, singular," Doc rumbled in a somber tone.

For once, Mildred agreed with the old man. In her travels with the others, she had witnessed far too many examples of Carl Jung's theory of the "group subconscious mind of humanity" for there to be any other explanation, in her opinion. All living things were bound together. It was only people who refused to accept the idea that life shared its dreams. Either that, or there was an unknown force in the world guiding everything and everybody along secret paths. Which was clearly ridiculous.

Easing their mounts to a stop just outside of arrow range, the companions let the animals catch their breaths for a few minutes. This also gave the sec men a chance to see them first, and spread the word. There was no reason to startle the guards and start a fight. Spilling blood wasn't a good way to start negotiations with the local baron.

Walking their mounts closer, the companions studied the gate. It was very impressive. The broad gap between two of the trailers had been bridged by a concrete lintel to form an arch. Set below that was a formidable gate made of the doors taken off wags and welded together into a single homogenous slab. It was as lumpy as oatmeal, and looked as impregnable as a redoubt blast door.

"A door of doors," Mildred muttered. "I wonder if their baron is a poet?"

Just then, a bright blue light of an alcohol lantern appeared, moving across the top of the wall and starting to come their way. To the east, dawn was rising. But the shadows were still thick across the world, and the bobbing lantern moved along like a lost star.

"We'll soon find out," Ryan replied, walking his horse a little bit closer.

Footsteps were heard, and a man carrying the lantern appeared at the edge of the metal wall. Wearing loose clothing and a leather vest, the sec man had a tremendous beard, pleated into two strands. As well as the lantern, he was also carrying a bolt-action longblaster, with a hand on the trigger.

Tromping over to the last trailer, the sec man stopped near a crude set of tremendous hinges that supported the colossal gate.

"Advance and give the password!" the sec man shouted down into the darkness.

"Sorry, don't know it," Ryan answered as his horse shifted its hooves on the ground. "We're strangers, rists, looking for a place to stay tonight."

"Yeah? What kind of jack ya got?"

"Brass, four rounds!"

"Packed with dirt, probably." The guard sneered in disdain. "Useless as tits on a turd."

In a smooth move, Ryan pulled the SIG-Sauer. "Be glad to show you," he offered in a voice of stone.

Shaking the reins, Krysty walked her horse closer between the two men. "What is the name of this place?" she added loudly.

Slowly, both of the men eased their aggressive stances. But their hands didn't stray far from their blasters.

"This be Broke Neck," the sec man replied with a touch of pride. "And where you folks from?"

"All over," Ryan answered truthfully. "Here and there, north and south."

"Yeah? A real son of Trader, are ya?" the man said, chuckling.

"We traveled with him some," J.B. replied over the nasal snorting of his horse.

There was a pause as a second guard appeared on top of the wall. The clean-shaven man was holding a loaded crossbow. The two sec men held a short conference.

"Now that might be flat-rock, or it could be a stretch," the first sec man said, stroking his beard thoughtfully.

"Either way, that's a lot of iron for a bunch of pilgrims," the clean-shaven sec man said.

"That's because we're not pilgrims," Ryan answered, slightly annoyed. "You folks interested in doing biz, or should we keep moving?"

The muffled footsteps on top of the trailer got louder as one of the sec men walked to the very edge and angled his lantern to make it shine on the companions. "Yeah, yeah, just keep your jets cool, rist," the sec man said gruffly. "I was just... Black dust, ya only got one eye! Clem, look! One eye, by thunder!"

The second guard rushed over. "It's Ryan!" he whispered in shock. "Gotta be! Look there, one of them is dark, another pale, she's got red hair, and that guy is wearing glass on his face. Never did understand that part before."

Already alert, the companions instantly drew

their assortment of blasters, snapping off safeties and working bolts without the slightest regard of being seen. Instantly, both guards leveled their weps.

Then the man with the beard slowly lowered his rifle and placed it on the wall. "Easy there, folks, easy now. We don't want any blood split between us."

"And what if my name is Ryan?" the Deathlands warrior asked, the SIG-Sauer tight in his grip.

"Then the baron will wanna talk to you right away," the other sec man replied, resting the crossbow on a shoulder. "We've been expecting ya for a long time, but thought you'd be coming from the south in the direction of the ocean gulf."

Mildred lifted both eyebrows at that, but said nothing. The rest of the companions followed suit. What was going on here? There was only one possible answer that made any sense.

"Seems like your doomie made a mistake," the physician stated.

The two sec men frowned at that. "Baron Harmond don't make many bad calls," he stated gruffly. "More likely you're lying."

"But even if ya are, don't matter," the other man added brusquely. "The baron wants to meet anybody with just one eye. If you're Ryan, good. If not, we can offer ya haven from the coldhearts hunting folks like you."

Haven. There was a word the companions hadn't heard, or been offered, for a very long time. Aside from Two-Son ville to the south, their reception in the Zone had been poor at best.

"We accept your offer of haven," Krysty said, her hair flexing gently around her shoulders. If there was any danger here, she couldn't sense it. But then, when dealing with a doomie, anything was possible.

"No offense, but I have never heard of a doomie baron before," Mildred shouted up to the guard.

"No offense taken. Baron Harmond is prob the only one around." The bearded sec man advanced a step, then lowered the lantern for a better look. "Your name Doc?" he asked.

Puzzled at first, Mildred started to speak, then realized the connection. Doc... "Close enough," she acknowledged warily. "But I prefer Mildred."

"Fair enough," the sec man muttered, looking her over closely. "Funny, you don't seem frozen to me."

That comment caught all of the companions by surprise. Way back in the twentieth century, Mildred had gone into the hospital for a simple operation, but there had been serious complications and the doctors had desperately attempted to save her life by using an experimental cryogenic freezer unit. The device had worked, and Mildred awoke a hundred years later, alive and healthy, but nearly a full century after the near-total destruction of civilization.

"Well, best get inside, there's muties out at night," the smooth-faced sec man stated. "And they love to eat people, if they can't get at our pigs."

"Pigs?" Jak asked, amused.

Shifting the crossbow, the man shrugged. "They go craz for them. They'll pass up a dying man to steal a pig. Damnedest thing ever seen."

"Something special about your pigs?"

"Well, they're not muties, iffen that is what ya mean."

"I hate pigs," Doc muttered softly, his expression unreadable.

Turning toward the ville, the bearded man cupped a hand to his face. "Open 'er up, Charlie! This be Ryan!"

If there was a reply, it couldn't be heard. But soon there came the sound of a sputtering engine and the massive gate began to sluggishly move in jerks until there was a wide enough passage for a single horse and rider to traverse.

Holstering his piece, Ryan took the lead and headed his horse inside, his every muscle tense and ready for betrayal. A doomie, a human mutie. Sometimes they could read minds as well as get glimpses of the future. Of course, once a person knew what the future was, since it hadn't happened yet, they could try to change it. So the main power of a doomie was keeping their visions quiet and working in secret. But this Baron Harmond had broadcast his visions to his sec men. Did the rest of the ville also know, or were they kept in the dark? he wondered.

As the rest of the companions rode through the formidable gate, Ryan glanced sideways and saw that J.B. had a hand buried in his munitions bag. Any trouble from the locals and that gate would be coming down louder than skydark. Past the gate was a wide strip of concrete that looked recent. The surface was roughly smooth, but seemed to sparkle in spots, casting tiny rainbows from the lanterns held by the armed sec men.

"Careful of that glass," a sec man shouted. "Even if your horses are shod, that'll cut them bad."

Thankful of the warning, the companions steered clear of the studded concrete. It seemed a poor barrier to stop horses. But what else could a field of glass be for?

"Escaping slaves," Doc stated, resting a hand on the LeMat, answering the unspoken question.

"Attacking muties," Jak countered, shaking the reins on his horse. The mare softly nickered in reply as if agreeing with her master.

Irregular rows of adobe buildings rose in the murky shadows past the lanterns, only a few windows were lit. Most of the wooden shutters were closed tight. There was the smell of frying onions and wood smoke in the chill morning air. Filling the sky, orange-glowing clouds rumbled ominously, a streak of purple zigzagged across the heavens and sheet lighting flashed somewhere in the murky distance.

"Must have been a lot of hard work laying out all of that glass," Ryan said, the statement poised as a question.

"Bet your ass," a fat sec man boasted, a revolver

shoved into his belt. "And sharp enough to rip the tires off any two-wheeler."

A reasonable enough explanation, even if it did sound a little rehearsed. "Get a lot of trouble from bikers?" J.B. asked, guiding his mount around the unusual trap. Most villes had pitfalls or sandbag nests for defenders to shoot from in safety. But this felt like something done as protection for a specific enemy.

"Nope, never even seen one," the man stated casually, starting along a dirt street. "This way, folks. We already sent word to the baron that you're coming."

"Thought was doomie," Jak said, impulsively scratching at the bandage on his head. The wound had to be nearly healed from the way it was itching constantly.

"Everybody sleeps, rist," another sec man replied with a touch of anger at the implied insult.

"They've never seen a bike," Krysty whispered to Ryan with a lot of meaning.

"No need to convince me after that freezer remark," Ryan answered, looking over the sleepy ville. The people were starting to stir. As window shutters swung open, the startled men and women began to point and stare at the companions. "Harmond is a doomie for sure, and, it seems, a triple-damn good one."

"That doesn't mean he's a good baron like your cousin in Front Royal, or Baron O'Connor back in Two-Son."

"You can load that into a blaster," Ryan said in total agreement as the strong resemblance of the ville to Front Royal was suddenly explained. The doomie had to have seen the ville, either in the mind of somebody passing through, or with the "long sight" that some of the mental muties possessed.

Suddenly the engine started once more and the gates began to ponderously rumble closed.

"Okay, we walk from here," Ryan ordered the others, sliding off his mount. "The horses are tired enough after that hard ride."

Besides, we'll need the horses to be rested if we have to race out of here with a mob of sec men coming after us, Ryan added privately. Exactly how much did this Baron Harmond know? Was the existence of the redoubts still a secret? Did he know why they were empty, and where the predark soldiers had gone? What about Dean, and The Trader? There were a lot of mysteries that a friendly doomie could answer. Trouble was, most of the mental muties were borderline crazy, and a lot of their answers didn't make any fragging sense. Like calling Mildred Doc and saying that J.B. had glass eyes. The answers could only be understood after you knew the truth.

Following after the fat sec man with the lantern, the companions led their horses through the wide streets, looking hard for any sign of recent combat or public executions. But Broke Neck seemed a peaceful enough ville. Windows were open on the second floor of most buildings, babies were crying, dogs barking, roosters crowing and the smell of cooking food became stronger every minute, until the stomachs of the companions rumbled in sympathy.

Much of the ville was like any other they had seen over the year: leather-working shop, couple taverns, one big blacksmith, an area for making more adobe bricks, a distillery for brewing alcohol and a fletcher who was already hard at work making arrows, a young assistant close by watching closely to learn the venerable craft. Blasters took a lot of tech to make and maintain. Arrows only needed skilled hands, some long wood soaked in salt water, glue made from boiled bones, chicken feathers for fletching, sharp stones for arrowheads and a ville was ready for combat. According to Doc and Mildred, most of the world had been conquered by folks using only bows and arrows, and the ancient weapon was most definitely making a big comeback in the Deathlands.

Every minute, more and more people were coming out of their homes to watch the companions pass by. A frowning wrinklie lifted a rock to throw, but a neighbor forced her to put it down. An Indian shaman wearing only a loincloth stepped out of a leather tent to bow at the procession. Ryan and Krysty exchanged glances at that, but had no idea what it meant.

Going through an open area covered with loose gravel, the companions passed a predark fountain that was dribbling water, a whipping post for criminals and then a predark bank. The granite building was obviously the barracks for the sec men. A sandbag wall protected the front entrance, every window was covered with thick wooden shutters, gunports covered the walls, and rusty barbed wire hung off the roof in endless coils as armed guards walked around on patrol.

"This is it," the fat sec man announced, coming to a halt at a flight of marble stairs. Worn and cracked, the steps led directly to the front of the building.

Stroking his horse's neck, Ryan looked the place over carefully. The portico of the bank was supported by a row of granite columns, and the front door seemed to be solid bronze, the shiny surface only slightly marred by a couple of gray streaks from bullet ricochets.

"Welcome to Broke Neck," a barrel-chested man said, stepping out from behind one of the pillars. "Obey the rules, and you'll leave alive."

The fellow was huge, both arms hanging slightly away from the chest from the thick layers of muscle. His eyes were hard diamonds set into concrete, but the rough features were softened with sideburns and a droopy mustache. The clothing was patched, and the locally made boots were new. A sawed-off scattergun rode in a holster on his hip as if it was a handblaster. There were only a few 12-gauge cartridges for the blaster in the loops of the belt, but they gleamed with protective oil. There was a long knife on his belt, and another jutted from the top of his left boot.

"Fair enough," Ryan said, brushing back his wealth of black hair. "You the baron?"

The crowd and the sec men smiled at that, and the big man laughed. "Shitfire, no! I'm just the sec chief, Glen Bateman." He jerked a thumb over a shoulder. "Baron Harmond will be here in a minute. Been expecting you all night."

Tightening his jaw, Ryan and the others exchanged glances at that, but refrained from comment.

Just then, the doors swung open and out walked four big sec men carrying a litter that supported a wicker chair. Sitting in the chair was a boy, certainly no more than ten or twelve. But he was wearing predark clothing in remarkably good condition, and a gunbelt with a sleek autoloader hung from the armrest of his chair. To Ryan and J.B., the blaster looked as if it had never been used.

As the four men carried the child down the flight of steps, Doc muttered something under his breath.

"Yes, it does look like something from the pages of Egyptian history," Mildred remarked out of the corner of her mouth. "And why not? Most of their leaders were physically weak from all of the damn in-breeding."

"Hope that isn't the case now," J.B. added, barely above a whisper.

As if he heard the remark, Baron Harmond raised his head and looked directly at the Armorer, sending a cold shiver of danger down his spine. Child or not, this was still the baron of the ville, and his word was the absolute law.

"So you have come, at last." Baron Harmond sighed, a faint smiling playing on his pale lips. "The casement begins anew. The future is dead, and the future is reborn."

Passing the reins of his horse to Krysty, Ryan scowled at that. Casement? What the nuke-blasting hell was the kid babbling about?

As the sec men placed the litter on the ground, Doc struggled to recall a faded memory, then his face cleared and he shrugged in resignation. The scholar had been in too many places, and too many times, to recall everything he had ever heard. It was an odd word though. Casement...

"Alternate realities," Mildred said out loud, then bit her tongue. "We studied it briefly in college." Maybe that's what's wrong with some doomies. They can see the different versions of this world, possibly even as it endlessly split apart to make and remake the future again and again.

"Ah, Dr. Mildred." Harmond chuckled softly, raising an open hand. "Long have we waited for you."

"Mildred will do, thanks," the physician replied. "And I thought Ryan was the important one."

"For others, yes, but not for me." The baron sighed

again, rubbing his head. "I'm in pain day and night. Nothing my healers do seems to help. But you can."

"Be glad to try," Mildred offered hesitantly. Taking the med kit off the pommel of her saddle, she started forward, but Bateman blocked her way with a raised hand, his other resting on the sawed-off blaster.

"Not so fast, outlander," he stated gruffly.

"She may pass, Glen," the baron said, waving a pale hand. "This healer does not chill unless necessary."

A growing crowd murmured at that as the chief sec man lowered his arm to make a sweeping gesture as if he was a cavalier from the Middle Ages doffing his plumed hat.

Resting the med kit on the granite steps, Mildred knelt by the pale child. Baron Harmond smiled weakly as she checked his pulse, and he obediently extended his tongue upon request. The crowd murmured unhappily at that, as if it was beneath the dignity of their baron. Then Mildred pressed her ear to his thin chest and finally stood back, chewing a lip.

"There's nothing wrong that I can find," she said pensively. "But from all of those cuts on your thumbs, and the lines around your eyes, you've been reading books, and a lot of them."

"I have that skill," the baron answered with a touch of pride. "And I have been going through the remains of the old library to find knowledge to help my people. We can make gunpowder, instead of crude black powder, know to boil bandages, and many important things."

Keeping their expressions neutral, Ryan and J.B. tried to hide their disappointment at the news. The secret of making gunpowder was their biggest trade item.

"Good for you," Mildred said. "But stop reading the books at night by candlelight. You're ruining your eyesight, and that's what is giving you headaches."

"The books are doing it?" Bateman growled.

"Calm down, my old friend," the baron ordered brusquely.

"Well, that combined with the fact that you're a doomie," Mildred said, undoing the canvas straps to rummage through her med kit. Thank God, Blaster Base One had been well stocked with medical supplies. These past few weeks had been a real test of her doctoring skills.

"Here," she said, passing over a plastic bottle wrapped in gray duct tape. "They're called aspirins. Take two when the pain gets bad. But no more! Just two, and never on an empty stomach."

"Thank you." The baron exhaled as if life itself had been given to him in the little container. "And the tape is for…?"

"Keeps out the sunlight, helps them last longer."

"Ah, yes, complex molecules break down quickly under the direct stimuli of external…" His voice faltered, and the boy wearily hung his head. "No, I can't remember the rest of the predark words. But

the ancient books spoke of sunlight hurting chems.
I…had always hoped that sunlight was repairing
our world," the baron said, looking at the toxic storm
clouds roiling and rumbling overhead.

"They will, sir, trust me," Doc said, resting both
hands on his ebony stick.

Clutching the bottle of aspirins to his heaving
chest, the doomie ever so slowly turned his head to
stare at Doc.

"Theophilus." The baron spoke in a clear voice.
"The message you bear is true."

Just then a sec man arrived with a bottle of water,
and the boy hurriedly started opening the cap, with
a little assistance from Mildred to figure out the
childproof top.

Curiously, Ryan looked at Doc and saw that his
friend was trembling, a hand clutching his chest as
if he was having a heart attack. Then Doc frantically
reached inside his frock coat to pull out an old
leather wallet. He looked at it for a long moment,
then gave the wallet a gentle kiss and tucked it away
again, mumbling something under his breath.

Surreptitiously as possible, J.B. shot Ryan a
glance, and the one-eyed man shrugged. The wallet
wasn't something he'd seen before. But then, everybody had secrets.

"I thank you, sir," Doc stated, standing taller.
"From the very bottom of my heart, sir. I thank you."

Tossing his head back, the baron swallowed the
aspirin, then wiped his mouth on a sleeve. "Please

do not mention it again," Harmond asked in a strained voice. "The matter is painful for me to think about. There is too much...no, say no more. That matter is closed."

Giving a slight bow, Doc nodded. "Of course, I understand."

"Do you?" Baron Harmond said, the words nearly rising to a shout. "Do you really?"

At the cry, every sec man shifted their stance, several of them openly drawing blasters. The companions moved protectively closer to Doc, but the boy slumped in the chair and waved a hand to dismiss the matter.

"I..." The baron stopped and blinked, the pained expression in his face easing somewhat. "By the blood of my fathers, the pain is getting less. No, it is not just eased, it is gone!"

"Hmm, interesting," Mildred said, musing over the quick reaction. The increased blood flow caused by the aspirin couldn't have affected the boy so quickly unless he had an amazingly fast metabolism. But that would mean...

Mildred snapped her head around to find the boy already looking at her. She tilted her head in a question, and he nodded.

"Yes," Baron Harmond said, addressing her directly. "Five years. Possibly ten now that I have these." He shook the aspirin bottle at the civies amassed below the stairs. "They do not know."

"Nor should they."

"Then you understand what the consequences would be? Good. We stand in agreement. I had hoped so."

Feeling the crowd and sec men watching her every move, Mildred closed the straps on the med kit and returned it to her horse. The little boy was ten years old, living every day in racking pain, and the mind that gave him such mental powers was also burning out his body. He was like a car engine running too hot. The child would be dead in ten years. Yet his every thought seemed to be directed toward making his ville healthy and strong, bigger, larger, more powerful.

Oh, shit, Mildred realized in shock. The kid knew something terrible was going to happen, some holocaust, and was preparing them for the time when he couldn't help them anymore. But what was coming, another nuke war? A plague? Famine? What fresh type of hell was going to be unleashed upon the world in ten years?

Spinning, Mildred started to speak, but the question became a muttered curse as she saw the litter already going back up the stairs toward the granite barracks.

"He fell asleep," Bateman explained, scratching at a sideburn. "Happens more and more these days."

"May Gaia protect the boy," Krysty said. "The young baron looks as if he carried the weight of the entire world."

"Perhaps he does," Mildred whispered as a cold

breeze from the dying night blew across the open area, chilling her to the bone.

"Come on, those horses need a stable. The riders, too, unless I miss my guess," Bateman announced. Then he frowned. "No, by thunder, frag that. Anybody who helps my baron isn't sleeping in the stable. You folks can stay in my home. I have the entire second floor above the tavern. Plenty of room for all of you." The frown became a hesitant smile. "The horses, too, in case you don't trust us."

"Above tavern. Put guests in brothel?" Jak drawled, putting a lot of negative feeling into the word.

"Used to be. The baron sent the girls to a building across town last year. Not my place, and guest rooms are for visiting folks deemed important enough. Other barons, traders and such," the sec chief said, starting to walk away. "The baron probably did it just for you folks, if you hadn't figured that out yet." He chuckled. "We plan for the future here at Broke Neck. Never understand half of what we're doing, but it all works out in the end."

"Always?" Ryan asked, matching his stride to that of the smaller norm.

"So far," Bateman stated with conviction.

Putting their horses in the ville stable, the companions hauled their backpacks up to their rooms. It had been a long night. As Broke Neck began another day of work, Ryan and the others settled in for some much needed sleep. Although it wasn't her turn, Krysty insisted on taking the first round of standing guard. This was a new ville, and friendly didn't always mean that the locals were friends.

Sitting in a wooden chair near the open window, watching the people below start their morning chores, the redheaded woman nervously kept touching the MP-5 rapidfire on her lap. She had the strangest feeling that somebody was watching the companions, but since they were outlanders in the ville, most of the people would naturally show an interest in them.

Nothing odd there, Krysty added privately, working the bolt on the rapidfire and easing it back again. Especially since their baron had foretold of our coming months ago.

The companions stirred in their sleep at the metallic noise, and Krysty stopped the fidgeting. But the uncomfortable sensation of being closely studied didn't leave her during the next hour, and she warned Ryan about the matter as he took over the watch. Something was wrong in Broke Neck, some hidden evil. The chain of events that had started with their controlled jump to Blaster Base One was drawing to a head. After which, Gaia alone knew what would happen next.

But Krysty felt sure it would all end in death.

Chapter Six

Surrounded by foul-colored clouds, the blazing sun was high in the sky as David and Sharon shuffled along the dirt road leading through the rocky desert. Covered with a fold of cloth, Manda was asleep in her mother's arms, but the two adults were panting from the rising temperatures of the direct sunlight, sweat dripping off their burning faces.

It had been a long night. After the stickies had finished their horrible meal, David had gotten down from the tree he had hidden in for refuge and gone back to the crater lake to get the slaver's handblaster. He'd found the tiny blaster lying in the mud along the shore and had carefully washed it clean. The wep was in fine shape, but empty. Reluctantly, David had rummaged through the gory remains of the slaver's clothing, trying not to be sick, and eventually found two live brass, along with a perfectly good pair of boots. Everything else was in utter ruins or coated with indescribable filth. Only the flies had seemed not to mind the tattered condition of the corpse, arriving in greater numbers every minute. Clutching his prizes, David had hurried away from the buzzing cloud of tiny scavengers as quickly as possible.

Reaching a safe distance, David had donned his new boots. They'd fit surprisingly well. Adjusting his two blasters, he'd begun to retrace his steps to hunt for his wife and daughter. Their steps were faint in the shifting sands, and often he'd had to proceed purely on guesswork. But he kept at the task, refusing to give up.

It was later in the afternoon before the exhausted man had finally located them sitting on the second floor of a crumbling predark building. The roof and facade were gone, the interior wide open to the wind. Loose sand covered everything. A sloping hill of hard sand gave access to the second floor, but that was blocked by a small wag. A couple of large black scorpions were feasting on the horde of small red ants taking apart the hairy corpse of a coyote. The skull of the stiff animal was smashed apart, the rock still lying there in the pinkish brains. From the sharp teeth of the coyote there fluttered a ripped piece of Sharon's dress. The sight had made David feel faint, then he'd heard a familiar cry, and looked up to see his wife rise into view from behind a desk on the second floor. Sharon had the baby in one arm, and held a rock in her other hand, ready to throw.

With a glad cry, David had rushed past the sand dune and climbed the broken ruins to reach the second floor. Embracing his wife and child, he'd covered them both with kisses until Manda started to giggle.

"Oh, beloved, you were gone so long that I thought you might be..." Sharon had begun in a rush.

Pressing a finger to her lips, David had stopped the words. "Hush," he'd whispered gently. "Never even say it. I'll always return to my family, no matter what."

Hugging the baby tighter, she'd blessed him with her eyes.

Reluctantly releasing the woman, David had set to work. Flipping the desk over with a crash, he'd shoved it down the sandy incline, crushing the battling insects and shoving aside the rotting corpse. Sharon and Manda were close behind.

Reaching level ground, the three moved away from the ruins, and David gave Sharon his old boots. He'd held the baby while she'd exchanged footwear, happily tossing away her ratty moccasins. Then the family moved way from the ruins and headed after the slaver's cart. Their supplies had been lost in the effort to escape, so at the moment, clean water was the most important thing in the world.

There was water in the blast crater, but that would be used only if there was no other choice. Even if the rads were gone, there could still be toxic chems in the water that would chill faster than a knife in the dark. On top of which, the bikers might return, and the family could make much better speed on a horse-drawn cart than on foot. There really was no other choice. They had to find the cart, or buy the farm.

Retracing their steps as much as possible, the family started doing a wide recce in gentle curves. Hours slowly passed. Then, cresting a low swell in the road, David heard the rattle of iron on wood long before he spotted the wag. Hidden by a sloping sand dune, the slaver's cart was off the road, the reins of the horses tangled in a clump of dried sagebrush. The frightened animals seemed in fine shape, aside from an array of nasty scratches on their legs from panicky efforts to get loose.

Incredibly, the wooden cart was undamaged, and inside the iron cage in the rear were several people holding a skinny man to the roof, where he was working at the lock on a hatch with a piece of what looked to be old bone.

"Well?" a scraggly woman demanded from the supporting crowd.

"Nothing yet," the man replied, his tongue sticking out as an aid to concentration. "Keep me still, will ya? This is a lot trickier than it looks."

"Just hurry up!"

"Doing the best I can!"

Just then, there was a loud crack, and the skinny man stared in horror as the bone shattered, the pieces falling away to rain down upon the dirty straw.

"Son of a bitch!" a bald man cursed from the bottom of the pile. "That was our last one!"

"Now what can we try?"

"How should I know?" the skinny man snarled

in reply, grabbing the hatch and violently shaking it until the heavy chains rattled. "Open, damn you. Fragging piece of mutie drek, open damn it!"

"Hello," David shouted, walking closer. The rusty revolver was tucked openly into his belt, but his left hand clutched the loaded handblaster in the pocket of his pants.

Holding the baby, Sharon stayed at the swell in the ground, watching and waiting to see what would happen. The knife in her hand was hidden behind the sleeping child.

Startled, the prisoners froze motionless at that, then burst into cries of delight when they saw the man approaching.

"Oh, thank heavens!" a woman gushed, tears on her face. "We were afraid that madman was going to leave us in here!"

"Open the lock and let us out!" a skinny man demanded. "The key is somewhere under the front seat. Get moving before he comes back!"

"Don't worry, he won't be coming back," David said solemnly, studying the cart and cage.

"Sharon, check the horses!"

Hurrying over, the woman balanced the baby in one arm as she carefully inspected the nervous animals.

"Rolph is aced for sure?" an old woman asked from inside the cage, hope flickering in her tired eyes.

"Eaten by stickies," David answered, bending to examine the wheels. A few of the spokes were splintery, but the wheels appeared to still be serviceable. "Was that his name, Rolph?"

"Yes, although he made us call him master."

"I see," David muttered, then lifted his head to call out. "How are the horses?"

"The poor things are exhausted, and have been whipped a lot, too much in my opinion," Sharon stated, starting to untangle the reins from the dried bush. It was difficult to do using just one hand, but she wasn't going to put the baby down for any reason. "But aside from that, they're in good shape. Fit for a baron!"

"Our lucky day," David said with a grin, standing to dust off his hands.

"Stop wasting time!" a young man barked irritably, grabbing hold of the iron bars, pressing his face against the metal. "Find the key and get us loose, ya damn feeb!"

Not bothering to reply, David went to the front of the cart. Placing his new boot on the wheel, he hoisted himself up and climbed into the seat of the buckboard. The reins were tied to a center post apparently built for just that purpose, and there was a hand-brake composed of a thick iron bar with a wad of leather on the end for pressing against the wheels. An old battered hat that reeked of sour sweat sat on the front seat, a single feather jutting to flutter in the breeze. The seat itself was more like a bench, with an old moth-eaten blanket tied down over a thick wad of dried grass to serve as a cushion. Rummaging under the bench, David unearthed a couple of plastic boxes lashed into place with rope. Inside one of them was a leather water bag, and a canvas sack full of wild grain stalk. Obviously food for the horses.

Gratefully, David took a small drink from the water bag, then passed it to his wife. Sharon gave the baby a little sip first, took a long drink herself, then passed the leather container through the iron bars to the prisoners. There was a brief commotion as they fought over who would get it first, but that was soon settled and the bag began its rounds, getting smaller and lighter at every person until it was drained.

"Thank you." A man sighed, sagging against the hot bars. "I really don't know how much longer we could have lasted without water."

"Well, it wouldn't be smart to get you all chilled, now would it?" Sharon said with a neutral expression.

"Smart?" the skinny man repeated in confusion. "What does that mean?"

At the front of the cart, David was laughing with pleasure at the sheer amount of items he was finding. Aside from the food and water for the horses, the second box had yielded a cornucopia of treasure. There were blankets, spare clothing, another crossbow and a quiver full of arrows with razor tips. Excellent! There was a bottle of shine, a ratty toothbrush, a plastic comb with several teeth missing, handcuffs, another whip, branding irons, some spare tack for the horses, a cracked glass jar full of what looked like tiny smoked fish with the heads still attached and two predark cans of food. It was a bonanza of wealth unheard of in his entire life.

"Let's eat," David said with a smile, using a knife to stab a series of slits in the top of a can to try to get the lid off. The knife wasn't very sharp, and it slipped once, cutting a finger. But the lid finally yielded and was bent upward.

As Sharon clumsily climbed onto the buckboard, David warily sniffed at the contents. His stomach grumbled eagerly at the aroma. It smelled like good beef mixed with veggies, and a gravy thicker than swamp mud. There was the faded pix of a dog on the side, so he could only assume this was dog meat. Good, that was one of his favs.

"You go ahead and start, dear. I better feed the baby first," Sharon said, settling onto the bench. Loosening the top of her blouse, she exposed a plump breast. Manda required little coaching to find the dark nipple and was soon sucking away contentedly.

"Hey, what about us?" a man demanded from the cage, grabbing the bars and trying to shake them. "Get us out of here! Then you bastards can stuff your fragging faces until ya explode for all we care. But open the nuking hatch first!"

Completely ignoring them, David slowly spooned the food out of the can, chewing it carefully to make every savory morsel last for as long as he could. Food out of a can, life doesn't get much better than this!

"So what are we going to do about them?" Sharon asked, jerking her head toward the cage.

Thoughtfully, David swallowed before answering. "Dunno," he answered honestly. "But there's gotta be a ville someplace that would trade for them. Trade big, too. Twelve slaves gotta be worth a lot."

The words so casually spoken hit the prisoners like blaster rounds, and they recoiled at every one.

"What was that?" The skinny man gasped, going pale. "No, you can't do this! You can't!"

"Sure we can," David replied calmly, taking a spoonful of the stew and offering it to his wife. Sharon opened her mouth to accept and sucked the spoon clean as it came away, not missing a drop.

"Black dust, that's good." She sighed, smacking her lips. "Is there much more?"

"Sure," David said softly, tilting the can to show her. "See? I saved most of it for you. You're eating for two, after all."

"You mutie-loving bastard!" a woman screamed, beating on the bars with her dirty fists. "Set us free! Set us free, or the first chance I get that fragging brat of yours will—"

"Shut up!" David yelled, whipping out the palm blaster and thumbing back the hammer. "The next one of you *slaves* utters a fragging word gets lead in the head, and that'll be all the food the others will have until you're sold. Get me?"

Silence answered the dire pronouncement, but their eyes burned with livid hatred.

"I said, do you savvy!" he roared, yanking the horsewhip loose from its post and letting the knotted length uncoil until the dangling tip rested on the sandy ground below. "Answer, or I start removing your hide, right now!"

"Yes, we understand…m-master," the skinny man muttered, his head bowing in shame.

Satisfied for the moment, David coiled the whip and tucked it away where it could be easily reached. Taking the baby from his wife, he cradled the cooing infant in his arms while Sharon ate. Afterward, they switched again, and David started the wag into motion while Sharon changed a dirty diaper with a ragged piece of cloth.

There were some rough bumps as David fought the heavy wag back onto the road. But soon the slave wag was rolling along the desert road at a respectable clip.

Whistling a tune, David shook the reins to increase their speed. Meanwhile, Sharon stuffed one of the wooden boxes full of blankets and laid the baby down for a nap. While Manda slept, Sharon tested the draw on the homie crossbow, then slung the quiver of steel-tipped arrows across her back.

Side by side, the happy family rode off into the desert while the slaves in the iron cage settled down into a morose silence, each of them lost in their own dark thoughts.

AS THE SUN BEGAN to set behind the guard towers of Broke Neck ville, there was a polite knock on the door of the baron's bedroom. When no answer came, the sec men worked the lock and stepped inside, carrying a tray of steaming food in good bowls.

"Baron?" a corporal called hesitantly, glancing around. "It's late, sir, and…" But he left the sentence unfinished.

The window shutters were closed, but enough light poured through the tiny cracks along the edges to show piles of predark books everywhere. The walls were lined with bookcases, tables piled high with leather-bound volumes, and more were scattered on the floor. A cluster of lanterns hung from the ceiling, the glass reservoirs drained, and wicks burned away to a charred stub. In the far corner, Baron Harmond lay mumbling in a huge predark bed.

Carefully, the corporal moved the bottle of aspirins to place the tray on a table, then rushed closer to catch every word. Sometimes, the boy's dreams foretold of things to come, both good and bad. Like that time he told them about a herd of cattle roaming the desert only a few miles away. The ville ate meat for a full season on that vision. Or the time a scav found a case of predark brass, and tried to trade the ammo to the ville, but the baron had dreamed that the brass was a boobie. The scav didn't believe the baron, loaded a brass into his own revolver and pulled the trigger. The explosion blew the blaster apart, and the scav was chilled by the shrapnel.

Twisting and turning in the sweat-damp sheets, Harmond mumbled something too soft to hear.

The corporal leaned in closer. "What was that again, Baron?"

"Traitor…walking among us…stinking coldheart," the baron whispered, giving a shiver. "Smiles… he smiles…but has a knife for a hand…traitor. Traitor!"

A knife for a hand?

"Who is it, Baron?" the sec man asked softly, trying not to awaken the boy.

"Don't…don't let them talk to the air," the boy said, his eyes focused on eternity. "Mustn't let them…talk to the air!"

Now what the nuking hell did that mean? "Tell me his name, Baron," the sec man begged. "Is it Ryan? A rist? One of our own men?"

With a deep sigh, the baron closed his eyes and fell asleep, his tortured features easing into a peaceful countenance. Whatever demons had been stalking his mind were temporarily gone.

Tenderly wiping the sweat from the boy's forehead, the corporal turned and walked across the room, pausing at the door to look backward.

"Don't worry, my lord," he whispered grimly. "We'll find the traitor. Have no fear of that. And the only air he'll talk to is when the bastard is dancing at the end of a rope!"

"No..." the baron whispered in warning, but it was already too late. The heavy door had closed and the sec man was running to report the dire news to the sec boss.

Chapter Seven

It was in the afternoon when the companions left the second story of the tavern and went to check their horses.

There wasn't a cloud in the sky and the sizzling streets were almost entirely deserted. A panting dog lay in the shade under an empty wheelbarrow. A few feet away, a cat was doing the exact same thing under a shovel propped against the wall.

Sitting near the ville well, a wrinklie was wearing a wide stray hat, the ragged ends fluttering like feelers in the breeze. Directly overhead, the wooden covering above the well was offering no shade, but the old man was small enough to hide in the shadow beneath his woven hat. Dripping sweat, a man was stitching together a pair of snakeskin moccasins, his hands moving with the stately grace of performing a task that he had accomplished a thousand times before.

"Morning, sir," Mildred said in greeting, shielding her face with a raised hand.

The man looked up from his work and grinned, displaying a lot of missing teeth. Then he went back to the task, the needle rising and falling in an endless rhythm.

"Been a long time since we haven't seen any clouds," Krysty said, rubbing the bandage on her left cheek. The wound was nearly healed, and itching badly.

"It's nice to not worry about acid rain for once," J.B. added, removing his fedora to straighten the brim and then place it back again. The harsh sunlight glinted off his glasses, casting a rainbow on his face. "Come on, let's get moving. The horses come first, then we hit the tavern for some breakfast."

"Dinner."

"Whatever."

"Probably dog," Jak drawled, glancing at the animal under the wheelbarrow.

"Hot dog." Mildred chuckled to herself.

"There is no reason for us to eat the local cuisine," Doc mumbled, mopping the back of his neck with his stained linen handkerchief. "We have plenty of MRE packs left."

"We have to save those for the trip back to Two-Son," Ryan said, starting along the dusty street. "After we find those bastard coldhearts, and figure out why they want me and Doc so badly."

Frowning pensively, Doc started to speak when there came the sound of multiple boots running along the hard streets. Instantly, the companions shifted their position into a defensive formation just

as Chief Bateman arrived with a squad of armed
sec men.

"Morning," the sec chief said, stopping a few
yards away.

Keeping his expression neutral, Ryan nodded in
reply. Fireblast, something was wrong. The sec man
had stopped just out of reach to shake hands, the
perfect distance for a blaster fight. Yesterday the
locals had greeted the companions with open arms,
today they seemed itching for a chance to unleash
some lead. Their faces were hard, and every hand
stayed near a wep. Whatever had occurred in the
past few hours, it seemed clear that the companions
had somehow worn out their welcome.

"How was the grub at the tavern?" Bateman
asked, trying to sound polite. In spite of what the
guard had reported, he had some difficulty believ-
ing that these rists were a threat to the ville. If so,
the baron would have seen it before this. No, there
had to be something else happening, and these
folks were just a part of it, but not the center of the
brewing storm.

"Haven't eaten yet," Ryan said honestly. "Wanted
to check the horses first."

"Fair enough," the sec chief responded, hitching
up his gunbelt. "Well, we're going that way. Keep
ya company."

Under guard, was more like it, Ryan realized as
the combined group started walking along the
street. What the nuking hell was going on here?

"So, hot enough for ya?" a fat sec man asked sourly, walking alongside the companions.

"It's not the heat, it's the humanity," Doc replied in sullen disharmony, resting his ebony walking stick on a shoulder.

"Huh? Now, what's that supposed to mean?" another sec man demanded angrily.

"Just a bit of simplistic jocularity," Doc replied with a big smile. "Nothing more. Merely a touch of jocundity. A spritely jape."

"Yeah, sure, I knew that," the fat sec man muttered, furrowing his brow in confusion.

"You'll get us all aced showing off like that," Mildred said softly, brushing back her explosion of beaded hair. "There are still places in the world where smart equals dead."

"Really now, madam, just because I once read a dictionary—"

"Got what in air?" Jak asked in a shocked tone. Then he spoiled the effect by grinning.

The rest of the companions shared a laugh, and even Bateman gave a little smirk of amusement.

"Crazy young coot." Mildred snorted in disdain. "At least you didn't talk about your thesaurus." But then she noticed that the sec men were relaxing some after the friendly banter. She guessed it was difficult to be suspicious of folks who were joking and laughing. Glancing sideways, the physician saw that Doc and Jak were studiously not looking at each other and realized the exchange had been deliberately staged. Smart, very smart.

Passing through a courtyard dotted with the shade from woven awnings, the companions saw it was filled with exhausted people fanning themselves, sipping gourds of water, and trying very hard not to move. The exhausted people smiled and waved as the companions and the sec men passed.

Which meant they didn't know what was going on, Ryan rationalized. So it was only the sec men who were worried. Which translated that the baron had done something, or said something, that made the guards nervous. But not enough for them to come charging in with blasters firing.

"How's the baron?" Krysty asked, obviously following a similar train of thought. She had her shirt unbuttoned about halfway from the stifling heat of the desert sun, and the swell of her breasts glistened with beads of sweat.

"He's sleeping, thank the gods," Bateman replied curtly, spreading the lapels of his own shirt collar. There were more tattoos under his clothing, some of them quite lewd. "And we have standing orders never to disturb him when he's doing something as important as that. Blind norad, knows Baron Harmond gets little enough sack time as it is, what with all of those headaches, and stuff."

"Didn't the aspirins help?" Mildred asked in concern.

The sec chief grunted. "Hell's bells yes! But—"

"Excuse me, healer?" a wrinklie called, hurrying toward the group from an alleyway between two tall buildings.

The sec men and the companions both stopped to meet the old man. Only Bateman and Ryan checked behind to see if this was a diversion to make them look in the wrong direction, but the alleyway across the street was clear, nobody was hiding behind the water trough or hitching post. However, the two men caught each other doing the recce and shared a smile. Then the moment passed and the unease returned like a cold wind in the night.

"Please, can you help me?" the wrinklie pleaded, rocking a bundle of rags in her arms. The collection of cloth wiggled and started to cry.

As the mother spoke softly to the baby, Mildred could see the woman wasn't really old, just worn down from a hard life.

"What's wrong with your child?" Mildred asked gently. The sun was blistering and she was starving, but this was her calling, the reason behind everything she did. Healer. The word meant so much more these days than the title of doctor.

"I…" The woman paused, then tried again, the words rushing out. "I heard what you did for the baron. Blessings be on ya for that."

"Thank you."

"And?" Bateman snapped impatiently. "Get on with it, Lucinda!"

The woman recoiled slightly at the outburst, then summoned her courage and rallied once more. "Can you fix my little one?" she finished with a nervous flutter, as if half expecting a blow.

"Show me," Mildred said, extending a hand.

But Bateman stepped between them and pulled back the blanket to scowl at the baby inside.

"Shitfire, Lucinda, you whelped another damn mutie," the sec chief growled, flicking the blanket back over the infant to take it from his sight. "Curse your guts, you know this was supposed to be chilled at birth."

The sec man had moved quickly to hide the offense, but Mildred had seen enough. "Good God, sir, its lip is merely a bit malformed. It's not a mutant!" the physician raged. "That is just a harelip, nothing more. It's trivial."

"Mebbe, but it is not a norm," Bateman said sternly. "So the mother is supposed to ace it. Or the father. Know who the father is this time, Lucinda?"

The woman said nothing, and looked uncomfortably at the brick street below her tattered sneakers.

"Yeah, I thought as much," the sec chief growled, rubbing his jaw. "Stop wasting our time, and bash in its mutie head."

Shaking all over, Lucinda burst into tears.

"It is *not* a mutation, Chief, and I won't allow you to harm a child!" Mildred stated, stepping between the sec man and the weeping mother.

Bateman glowered at the healer, his jaw working on the matter. Suddenly the fat sec man lashed out with a longblaster. The wooden stock hit Mildred in the mouth and she toppled to the bricks with blood on her face.

"Obey the chief!" he snarled, reversing the long-blaster and working the bolt to chamber a round.

Sputtering in rage, J.B. started to charge, but Ryan drew his SIG-Sauer. "Freeze, lard ass!" he demanded. But then a shot rang out and the blaster went flying to land yards away with a clatter.

"Nobody move!" Bateman commanded, gesturing with his smoking revolver. "Back off, Ryan, this is not your concern."

Suddenly alert, Jak made a gesture and a knife dropped into his palm, but Doc moved first by simply dropping his ebony stick. As it hit the street, everybody flicked their eyes that way, and when the sec men looked back, Ryan was pulling the pin from a gren. The sec chief gasped as Ryan flipped it away and the pin hit the ground with a musical tingling.

"Your move," Ryan snarled as J.B. worked the bolt on the Uzi rapidfire.

Grimly, Bateman leveled his blaster as the rest of the companions drew weapons and the sec men brought up their assortment of crossbows and scatterguns. In the background, Lucinda slipped way from the heavily armed people.

"The thing is a mutie, so who gives a drek if it

lives?" Bateman demanded hotly. Was this what the baron had foreseen? Was this the betrayal?

"We do," Krysty replied, the MP-5 held tight in both slim hands.

"And your guy started this, not us," J.B. added tersely.

"Nukeshit! Why—"

"Sir, it's true," a young sec man stated, a black-powder revolver tight in his fist. "Fats did strike the healer first."

Although the teen's blaster was rock-steady, the hammer wasn't cocked, and the barrel was noticeably not pointing anywhere near the companions. If anything, it was closer to Fats, who was sweating profusely. His longblaster was still pointed at Mildred, but her Czech ZKR target pistol was aimed right back at him, her finger already putting pressure on the trigger.

A long minute passed with nobody moving or talking, the tension in the air thick enough to patch a breached ville wall. Thankfully, the baby had stopped crying and the only sound was the soft weeping of Lucinda, which only seemed to heighten the awkward silence.

"Yeah, so he did," Bateman finally relented, seeming almost disappointed. Slowly, he eased down the hammer on his piece. "Must be this fragging heat. This time of day, the sun can fry a man's brain. Makes folks do all sorts of stupe stuff. You gotta stay inside when there are no clouds. Just too damn hot."

Scowling, Ryan said nothing, the gren tight in his fist.

"All right, stand down, boys," Bateman said, holstering his blaster. "Put those hoglegs away."

Relaxing their postures, the sec men did as they were ordered, and the companions lowered their own weps. After a few seconds, Ryan knelt to get the pin, carefully disarmed the explos charge, and tucked it into a pocket once more. Everybody sighed in relief at the sight of that.

"As for Fats," Bateman said, staring at the overweight sec man. "You're on shitter duty for a week. Get going, and start digging."

"But, sir...!" the sec man began askance.

"Move that lard, feeb!" the sec chief bellowed, brandishing a fist. "Or I'll make that fifty lashes, and an entire moon digging new holes for the shitters!"

Going pale, the sec man hurriedly tucked his blaster into a holster, almost dropping it in the process.

"Well done, sir," Doc said, retrieving his stick.

Complacently, Bateman gave a shrug. Everybody screwed up now and then. The trick was learning how to keep sucking air afterward.

Going after his blaster, Ryan found the weapon alongside an adobe wall. The soft lead ball from the black-powder blaster had not done any damage to the steel frame of the predark autoloader, aside from leaving a small gray streak where it ricocheted off.

Working the slide a few times to check the action, Ryan tucked the handblaster away when he was satisfied that it was in working condition. Privately, he was impressed, and annoyed. Nobody had ever outdrawn him before. It was a disturbing event. It was the wound in his arm that was still slowing him down. If things ever went bad in the ville, Ryan couldn't take a chance facing down the sec chief in a fair fight. He'd have to ace the big man on sight, hopefully from a distance. Even better, in the back.

"Okay, healer, go fix the brat." Bateman sighed, removing his hat to wipe down the inside, then tuck it back into place once more. "If you can, that is. We'll wait."

Correct a harelip on a street corner?

"Whoa there, Chief!" Mildred said, holding up a restraining hand. "I can do the surgery, but not until the baby is older."

"Fair enough, how much older?" he replied grumpily. "Couple weeks?"

"A couple winters is more like it. Mebbe more."

"More?"

"Don't concern yourself over the matter anymore," Krysty whispered, closing her eyes. "The matter has been closed."

"Now what the nuking hell does that mean?" Bateman demanded, resting a fist on his hip.

"Oh, no," Doc whispered.

Feeling as if the world were slowing down,

Mildred turned to see Lucinda kneeling alongside the water trough. Her hands were dripping wet, and the bundle of rags was nowhere in sight.

"Sweet Jesus!" Mildred screamed, rushing to the horse trough.

Pushing Lucinda aside, the physician saw the cloth bundle lying unnaturally still on the bottom, a tiny pink fist showing from within the soaked cloth. Giving an inarticulate cry, Mildred yanked the swaddling mass out of the shallow water and tore the cloth apart, exposing the still form of the aced child. But as she frantically tried to do CPR on the body, Mildred realized that it was much too late.

"You heartless bitch," Mildred breathed, barely able to control her emotions as she folded the blanket over the tiny corpse. Then jerking her head up, the physician stared in feral hatred at the frightened woman. "Why? Why in the name of God, did you chill your own child?"

"But he said to," Lucinda stated, pointing a trembling finger at the crowd of armed people standing in the sunny street.

"Idiot!" Bateman roared furiously. "No decision had been made yet!"

Confused and terrified, Lucinda raised her hands as if in prayer. "Forgive me, sir! I only wanted to obey the law!"

"Liar!" Bateman barked, the word echoing along the street like the crack of a whip. "You only wanted to escape from being punished for breaking the law and not chilling it in the first place!"

"Sir, I—"

"Silence! I should send you to the post for this!" Bateman stormed. "But since you took a life, you owe a life."

"Sir?"

Bateman turned on a boot heel. "You there! Healer! The one called Mildred!"

"Yeah?" Mildred answered listlessly. Every emotion seemed to have drained out of the physician. She wasn't angry anymore, or sickened, or anything. She felt numb, as if something had died inside her along with the baby.

"This woman is now your property," the sec chief declared in a loud voice. "Do with her as you please."

Caught by surprise, Ryan scowled at the pronouncement as if not sure that he had heard it correctly.

"Eh? What was that again, sir?" Doc demanded.

"I thought there were no slaves in this ville," J.B. added with a frown, a hand resting on the Uzi.

"There aren't," Bateman agreed. "This is a punishment detail. The healer can do anything she likes to the gaudy slut."

"A rose by any other name, sir!" Doc retorted hotly.

"Stuff a sock in it, Doc," Mildred snapped. "Okay, just to make sure that I have this right, Lucinda is mine. I have total control."

"Within reason," Bateman added grudgingly.

"Meaning?" Ryan asked, crossing his arms.

"Mildred can't chill her, or make her act against the baron, or the ville."

"Okay, it's a deal."

Standing erect, Mildred offered a hand to Lucinda and hauled the woman to her feet. "Then go home. I set you free."

As the ville sec men gasped, Lucinda threw off the helping hand as if it were covered with suckers.

"Now just wait a nuke-sucking tick," a sec man said, starting closer. But Ryan and J.B. got in the way, and the man stopped uneasily, not sure of what to do. The companions and the sec men started glaring at each other again, and it was clear that a confrontation was only heartbeats away from erupting into bloodshed.

"Well, Chief, is she mine, or not?" Mildred demanded.

"She is yours," Bateman admitted reluctantly. "Although why you would do such a thing I have no idea."

"Didn't think you would," Mildred said. Picking up the soggy bundle of rags, she thrust it back at the startled woman. "Here! Go home and bury your son properly. You've suffered enough today. I set you free."

Hesitantly accepting the bundle, Lucinda ran away to disappear around a corner, all the while sobbing hysterically.

"Poor thing." Mildred sighed. "Maybe she'll feel better tomorrow."

"She'll be on the last train west by tomorrow," Bateman stated, viewing the water trough in stern disapproval. "Come on, let's see to those horses."

"The last train… You think she'll ace herself?" Mildred demanded in astonishment. She took a step after the fleeing woman. "Maybe I can help."

"Already done enough," Ryan chided sternly. "More than enough. You didn't mean to, but that's no help now. Let her buy the farm in peace."

"The blessings of Gaia upon her soul," Krysty said softly.

"Amen," Doc whispered, bowing his head.

Totally confused, Mildred looked around. "But…"

"You shamed her publicly," a large bald sec man related, using a forearm to wipe the sweat from his face. "It was bad enough she gave birth to a mutie, that happens sometimes. But then a rist refused to even have her as a slave?" He shrugged. "That was too much for anybody to stomach."

"And you think that she'll…but I didn't want a slave!" Mildred exclaimed, spreading her arms wide. "You of all the people here should understand that!"

The bald sec man furrowed his black face. "Why is that?" he asked, puzzled, extending an arm to show there were no scars on his wrist. "I've never worn iron."

As the others started to walk away, Mildred opened her mouth to try to explain, but then saw the hopelessness of the situation. How could she possibly explain the eighteenth-century slave trade to a free man born in the Deathlands? Nobody treated blacks like second-class citizens anyway. Racism had died in the nuke war. Yet, ironically, Mildred felt that some small part of her heritage was also gone forever, and she wasn't quite sure how to feel about that yet. People were just people these days. Most folks didn't care about skin color or religion. Only muties were despised and shot on sight.

"Better get moving or they'll be serving dinner by the time we're done with the horses," Ryan said as the combined group started along the street once more.

A sec man stooped over to retrieve the single brass shell lying on the street, leaving nothing behind but an emptiness in the air and a few damp spots on the ground that were already drying from the searing rays of the relentless sun. Soon there wouldn't be any signs of the event remaining.

"Damn, it's hot today," Bateman commented as they turned a corner.

Ryan didn't reply, but kept a hand near his blaster until the stables came into view. He felt as though he were in the crosshairs of a longblaster, but couldn't quite figure out whose hand was on the trigger.

HIGH ON A NEARBY ROOFTOP, the man lowered the longblaster and moved away from the edge in frustration. There had been too many sec men below for him to try a shot. But soon now. Very soon…

Chapter Eight

At the stables, Bateman and the other sec man left the companions and set off to resume a security sweep of the ville.

"Looks like they're expecting trouble," J.B. said, finally releasing his hold on the pistol-grip safety of the Uzi. "Then again, good sec men are always ready for a shit storm."

"Comes with the job," Ryan agreed, watching the group of armed men stroll away until they were out of sight. Casting a glance at the ville wall, the one-eyed man saw the guards slowly walking along the top of the rusty trailers, crossbows in their hands. The guards were smoking and talking to one another, and their faces were turned toward the desolate farmland surrounding the ville and the endless shifting sands of the New Mex desert. Somewhere in the distance, thunder rumbled, but there wasn't a cloud in the sky.

"Apparently the rank and file are not aware that something is wrong inside the ville," Doc espoused thoughtfully. "That would seem to make it a purely executive concern."

"That's bad for the ville, but good for us," Krysty said, glancing at Mildred. "You okay?"

Looking at the ground, Mildred shrugged, unable to express the mixture of emotions that filled her mind.

"Come on," Ryan directed, heading for the stable. "Mad dogs and Englishman, you know."

Doc shot the man a startled look.

"Heard it from you."

"Ah!"

Stepping out of the sun, the companions stood for a moment in the cool shadows to breathe in the richly scented air. It was filled with the pungent smells of horses, sweat, soap, leather and manure. Low dividers of adobe bricks had sectioned the warehouse into individual stalls, and the rear of the stable was stacked high with bales of green hay and a loose mound of dry yellow straw. A crude wall of bright orange highway crash barrels separated the edible hay from the straw, a lot of which was spread across the floor. Sunk into the concrete floor, steel girders supported a corrugated aluminum ceiling high enough to give proper ventilation, and the predark fluorescent light had been replaced with clusters of alcohol lanterns hanging by rusty chains. None of the lanterns was on, the bright sunshine coming through the front doors more than enough to illuminate the interior.

Surveying the place, Ryan saw only horses in the stalls, and a ratty-looking camel. But no wags of any kind. Strange.

"Yeah?" a burly man shouted in crude greeting,

a dirty wooden pitchfork in his wide hands. The fellow was in loose pants that seemed to be composed entirely of patches, and a sweat-stained T-shirt that clung to his muscular chest as if painted onto the skin. "And just who the frag are you?"

Then he blinked and gave a smile. "Oh, it's the rists! Welcome! Been waiting for you! Come on, your animals are over here!"

As the beefy stable hand walked away in a rolling gait more seemingly for a sailor, Doc nudged J.B. with an elbow.

"We seem to have been expected," Doc mumbled with ill-hidden meaning.

"Not take doomie to figure that," Jak said, brushing back his snow-white hair. "Not much more important than horse."

"Here they are," the stable hand announced, casually waving the pitchfork. "Baron Harmond said only the best, so I took care of them myself."

Going to their horses, the companions checked over the animals and were pleased to see that the man appeared to be telling the truth. The horses were in fine shape, watered, fed and curried clean. Even the saddles had been rubbed down with fresh oil. Ryan didn't know if that was a courtesy for helping the doomie, or his subtle way of suggesting they might need to leave soon. But either way, the companions were pleased with the attention the horses were receiving.

"The palomino had a stone bruise," the stable hand said. "But I took care of that."

Hanging his leather jacket on a wooden peg sticking out of the adobe wall, Jak went to his mare and ever-so-gently got the horse to lift her rear hoof. There was some minor discoloration there, but nothing serious.

"How fix?" Jak asked, easing the hoof down again.

The stable hand snorted in amusement at that, and the teen nodded in understanding. Check. Trade secret. Just like J.B. with blasters, and his own knowledge of making shine. Some things you talk to folks about, but other stuff you carry to the grave. When most people knew jackshit, even one little bit of smart could keep grub on the table for a lifetime.

"They're all in excellent shape," Krysty commented, scratching her roan mare behind the ear. The horses preened under the touch, nickering softly.

With the saddle and blanket removed, she could now see all of the scars on the hide of the poor animal. This had been a sec man's war horse, the survivor of a hundred battles, a veteran who had been ready to be slaughtered for the dinner table before she'd taken ownership.

The stable hand waved that away. "Just doing my job."

"Well, thank you anyway..." Krysty left the sentence hanging.

"Armand." The man smiled, leaning on the pitchfork. "Don't bother to tell me your names, I know them already. Hot rain, everybody in the ville did long before you arrived."

"About that," Ryan said, walking over, his combat boots crunching where the straw was dry, and squishing in other locations.

"Yeah?" Armand asked curiously, his tone pleasant. "If you're gonna ask what else he said about you, save your wind. Ever talk with a doomie before?"

"Some," Ryan admitted honestly. Aced a few, too.

"Well, then, you know, they don't talk from the hip," the stable hand explained with a snort. A horse copied as if in agreement. Armand chuckled, then continued. "You gotta listen to what they don't say, just as much as what they blabber about."

"Just like figuring out what's wrong with a horse," Mildred added, meandering her way through the steaming piles as she walked closer.

Caught totally by surprise, Armand shot up both eyebrows. Well, nuke me running, she understood!

"Yes, ma'am," he replied. "There was this time when the baron was little, when he told about his father's death and warned of the fringed traitor. We had no idea what the hell that meant. But a couple hours later, the sec chief rode back alone, saying a mutie got the baron. Chief Bateman, he was just a corporal then, spots the fringe on the saddle bag of the chief's horse and shoots it with his blaster."

Armand shook his head. "The blast damn near blew down the ville gate even though it was fifty yards away. The bag was full of predark explos. Took us a week of hard digging to fill the fragging hole, I can tell you. Any closer and the wall would have been down for good. Well, the sec men declared Junior the baron that very night, and the first thing Harmond did was make Bateman the new chief."

"Junior?" Doc asked.

The stablehand gave a rueful grin. "That's his name, Junior Harmond. Odd name, don't you think?"

"Absolutely," J.B. agreed. "But then, barons are strange, doomies even more so."

"Fucking aces." Armand laughed. "About two winters ago, the baron awoke at dawn and ordered everybody onto the roof with any weapons they had—blasters, crossbows, knives, rocks bottles, axes, anything! Then he threw open the ville gates and we all just waited, sitting there, freezing in the cold. Some of us naked as a piglet. Couple hours later, a small army of coldhearts arrived, dragging along a predark cannon they called a howitzer. The ville wall is strong, nuke yes, but that mil wep would have punched holes in it like pissing in snow."

A wind blew hot air into the cool stable through the open doors just as Armand continued. "The coldhearts seemed puzzled finding the gate open, but they strolled inside anyway and started wandering around, getting more and more scared that mebbe this was a plague ville with everybody aced, and just as they started to panic, the baron stands up in plain sight and orders the attack."

"Must have shit pants," Jak said in amusement.

"Yes, sir, we caught them totally by surprise. Chilled them all, down to the last son of a bitch," Armand said proudly, patting the leather sheath on his hip. "He saved this ville, sure as Mohawk is a mantrap. The sec men got the howitzer, and I got a new knife."

Mohawk? Oh, yes, the western mountain range.

"Any trouble since then?" Ryan asked, probing for additional information.

It wasn't gossip they wanted, but some sort of idea what to expect from the baron. Was he really on their side against this common enemy, or was he planning to use the companions as bait in a trap to save the ville, and to hell with the outlanders? This is what the Trader used to call "chewing" a ville. Just keep smiling and asking for stories and a smart person could discover all sorts of important things.

Appreciative of the willing audience, Armand gave a hard smile. The others in the ville knew all of the old stories. But he enjoyed telling them again and again to the rists and pilgrims who wandered in from the Zone.

"Trouble? Yeah, sure, some," he admitted, stabbing the pitchfork into a pile of straw. "But we get them more times than they do us, that's for fragging sure." Leaning against an adobe wall, the stable hand pulled out a piece of jerky and tore off a chunk to start chewing. He would have preferred to smoke some maryjane in his corncob pipe, but the horses hated smoke more than the colic. Couldn't blame them, either, not really. Not much worse than a fire in the stable.

"And what did Baron Harmond say about us?" Ryan finally asked, getting to the point.

Biting off another chew, Armand shifted uneasily under the man's gaze. "Well...he said to give you anything you want, and stay the fuck out of the way."

"Any reason?" Mildred asked suspiciously.

"All those folks coming after you. Coldhearts with all sorts of predark drek. Lots of people are gonna die."

"Then why let us in?" J.B. demanded, tilting back his fedora.

He shrugged. "Even more get aced if we don't," Armand answered in blunt honesty.

"More? Who among us will get aced?" Krysty asked, her hair flexing anxiously.

"Dunno that." Armand tilted his head toward the ville. "We lost our healer last week."

"Was your healer like me?" Ryan asked, touching his scarred face.

The stablehand studied him before replying. "Yeah, only had the one eye. But no accident like yours. I can see the scar. Jerry was just born that way. Not a mutie, mind you!" he hastily added, raising both hands. "The other just wasn't there. Only an empty socket."

"Black Cough," Mildred said, frowning. "His mother must have had the Black Cough when she was in term. A lot of the women who survive the disease gave birth to children with facial deformities."

"The cough, eh?" Armand said, mulling it over. "Yeah, I think you're right about that." Then his face brightened. "Oh, yeah, and one more thing. We're supposed to tell you the stew is fresh at the Broke Neck tavern."

"Is it? Ryan asked suspiciously.

The stable hand shrugged again. "I eat with the sec men. That place is for villagers. I have no idea."

"Interesting," Doc uttered, worrying the sword-stick in his hands. There was a snap, and the silver lion's head came away from the shaft, exposing a couple inches of the steel sword hidden inside. Then the scholar shoved them back together with a solid click. "And when did the illustrious baron order you to tell us this?"

"About a month ago, I guess. Mebbe five weeks."

Just when we arrived at Blaster Base One in southern part of New Mex, Ryan realized. Could be a coincidence, but he didn't think so. Wheels within wheels, as Mildred liked to say. Bateman had guided them here so that Armand could tell them to go to the tavern. Ryan felt a rush of blind rage start to well from within, and he forced the chilling fury under control. Fireblasting hell, were they being played for feebs by the teenage doomie? Or was this Harmond's way of helping them? Only one way to find out.

"Arnie?" somebody shouted.

With hands on blasters, the companions turned just as a young woman walked into the doorway of the stable. Dressed in a tattered white dress with her blond hair cascading to trim hips, the busty teen paused in the opening and hesitantly smiled. With the bright sun streaming from behind, the thin fabric of her white dress was rendered translucent, nearly transparent, and it was shockingly obvious that the girl was wearing only skin underneath.

"Hey, Danni," Armand said, hurriedly tucking the piece of jerky away into a pocket and smoothing back his hair. "Just let me take care of these people, and I'll give you that riding lesson I promised."

"A riding lesson?" Danni replied, puzzled. Then she caught on. "Of course, Arnie. No prob, I'll wait over here till you're done."

"Thanks," the stable hand said with a forced smile, then turned to look at the companions with a pitiful expression. "Anything else I can help you with?"

"No, thanks. We'll be going now," Ryan said, fighting back a bemused grin. From the way the two of them were acting, he'd assume that she was the only child of either Chief Bateman, or some villager with a nuke-hot temper and a working blaster.

As the companions left the stable, the young woman rushed in and Armand closed the plywood doors. As the locking bar was noisily dropped into place, there instantly came a feminine squeal of delight and then profound silence.

"Lucky Armand," Jak said, casting a glance back at the warehouse. It had been a long time since the Cajun had knocked boots, and that view of the teenage girl standing in the bright stable doorway had been mighty close to heaven in his opinion.

"Not my type," J.B. replied nonchalantly, removing his glasses to start rubbing them with a soft cloth taken from an inside pocket. "Too young, too blond and I'll bet she doesn't know anything about cutting up the innards of people and sewing them back together."

Frowning slightly at that comment, Mildred glanced at the short man who was industriously cleaning his glasses. She walked over to bump him with a hip.

Donning his specs, J.B. smiled in reply, and the two of them walked side by side, sharing a private moment on the hot and dusty street. When you were with the right person, some things didn't need to be said out loud.

"What now, lover?" Krysty asked, checking the load in her revolver.

"It's time we did a recce on that tavern," Ryan answered, his stomach rumbling. "And get some bastard chow, too."

"Sounds good," Jak added, slipping off his camou jacket to tie the arms around his waist. The day was brutally hot, and the jacket weighed a lot with all of the knives hidden up the sleeves and the bits of razor and glass sewn into it.

"And afterward?" Krysty prompted, tucking away her weapon.

"Then we go see the baron," Ryan intoned dangerously. "The doomie knows a lot more than he's telling, and I'm starting to feel like a pawn in that game Doc once tried to teach me."

"Ah, chess!" Doc quipped in exclamation. "I concur, my dear Ryan. The baron may even know who is behind all of the mysterious events that brought us here."

"Could be anybody," Ryan agreed, cracking his knuckles. A hundred names went through his mind like windblown leaves in autumn.

"Gaia knows, we've made enough enemies," Krysty remarked, brushing back her wildly flexing hair. For every baron they blasted, there always seemed to be some distant kin out for revenge. It didn't matter that the folks they aced were mad-dog evil, druggie cowards or completely insane. Some distant relative always seemed to want revenge. The world was ruled by the crazy, and there wasn't much a person could do about the matter, but fight to stay alive.

IN THE FOREST GLEN, the door to the blockhouse was wide open, held in place by a tree branch. Sitting on some ammo boxes in the shade, the Rogan brothers were cleaning their weapons. Walking across the warm grass, Lily stopped near the doorway and bowed her head.

The barefoot woman said nothing, waiting until they spoke first. Sometimes, they didn't and let her stand there all day while they played cards or slept. She fervently hoped this wasn't going to be one of those days because their anger over finding out what they missed would be incalculable.

The big men saw her, but continued their work. Softly in the background could be heard the gentle splashing of the little waterfall, the soft crackle of the campfire.

"What's the bitch cooking at high noon?" Robert muttered in his twisted voice, clumsily sighting down the barrel of his rapidfire to make sure it was thoroughly clean. His left arm was wrapped in bandages from the arrow they had removed. "Bitch is going to faint from the heat, fall in and cook herself."

"Gotta taste better than everything she cooks," Edward drawled, thumbing loose predark rounds into an empty clip. Each live brass went firmly into place with a satisfying click.

"There is no fire," Lily said quickly in relief. "That's the…the radio." The tech word tasted like shit in her mouth.

Instantly, the three men dropped the disassembled rapidfires and plowed out of the blockhouse, pushing Lily aside. Charging across the sunny glen, the brothers could now clearly hear the crackle coming from their bikes. Muffled by the sound of the waterfall, the bursts of static coming from the radio built into the two-wheelers sounded almost exactly like a fire burning green wood.

"...ello?" a voice called out. "You assholes awake? Repeat, anybody..." A burst of hash came from the radio blocking the rest of the message.

"Alan?" John demanded, grabbing a mike and thumbing the transmit switch. "That you, bro?"

Whatever came next was lost in a burst of hash, but eventually it cleared. "...epeat, well, it ain't our sister!" the fourth Rogan snarled. "But good news! They're here. Arrived last night."

"All of them?" Edward retorted, the mike almost lost in his massive fingers.

More static almost blanketed the positive reply.

"Where are you?" Robert demanded over the shoulder of the elder Rogan. "The ruins? The water hole? Broke Neck? Iron Mesa?"

"Broke Neck," Alan answered, the reply wavering in tone and strength as the com link automatically battled the rippling flow of radioactive isotopes in the atmosphere. "Repeat, I'm in Broke Neck. That fragging little mutie baron was right! But more importantly..." The voice faded into silence, and there only came a soft hiss from the speakers like a tire deflating, but it went on and on forever.

Impatiently, John reached out a hand, but then stayed the urge to fiddle with the controls. The fancy equipment handled such things all by itself, and didn't need any help, strange as that sounded. Until today, the elder Rogan would have sworn that radios were only good for a couple hundred feet under ideal conditions, often a nuking lot less. But these models that Delphi had given them could cover miles in open territory. Miles! Even more at night, although he didn't know why. Did the sun interfere with a radio?

Long-range communications. It was a whole new idea to the Rogans, and had opened a wealth of recce possibilities in their hunt for the outlanders. Plus, there now was the potential of rebellion against their hated master. They knew that Delphi listened to every word they said on the device, and could track the bikes by some kind of predark tech totally beyond their understanding. But knowing that he listened to them, the brothers had worked out a plan to get some revenge should the opportunity present itself.

"Alan?" the elder Rogan shouted into the hand mike. "We can't hear you anymore. Still there, boy?"

Stutters, chirps and high-pitched howls came from the speakers on the three motorcycles in perfect unison. Suddenly the static vanished as if a switch had been thrown and there was only a low powerful hum coming from the radio speakers.

"He said that Ryan and Doc are at Broke Neck ville," Delphi said in a deceptively calm voice. "Now go get them, and do not fail. I would be most displeased." There followed a moment of silence. "Goodbye for now."

Pressing the transmit button on the side of the mike, John started to ask a question when there came a loud snap from the speakers and all of the radios went silent.

"Dead as dirt," Robert said, rubbing his wounded arm. "I guess they ain't needed no more."

"And the same thing will happen to us after Delphi has what he wants," Edward proclaimed, returning his mike to a clip on the dashboard. He watched as the cord was automatically drawn inside to vanish from sight.

"I know that!" Robert barked.

Glancing skyward at the fiery sun, John ran a thoughtful hand across the satiny paint of the predark machine. The black metal was cool to the touch, and he remembered Delphi saying something about the bikes needing to absorb sunlight to charge the electric engines. Were heat and light the same thing? Mebbe. Interesting.

"What now, brother?" Edward asked, cracking the knuckles of his oversize hands. "Should we wait for dark, or—"

"We ride," John said, climbing onto the two-wheeler and twisting the grips on the handlebar. The big engine began to softly hum, the dashboard coming to life with a dozen glowing meters and gauges. "Ed, get the blasters. Robert, lock Lily in the blockhouse, and give her some water this time. I don't know when we're coming back."

Lily said nothing, waiting for her fate.

As his brothers got busy. John reached inside his shirt to pull out a heavy revolver, a blaster not given to them by Delphi but taken from a one-eyed baron before they'd nailed him screaming to a cross. Each of the brothers had a secret arsenal of weps taken from their victims—handblasters, plas charges, switchblade knives, even an implo gren! Yeah, all sorts of things. From the very beginning, Delphi had treated them like dogs, stupe animals to be whipped and trained.

But old dogs could learn new tricks, John added with a grim expression. When the Rogans delivered Doc Tanner alive to Delphi, he'd go crazy with delight. Which made it the perfect time to strike back at their hated master. And the first move would be to distract Delphi by chilling Tanner.

Chapter Nine

The Broke Neck tavern was located near the market-place and the whipping post, a grim reminder of the painful fate that would befall any sec man found drunk on duty. Ryan approved of the iron-fisted subtlety.

Whatever the building had been in the past was gone under decades of sandblasting from the desert winds and the addition of adobe brick walls to support the exterior of the structure.

A poorly carved wooden bottle hung above the front door to let folks know this was a tavern, and there was also a rather surprisingly good painting across the front of the mud bricks showing laughing people with huge frothy mugs raised high as beautiful topless women danced on tabletops laden with steaming food.

Shifting the med kit slung over her shoulder, Mildred snorted. So advertising had finally crawled from the grave of the nuclear war, she thought. Pity.

There was no porch, but a tattered awning stretched out from the roof to offer some small measure of shade to the couple of men sitting on plastic milk crates in front of the building. A middle-aged man was whittling on a dried gourd, every now and then blowing into the stem to produce musical tones. But he'd frown unhappily with the result and return to carefully carving on the husk some more. Smoking a hand-rolled cig, the young man was dressed in only denim shorts, his lean body rippling with hard muscle.

Outside of the small patch of shade was a swayback horse and a bicycle, both lashed securely to a piece of lead pipe sticking out of the ground. The rusty bike seemed to have been there for years, and the horse had seen better days. Its back was deeply bowed, and the coat dappled with scars. The chestnut mare was trembling from the tremendous effort of simply standing upright. It was plain to see that soon the beast would get aced from sheer age to become boots and belts, the flesh smoked into jerky, and the bones boiled down into glue for the crossbow arrows. Even in death, the horse would serve its owners.

As the companions pushed open the screen door, the young man waved his cig in greeting, and Jak caught a whiff of the smoke, some awful mix of cornsilk and maryjane. Obviously a local taste.

The interior of the tavern was dark. The windows were boarded shut, probably to keep out the wind-blown sand and to prevent drunks from smashing the irreplaceable sheets of predark glass. The cool air was smoky from the fumes of the lamps on the tables. In the flickering glow of the lanterns, the companions could see that the tavern was nearly empty. Aside from a couple of scantily dressed gaudy sluts sitting at a table near the bar. One of the table legs was short, and supported by an adobe brick to make the piece of furniture stay level.

Flashing fake smiles, the women perked up as the companions entered. But when none of the outlanders seemed interested, the women let the expressions fade away, then went back to playing a game of dominos and smoking their cigs. Behind them, a flight of stairs leading to the second floor from where there came the unmistakable sounds of couples having enthusiastic sexual intercourse.

Warily glancing around, Ryan saw that the walls were made of the original redbrick, and displayed a lot of predark posters of different cities from around the world. Obviously, loot from a travel agency. The posters were torn and faded, but Mildred felt a lump form in her throat at the sight of New York and the mighty Empire State Building, London and Big Ben, San Francisco and the Golden Gate Bridge, the ultramodern Opera House in Sydney Australia...

With a sigh, Mildred turned away from the depressing sight. Gone. All of the once-great cities were long gone now, either crumbling into ruins or merely radioactive holes in the fused ground.

Across the tavern was an ornate grandfather clock in the far corner, softly clicking, and nearby stood a huge grand piano. Not an upright, or spinet, or even a baby grand, but a full-size, concert-class grand piano. Then the physician did a double take. The damn thing was enormous! The black veneer had peeled away in spots, exposing the dark wood underneath, but the lid was raised showing that all of the strings were still intact. Just incredible.

"How get in?" Jak asked, glancing at the man-size front door.

"Must have been here originally," Krysty theorized. "Or else one of the rear walls was missing and they hauled it inside before putting up the adobe bricks."

The teen nodded. Yep, made sense. The simple answers were usually correct.

The tables in the tavern were everything from an office desk to a wooden door placed on top of a refrigerator lying sideways on the floor. At the far end of the room was a counter made of wooden boards laid on more orange highway crash barrels. A bald man in an apron was wiping down the counter with a rag. His shirt was cut off at the shoulders, displaying numerous tattoos, including a vaguely familiar compass and square. It took Doc a minute before he recognized the ancient symbol of the Freemasons. The ancient fraternity had survived the nuke war? Well, well, his father would have been highly pleased to know that. God rest his soul.

Filling the wall behind the bartender was a jigsaw mirror composed of countless shapes and sizes, but the reflection made the tavern seem brighter and larger. Wooden shelves around the mirror were lined with drinking containers of every type imaginable—glass tumblers, ceramic mugs, crystal goblets and plastic cups bearing the colorful logos of famous football teams. The warriors of the gridiron reduced to amusing figures for the grim soldiers of the Deathlands to puzzle over.

With Ryan leading the way, the companions choose a large redwood table that had formerly been a spool of industrial cable. The round table was situated near the empty fireplace where they could keep a watch on the front door. Taking chairs from other tables, the companions sat and placed their blasters on the tabletop to deter any trouble from drunks.

"Hey, Gertie!" the bartender hollered, still rubbing the counter. "Customers!"

From out of a back room exploded a mannish woman with a broken nose, tattoos and close-cropped blond hair. Her dress was made of a hundred different squares of material in a bewildering array of colors. Gertie was also wearing a greasy apron more suitable for arc welding than serving. Then to belie the rough demeanor, the woman boasted a tremendous bosom. It was absolutely colossal, barely contained in the patchwork dress. Every man in the room sneaked an appreciative glance, and every woman gave an expression of sympathy. Her back had to be in agony at the end of the day from hauling around that amount of jiggling weight.

"Oh, it's you folks," Gertie said, frowning as she approached the companions. "Thought you'd be eating with the baron."

"Not today. What do you have?" Ryan asked, sidestepping the issue. The less folks knew about their biz, the better.

"Whaddaya got?" she shot back, resting a fist on her hip in the style of every waitress in the history of the world.

Reaching into a pocket, Ryan laid a couple live rounds of brass on the table. They were .22-caliber shells, a size that didn't fit any of the weapons used by the companions. But for most of the Deathlands, ammo was the only currency that mattered, and it always got the best exchange rate.

In frank appreciation, the woman greedily stared at the brass, then sighed. "Ain't worth shit here," Gertie stated, scratching her head. "Sorry. Just wanted to see if you were trying to pull rank or something. But we heard what ya did for the baron. The meal's on the house."

Across the room, the gaudy sluts looked up at that, their cigs drooping in stern disapproval.

"Of course, that doesn't cover shine or sluts," Gertie hastily amended. "We love the boy, but we gotta make a living, ya know?"

"No problem," Ryan said, rolling the cartridge across the wooden surface. "Food and shine."

Gertie made the catch with one hand and bit the cartridge to make sure it wasn't corroded or varnished wood. Satisfied, she tucked it away between her ample breasts.

With the amount of sheer cleavage on display, J.B. casually wondered what else was hidden there. Mebbe a couple war wags, or a small ville?

"For chow, we got some roast prairie dog, very nice. Then lizard stew and fried rabbit. Plus, there's some roast horse that probably won't ace you too quickly if you're strong."

"We'll have the rabbit," Mildred decided. There were a lot of unsavory things that could be tossed into a stew to make it last longer, some of them extremely unhealthy.

"Smart choice. This ain't the baron's table, and sure as drek ain't no redoubt." Gertie smiled generously, scratching under a breast. "But the rabbit is fresh, and it wasn't a mutie. Well, not much of one, anyway. What's a couple legs among friends, eh?"

Galvanized motionless, the companions said nothing as the soft hissing of the alcohol lantern ruled the table, the noise seeming unnaturally loud. Then Ryan slowly looked up at the woman.

"What was that word you used?" Ryan demanded, trying to fake indifference.

Puzzled, Gertie started to repeat the old joke about extra legs, then realized it was the other part they meant. "Shitfire, ain't you folks ever heard the legend of the redoubts?" She laughed, her plump breasts jiggling outrageously.

None of the companions spoke or moved.

"Guess not," Gertie muttered. "Well, the short version is that there's some sorta underground fort up in the Mohawk Mountains near a bridge, and it's filled with blasters and bread, and wags and all sort of wonderful drek."

Placing both hands on the table, she leaned forward, the position straining her dress to the breaking point. "Guarded by armored muties, of course." She grinned, enjoying their stunned reactions. The stupe bastards were listening as if this was important. Nobody was even looking down her dress. "And even the black doors chills ya if you touch it wrong. Zap! You're ash in the wind."

"Really? Sounds fascinating," Doc whispered, his hands knuckle-white on his ebony walking stick. "And, uh, where was that again, dear lady?"

Standing straight, Gertie shifted her stance to ease her aching lower back. "Dunno, just somewhere in the hills. Near a bridge, I think. Or was it a mine?" She jerked a thumb at the bartender. "Buy him a couple drinks, and Cougar will tell ya all sorts of stuff."

"You bet I will!" Cougar promised from behind the counter, crossing his herculean arms. "Supposed to have booze by the gallon, and barrels of brass!"

"And dancing girls!" a drunk shouted from a corner table. "And clean water! And boots made of silk!"

In short order, the rest of the people in the place

took up the cry, adding wonders and delights, until the place roared with laughter. Only the companions stayed quiet at their table, an island of silence in the boisterous tavern. Realizing that they were starting to stand out from the crowd, the companions joined in with the rest, and started making up impossible things. Solid-gold blasters! Air wags! Vids! Medicine that could cure rad sickness! Toothpaste!

"Sounds aces to me," Ryan said when the laughter slowed down at last. "So why are you here, and not searching for this redoubt?"

"Oh, lots of folks have gone looking," Cougar said, giving a wink. "But nobody ever came back."

"Where was that again, the More-Walk Mountains?" J.B. asked, deliberately getting the name wrong to test their reaction.

"No, the Mohawk Mountains," a gaudy slut added. "They're just to the west and north of here. Can't miss 'em."

"Thanks," Cougar jeered, giving the woman a dirty look. He had been planning to string the outlanders along into buying drinks for the rest of the night with that bit of info.

"Mutie shit, I say," Gertie added with a rude snort, turning to walk away. Then she added over a shoulder, "Underground forts, metal doors…blind norad, what a load of drek!" Still laughing, the waitress went into the back room, and there came the sound of rattling pots and pans.

"Mother Gaia, how is this possible?" Krysty

asked urgently, her voice hard with tension. "Think somebody found a redoubt?"

"Lots of people have before," Ryan admitted. "But they generally end up chilling each other and that keeps the bases secret."

"Still, this gives us the option of climbing, rather than trying to swim upstream to reach Blaster Base One," Mildred added softly.

"Don't like this," Ryan confessed, worrying a fist into his palm. "Anything that seems too good to be true, most often is. I'm just wondering if this is a lucky break or another damn trap."

"Baron Harmond would know," Doc added succinctly.

"Mebbe this is why he had the stable hand send us here."

"Mebbe."

Just then Gertie appeared, carrying a wooden board stacked with hubcaps piled with steaming meat. There was also a ceramic jug with a cork in the top, and a collection of coffee mugs.

"Eat fast," Ryan directed. "Then we go see the baron."

"I'll be fragging delighted when we leave his pesthole," J.B. added with unaccustomed vehemence. "There are just too damn many odd things going on here, and I'll be a lot happier once Broke Neck is growing small behind us."

"Amen to that," Doc mumbled, stoically digging into his meal.

Chapter Ten

Whistling a tune, the mountain man strolled along the predark bridge. The asphalt was barely cracked, and the structure was as strong as ever. Down below on either side were only misty depths, the bottom of the canyon lost from sight.

Thankfully, the metal girders didn't shake in the least as he walked along, even with a heavy haunch of dripping meat draped across his broad shoulders. The hunting had been excellent that day and he'd aced a norm deer. The man smacked his lips in delight. With proper curing, this much meat meant that he would live through the coming winter. The flatlanders often bitched about the acid rain. Moose crap. Let them try living through a season of acid snow!

Reaching the other side of the bridge, the hunter suddenly paused, every nerve tingling with danger. Swiftly his eyes swept back and forth, but there was nothing to be seen but the bare rocks of the mountain pass and a few scraggy bushes.

With a curse, he shrugged off the carcass and drew both of his blasters, a remade predark and a homie. There was something inside the bushes that reflected something shiny.

At the sight of the weapons, the basilisk rose to its full height and towered over the horrified man. Almost dropping his blasters, the hunter stared in horror at the twinkling lights and flexing steel armature inside the pulsating gelatinous mass. What the nuking hell kind of mutie was this?

Sensing the target was disorientated, the basilisk fell upon the man, covering him completely. Surrounded by purplish jelly, the hunter fired both blasters, the lead rounds tearing through the translucent material and hitting the nearby rocks to ricochet away into the canyon.

In response, the basilisk started to tighten around the man, its acidic flesh dissolving his outer layer of clothing and hair. Holding his breath inside the hardening ooze, the hunter fired again and again at the twinkling lights set into the flexible skeleton running through the creature. Then he abruptly stopped as his eyesight vanished, the orbs in his sizzling head gone completely white. Opening his mouth to scream, the man felt the ooze fill his mouth and force itself down his throat. A horrible burning sensation filled his world, and the blasters spoke one last time, the pitted muzzles pressed tight against the man's heaving chest.

Moving back behind the bushes, the basilisk-class guardian settled down to digest the meal.

Abandoned on the rocky ledge, the haunch of

deer soon became covered with black ants, the horde of busy insects effectively doing to the piece of deer the exact same thing that the basilisk was doing to the man in its belly.

On the nameless bridge, the cold winds moaned softly, as a small vid cam hidden in the bushes recording everything and transmitting the encoded signal into the overcast sky.

IN BROKE NECK VILLE, Baron Harmond sat bolt upright in his bed and screamed. "Traitor!" the boy cried, clutching his throbbing temples. Blood trickled from his nose. "Guards! Sound the alarm! Guards!"

Instantly, the heavy door to the bedroom was thrown open by several sec men waving blasters.

"What is it, Baron?" one asked, looking around for any sign of an attacker. But the books and the room seemed normal and undisturbed.

"Too late." The boy sighed, covering his face with both hands. Tears started rolling down his cheeks. "It's too late. It's already here."

"Who is, my lord?"

Raising his anguished face to the window, Baron Harmond looked down upon the ville for the last time. "Death," he replied simply, the word seeming to fill the room.

THE COMPANIONS WERE finishing their meal when the screen door to the tavern slammed open and a sec man staggered inside. He went directly to the counter and grabbed on to the planks as if he were drowning at sea.

"This could be trouble," Ryan said, laying aside his knife.

Wiping his hubcap clean with a piece of corn bread, Jak stuffed the morsel into his mouth. "Ain't bleeding," he mumbled. "Blood on boots."

"So somebody else is aced," Mildred said with a frown.

"Looks like, yeah."

Under the table, J.B. moved his hands and racked the bolt on his Uzi machine pistol. "Mebbe our coldhearts got tired of waiting and have come hunting for us."

"Good," Ryan growled, wiping the blade clean before tucking it away. "Let them come. We'll settle this in lead."

"Be careful what you wish for, my dear friend," Doc rumbled. "You may get it."

"Hi, Dave, what'll it be?" Cougar said, his friendly greeting fading as he studied the guard.

"Shine," Dave gasped, then shouted, "I said shine, ya nuking feeb!"

Startled by the outburst, Cougar laid down his rag and took a full bottle off a shelf, along with a cracked shotglass.

"Shitfire, what's the matter with you?" the bartender asked, placing both items on the counter.

Grabbing the bottle, the sec man smacked the

glass away. It tumbled off the counter and went flying to shatter on the floor. Biting out the cork on top, Dave chugged the bottle's contents until his face began to turn red for lack of air, then he slammed it down so hard the glasses behind the counter rattled.

"Harry is chilled," he gasped. "I—I was on recce outside the wall when I found him…it…him. Blind norad, there he was tied spread-eagle to a boulder, his hands and feet lashed behind the rock, leaving him helpless as a blind kitten."

"Is he…"

The sec man nodded.

"Was it cannies?" the bartender asked, taking the guard by the shoulder. "Or was it muties? Talk, man! What happened to Harry?"

"Everything," David whispered, shuddering. "He was taken apart like you was cleaning a blaster, each…piece…was sitting in a bowl of blood, some of them still…attached…"

As the guard took another long drink from the bottle, everybody in the tavern rushed closer to hear more of the grisly details.

"Okay, it's them, all right," Ryan declared, pulling out the SIG-Sauer to rack the slide. "Let's go."

Pushing away their chairs, the companions moved through the tavern and into the bright sunlight.

"How could any human being do such things to another?" Krysty muttered. Then the woman realized that she had just answered her own question. When coldhearts acted like this, they weren't normal people anymore, just beasts drunk on human blood.

An alarm bell started to ring, and the companions could see sec men running along the top of the wall, loading longblasters, waving crossbows and shouting orders.

"Something wrong about this," Mildred said, pulling out the clip from her MP-5 rapidfire to check the load, then slapping it back in again. "These assholes usually only do nightcreeps."

"Change how do, means dif goal," Jak stated, shrugging his jacket into a more comfortable position.

"Which means they know we are here," Doc concluded, pulling out the Ruger and LeMat.

"Let's try to save one for questioning," J.B. suggested.

"No promises," Krysty said, yanking the bolt on her MP-5. The rapidfire was down to its last clip, but she flipped the selector to full-auto. The woman wasn't going to take any chances with these coldhearts. There was a strange feeling in her mind, a growing sense of unease. She wasn't exactly sure what that meant, and that worried her a great deal.

Clenching his fists, Ryan felt a stab of pain from the bandaged wound in his right forearm. Damn, not fully healed yet. He had been afraid of that.

Holstering the blaster, Ryan whistled sharply

and held out a hand. J.B. released the Uzi, letting it hang from the canvas strap as he took the scatter-gun from behind his back and tossed it to his friend.

Deftly, Ryan made the catch with his left hand, then worked the pump-action and started to remove 12-gauge cartridges from the loops on the sling and stuffing them into the belly port.

"Okay, let's get the horses," Ryan declared, resting the scattergun on a shoulder and heading for the stables.

As the armed companions started along the sunny street, a muffled explosion came from the direction of the front gate. Swiftly changing course, the companions broke into a run. As they got close, a sec man on the wall above the gate snarled a curse and aimed his longblaster at something outside the ville.

But before he could shoot, there came the sound of a hundred blasters banging away in tight unison. The sec man was torn apart by the fusillade, his riddled body flying off the top of the trailer to sail into the ville and fall onto the hard ground with a sickening crunch of breaking bones.

"Rapidfires!" Ryan cursed, swinging up the shotgun to brace it with both hands. "That has to be them!"

Suddenly, a muffled thump sounded from beyond the gate. The telltale noise sent chills down the spines of the companions.

"Down!" J.B. yelled, diving for the ground.

The rest of the group did the same, and a few

ticks later the roof of a nearby building loudly erupted in fiery explosion. The sides of the structure cracked apart, and in ragged stages the building broke into pieces and collapsed into the street, screaming people and broken masonry tumbling down to mix together in a hellish avalanche.

"Gren launcher!" Jak snarled, rising to his knees. The alarm bell was still ringing, but scattered shots could now be heard from all over the ville. The dull roar of the black powder weapons punctuated by the sharp rattle of the predark rapidfires.

"Worse than that," J.B. corrected, "I'd say it was a combo."

"A working combo?" Krysty demanded, her hair flexing wildly in every direction.

"Gotta be," Ryan said calmly, twisting his grip on the scattergun. A combo—the Trader used to have one of those mil blasters, but only one, and he'd saved it for triple-bad emergencies. The damn thing was the deadly mix of an M-16 rapidfire with a big-ass 40 mm gren launcher slung underneath. The Deathlands warrior had faced a lot of iron in his travels, but those were the worst. It was no wonder that they had been the standard wep of the predark army.

"Okay, the coldhearts found a functioning M-16/M-203," Mildred said, staying in a crouch. "But there's no way they have more than a couple grens."

Over the clanging of the bell, and the assorted yelling, there came four muffled thumps, evenly spaced apart. The companions took cover again, and several more adobe buildings were blown apart. Screaming people filled the smoky air. Only now, reddish flames started rising from the smashed masonry, huge volumes of thick black smoke rising into the sky to blot out the blazing sun.

"Willie peter?" Jak asked, blinking from the acrid fumes.

"That was thermite," J.B. corrected, swallowing with some difficulty. "Dark night, even I don't have one of those anymore!"

"Stables?" Krysty asked, putting a wealth of urgency into the word.

"Not yet," Ryan snapped, reaching out to grab a sec man running past.

"Where's the mill?" he demanded, shaking the guard.

"The what?" the terrified sec man asked, struggling to get loose. "Let go ya idiot! We need everybody on the wall! Coldhearts are attacking!"

"Mill!" Ryan repeated, tightening his grip. "Where's the bastard powder mill? The secret place that Bateman makes his gunpowder?"

"I don't know where it is," the sec man lied, flicking his eyes to the right for only a heartbeat.

But Ryan caught the motion and released the man. So the gunpowder mill was hidden at the south side of the ville, eh? Good. With any luck, that might just be far enough away from the front gate to not be hit.

The multiple combos chattered again outside

the ville, and more guards tumbled from the wall. As the screaming and shouting grew louder, J.B. frowned in concentration. The combos didn't sound exactly the same as they had the last time they fired. Altered somehow.

"Hot pipe, how many coldhearts are there?" the sec man gasped, working the bolt on his longblaster with shaking hands.

"Go see for yourself," Ryan barked, giving him a shove. "Get moving! Protect the baron!"

The sec man seemed confused at first, then he took off at a run, starting for the front gate, then curving away to sprint for the barracks.

"They're using different ammo," J.B. stated. "Not soft lead or hardball rounds anymore. Mebbe armor-piercing."

"My guts tell me that this is just a diversion," Ryan stated with conviction. "I'm betting that they'll hit the mill next. That will blow half the ville to hell. In the smoke and confusion, they can easily break inside, and there will be nobody to stop them."

"Except us," Doc said, thumbing back the hammers on both of his big-bore handblasters.

"Attack a ville with only four blasters?" J.B. snorted, hunching his shoulders as a cloud of smoke moved along the ground, hiding him for a moment. "Even with combos, that's crazy talk!"

"We did once," Jak reminded as there came a flash of light brighter than the sun from the south side of the ville.

Frantically, the companions dived to the dirt again and covered their ears. A split second later the deafening concussion of the exploding gunpowder mill rolled along the streets, blowing out glass windows and ripping off roof tiles. Sec men sailed off the wall to fly out of sight, their death screams lost in the strident blast.

Groaning as if in pain, several of the trailers shook, then came free from their moorings and fell sideways to start rolling across into the croplands, leaving huge gaps in the ville perimeter. The ground shook, horses screamed, a column of fire rose from somewhere to the north, and then a dense cloud of black smoke rolled across the ville, turning the afternoon into midnight.

Moving quickly, the companions took cover under a stone archway just as the expected rain of debris arrived. An assortment of objects dropped from the murky sky—broken bits of machinery, smoking sand bags, a bucket, a shoe and countless body parts.

"Gaia!" Krysty coughed, waving away the smoke and dust. "They're blowing the whole ville apart!"

Just then, four black shapes appeared from out of the billowing fumes, the figures moving slowly.

"Bikes!" J.B. cursed, swinging up the Uzi. "Ace them!"

The companions cut loose with their blasters, sending out a hellstorm of lead. But the shapes kept moving past them without slowing or deviating from the course. As the two-wheelers came closer, Ryan cursed at the sight of the four riderless bikes rolling along, the black frames marked with ricochets but otherwise unharmed. Tricked!

"Everybody, head for the stables!" Ryan bellowed. "We have to get those horses!"

Taking off in the opposite direction, Mildred glanced backward to see two men step into the street from an alleyway, each holding the unmistakable outline of an M-16/M-203 combination rapidfire.

Mildred opened her mouth to shout a warning when somebody dressed in rags and holding a raised knife charged out of a doorway.

"Die, rist!" Lucinda screamed, rushing forward.

The two men turned at the cry and cut loose with their weps, the converging barrage of hot lead cutting Lucinda down before she could take another step.

Time seemed to slow as Mildred stared in shock at the still body of the woman who had just saved her life by trying to end it. No words came to mind, but in a rush of emotion, the physician braced her MP-5 against a hip just as the rest of the companions spun, leveling their blasters and started firing.

The yammering fusillade knocked down the two outlanders, but they incredibly got back up and took refuge behind a pile of rubble.

"Sons of bitches are wearing body armor!" J.B. cursed, unfolding the wire stock of the Uzi and tucking it under an arm. "Aim for their heads!"

But even before the others could react, there was a motion in the air and something large fluttered down from the smoky sky.

With the instincts honed in a thousand battles, Ryan dived to the side and hit the ground rolling. Jak and J.B. were only a split second behind the man, and the descending net only draped over Mildred, Krysty and Doc.

"By the Three Kennedys!" Doc snarled, swatting at the strands with his handblasters. He fired twice into the air, but couldn't aim the blasters at the sticky net. The ebony walking stick was thrust into his belt, but the net made it impossible for him to holster the weps to reach it.

Burping the Heckler & Koch MP-5, Mildred tried to shoot the net, but the vibrating rapidfire wasn't designed for precision aiming, and she only hit a nearby wall, a spray of stone chips from the impacting lead striking her in the face. As the rapidfire ran out of ammo, she let it drop and fought to reach her Czech-made ZKR target pistol. Radio-controlled, electric motorcycles, rapidfires, bulletproof body armor, maybe these attackers really were agents of Operation Chronos like Doc had suggested! It was a chilling thought, and the physician redoubled her efforts to reach the revolver.

The two outlanders popped up from behind the rubble and sent short bursts of autofire at Ryan and J.B, while Jak whipped out a knife and slid it across the ground to the trapped people. Krysty grabbed the blade and started slashing at the restraining net. But then a second net fluttered down on top of the three captives, closely followed by a third that knocked the knife from her grip.

The heavy weight of the multiple nets was making it difficult for the three companions to move, and with the clouds of smoke drifting along the street it was now impossible for them to get a clear view of what was happening. Trapped, but still armed, the men couldn't risk shooting any more for fear of acing their own people.

The Uzi cut loose with a blast, followed by the roar of the scattergun, then the telltale boom of Jak's big .357 Magnum Colt. Those were answered by the chatter of an M-16, the sound of the rounds hitting, and the wild ricochets mixing with the musical ringing of the spent brass hitting the cobblestone road to bounce around.

"Mother Gaia, help me now!" Krysty intoned in a desperate prayer, and cold strength flowed into the woman like silver waters.

Standing easily, the redhead grasped the net and started to pull apart the resilient black nylon cord as if it were sewing thread. Squirming sideways, Mildred got an arm loose and started to bang away at the outlanders down the street. Warily, she also tried to keep a watch above for any more nets. Although what the physician would do if one appeared, she had no idea.

The combo rapidfires spoke again in unison. Somewhere a man cried out in pain, followed by a woman's scream. The weapons of the companions answered, but farther away this time.

Suddenly in motion, Doc was alongside Krysty and together they started to widen the rip in the nets. With a curse, Mildred lowered her empty blaster just as a familiar-looking canister came bouncing along the ground, spewing thick trails of green smoke.

"Grenade!" Mildred cried, frantically throwing the revolver. The ZKR hit the canister, and it rolled back toward the pile of rubble.

But then a second canister hit the ground directly in front of them and a fourth net fluttered from the sky.

As the oily green fumes flowed over them, Mildred fought to reach the gren as Doc and Krysty continued to try to get free. But at the first whiff, the physician became dizzy and a rush of relaxing warmth spread through her body. What the…that wasn't a smoke gren, but sleep gas!

"Cover your mouths!" Mildred shouted in warning as the fumes swirled thick around them. "Breath through a sleeve!"

However, it was already too late. The three companions were starting to move more slowly, more clumsily, their breathing labored and shallow. Even Krysty's enhanced strength had no power over the gas. Somewhere in the roiling banks of black smoke and green chem fumes, four M-16 rapidfires chattered out a long burst. Glass shattered, a dog began to howl, voices cursed, the Uzi spoke from far away, then the Steyr answered.

Reeling from the airborne drugs, Mildred dropped to her knees as Krysty shuddered all over and toppled to the ground, the brief charge of strength neutralized by the mil gas.

As the world got hazy, furious anger welled within Doc, only to be replaced by a terrible numbness, and the scholar felt himself unwillingly slide into the artificial sleep of chemical intoxication. His final conscious thoughts were of rage, then fear, and the terrible absolute certainty that after all of these long years, Operation Chronos finally had their hands on him once again.

Chapter Eleven

Studying the hooting mob of stickies pounding their suckers against the immaterial boundary of his forcefield, Delphi tried not to sigh. Back to square one again. So be it.

Pulling a crystal rod from within the voluminous sleeve of his spotless white garment, the cyborg extended it toward the slavering creatures and pressed hard with a thumb. A beam of soft green light extended to wash over the stickies and fully half of them ceased to pound on the shield.

"Excellent!" Delphi breathed, feeling a rush of excitement. This pack of mutants was responding even better than that group in Tucson. There was hope for the great project yet!

The angry hoots changed into expressions of curiosity, and Delphi eagerly upped the data flow, sending pictures into their twisted minds. One of the larger males picked up a stick and began to wave it around like a baton. Another did the same, except that he hit a nearby rock with the crude club, the images filling his mind showing the results if that had been the head of a norm.

Squatting in the hot sand, a female gathered two rocks and hit them together. She hooted at the pretty sparks, then paused and moved to a clump of dry weeds. She banged the rocks once more and the dead plants smoldered, then burst into flames.

Instantly, all of the stickies rushed to the little fire and hooted in delight. But none of them rushed into the crackling flames. Instead they stayed just outside the area of conflagration, watching the dancing firelight, the images growing stronger and more clear in their minds. Fire…was a friend. Wooden sticks would become spears with fire, and torches could light the night, allowing them to endlessly pursue two-legs. Use the torches to find the norms, then hit with clubs. This would yield much food for the little ones! No more starvation! The family would grow, become big, strong, rulers of the Deathlands!

"Yes, that's it, my pretties." Delphi chortled, increasing the power. The glow of the crystal rod illuminated his twisted face in hellish reflection. "Learn, my children. Learn!"

One of the stickies crumpled unconscious to the desert sand, and a baby went still, watery fluids dribbling from the misshapen mouth. But the rest seemed to stand taller and more aggressively as they tossed little sticks onto the burning weeds to create their very first campfire.

RIPPING…TEARING…cold laughter. Sluggishly, Doc came awake to the sound of rending cloth. Blinking hard to clear his vision, the scholar realized that he was lying on a field of grass. The air was cool, and the sun was setting, the cloudy sky dark and rumbling dangerously. How long had he been unconscious?

Trying to sit up, Doc discovered his wrists were bound with steel handcuffs. What in the world? Cold adrenaline filled Doc as he nervously looked around. The old man was in some sort of a glade, or perhaps a glen, surrounded by trees, with a little waterfall off to the side flowing right out of a large boulder as big as a house. Mildred lay nearby, her face slack in deep sleep. That was when he noticed his gunbelt was gone, along with his swordstick, and even his boots. A quick glance showed that Mildred was the same, stripped of everything that could possibly be used as an offensive wep. But if they were prisoners of Overproject Whisper, then why weren't they inside a redoubt? Something was very wrong here.

The sound of ripping material came again. Doc squinted to see into the shadows. In the center of the glen was a small campfire, and in the dancing red light he saw four men standing around a body lying supine on the grass. One of the men made a throwing motion, and something landed with a soft thud nearby. It was a blue cowboy boot with a steel toe.

Mouthing a curse, Doc felt unbridled outrage flood his tired body, burning away the sleepiness of the mil gas. That was Krysty's boot! In dread certainty, the Vermont scholar knew what the men were planning for his friend, and he rallied savagely against his steel bonds. He had to help her! But it was hopeless. There was no way he could escape his bonds.

As another boot landed in the soft grass, Doc heard Mildred mutter a foul expression not typical of the mild-mannered physician. He knew if the two of them didn't do something quickly…

The cruel laughter of the four men rose, and Doc tasted sour bile in his throat. Krysty was helpless. She had used the special strength that Gaia gave her in times of true emergency, but afterward the woman was totally drained, completely exhausted. Mix that with the mil sleep gas, and she would probably sleep through her entire ordeal. Until they aced her in the end when their lust was sated.

Looking frantically around for something to use, some trick to play, Doc saw only a concrete blockhouse across the grassy field, and four sleek motorcycles parked near a barbed-wire gate in the bushes. That was the exit! But it might as well be on the moon for all the good it would do them at the moment. Then he saw a pile of objects and recognized their blasters and other possessions. The stack was several yards away, brightly lit by the campfire. There was no way to sneak over there without being seen. More cloth was ripped and the laughter sounded again, lower, more guttural in tone.

Hawking softly, Mildred spit and started grunting softly. Doc saw that the woman was twisting a wrist against the handcuffs, red blood starting to show from her efforts. He whistled softly, and she stopped to stare at him quizzically. Doc nodded at her, then tilted his head toward the grass. After a moment Mildred's face brightened in comprehension. She grimly nodded in agreement, and lay down as if she were still unconscious, tilting her face so that the flicking light from the campfire cast a shadow across her features and hid her eyes.

Biting a lip, Doc started to think about his wife Emily, his children, and life before Operation Chronos took him away from his friends, and family. Memories started clouding his mind, and he felt madness start to overtake him, but the scholar fought it back with all of his will, and concentrated on how much he loved his wife. His Emily, his sweet dear Emily.... Suddenly a breath caught in his throat, and the time traveler started to weep uncontrollably, huge racking sobs shaking his body.

"What the fragging hell is that drek?" a voice said from the group, and a young man walked over to him, his shirt partially unbuttoned.

Maintaining the caterwauling, Doc was privately startled to recognize the man as the drunk from the tavern. So, there had been a spy in town, eh? The filthy traitor. That did explain a lot.

"Cut the drek, Tanner, or I'll beat you to death!" Alan Rogan ordered, brandishing a clenched fist.

Doc felt the full force of his misery flow out in

Get FREE BOOKS and a FREE GIFT when you play the...

LAS VEGAS

GAME

7

*Just scratch off
the gold box with a coin.
Then check below to see
the gifts you get!*

YES! I have scratched off the gold box. Please send me my **2 FREE BOOKS** and **gift for which I qualify.** I understand that I am under no obligation to purchase any books as explained on the back of this card.

If offer card is missing write to: Gold Eagle Reader Service, 3010 Walden Ave., P.O. Box 1867, Buffalo NY 14240-1867

BUSINESS REPLY MAIL
FIRST-CLASS MAIL   PERMIT NO. 717-003   BUFFALO, NY

POSTAGE WILL BE PAID BY ADDRESSEE

GOLD EAGLE READER SERVICE
3010 WALDEN AVE
PO BOX 1867
BUFFALO NY 14240-9952

NO POSTAGE
NECESSARY
IF MAILED
IN THE
UNITED STATES

a wail of despair, the tears flowing down his face. "My pills," he moaned. "My heart...the pills...I need my medication!"

"Pills? What pills?" Alan snarled, lowering the fist. "What in hell are you blubbering about, ya feeb?"

"Bad...heart..." Doc wheezed, tears flowing down his cheeks. "Can't breathe...must have... pills..." He then started to hyperventilate, breathing as fast as he could.

Alan started to reach for the old man, then drew back his hand in fright. Nuking hell, was the wrinklie sick? He looked okay. But he had also seen many old men just keel over and die, clutching their chests. Did Tanner have a bad heart? Or was it the Red Death?

"Okay, stay calm. Where are the fucking pills?" Alan demanded.

"Cane...in my cane..." Doc panted, trying to drool.

"In the cane?" Licking dry lips, Alan stared at the twitching wrinklie, then at the ebony walking stick lying on top of the pile of the weps and possessions they had taken from the unconscious outlanders. It was just a black cane the wrinklie used for walking. Certainly no damn wep. Alan could break it between his fingers! On the other hand, he was annoyed at being interrupted before the fun started, and saw no fragging reason to give the old man anything.

"Stuff it, or get chilled," Alan warned, drawing a blaster.

For Doc, this was the deciding moment. The

rumors were that these people chilled anybody who looked like Ryan, but captured people that resembled Doc alive. Until they were sure that person wasn't Doc. If they truly wanted him alive, they wouldn't hurt him. They'd threaten and bluster, but it would be a bluff. There was no other choice. Doc would have to gamble his life to save his friend. So be it.

Throwing back his head, Doc howled in misery at the darkening sky, raising both hands to rattle the cuffs. Then he began to cough, loud and hard.

Make it real, Doc commanded himself. You only have one chance at this.

"Cut that drek out!" snapped an inhuman voice from the three partially dressed men kneeling by the woman on the ground. Krysty was nearly naked from the waist up, her hair unmoving around her slack face.

"And right fragging now!" John added grimly, undoing his gunbelt.

Tightening his grip on the blaster, Alan debated the matter. He couldn't beat the old man unconscious or Delphi would have their beating hearts on a plate. And it sure didn't seem like he could frighten the wrinklie into submission. A gag would stop the screaming, but if the man really did need his pills for some sickness, then he might climb onboard the last train west. Delphi would then put the Rogans on right after him.

"Shitfire!" Alan growled, holstering the piece. "Just wait a tick, I'll get your damn pills!"

Giving no reply, Doc continued to heave with a racking cough.

Furiously, Alan walked over to the pile and lifted the stick. It was too light to make a good club, and the silver head was too small to do any real damage to a person, much less to a Rogan! Taking it by the end, Alan swung the stick a few times, getting a feeling for its weight and offensive capabilities. Which were zero. It was just a fucking cane the wrinklie used to walk. But he didn't see any pills attached. Mebbe inside?

"Here!" Alan snapped, tossing the stick to the crying man. "Open it, and shut the fuck up, or in spite of what Delphi says, I'll kick in your teeth!"

"My cane," Doc panted, cradling the stick. Then he smiled at the disgusted coldheart. "Thank you. But if I do say so, sir, I believe that these handcuffs are far more intelligent than yourself."

Startled by the abrupt transformation in speech, Alan could only gasp as the wrinklie twisted the silver lion head of the stick, pulled out a steel sword and buried it in his throat.

Blind from the pain, Alan clutched at his neck, cutting his fingers on the razor-sharp length of Spanish steel. Rising smoothly, Doc shoved the sword in deeper until the tip came out the other side, red blood gushing from the front and back of the dying coldheart.

Gurgling and choking, Alan fought for air as he started drowning in his own blood. Clawing for his blaster, Alan found it was gone, and on impulse jerked backward to free himself. Spraying blood with every beat of his weakening heart, Alan opened his mouth to call for help when Mildred rose and slammed the butt of the blaster directly onto the rear *lambdoid fissure* of his skull with surgical precision. There was a soft crunch of bones, and Alan shook violently all over as if struck by lightning. Exhaling his last long breath, he fell to the ground, dead before he landed on the soft green grass.

Frantically, Doc started searching the clothing of the corpse for a key, while Mildred braced the bulky revolver in both of her sticky hands. Her fingers were covered with her own blood, making the grip slippery, so she spit on the blaster and managed to thumb back the hammer. Damnedest thing, though, the gun felt satiny-smooth, as if it was brand-spanking new and right out of the manufacturer's box.

"Well?" Mildred whispered impatiently.

"I found some brass," Doc confirmed, displaying a fistful of speed loaders. "But he doesn't have the key."

"Damn! Well, then, it's been nice knowing ya, Theophilus."

"You, too, Millie."

As the laughing men began to drag off Krysty's pants, Mildred leveled the weapon, testing its weight. Gauging the gentle breeze on her cheek, she noted the placement of the campfire, took the rising air thermals into account, made one last adjustment for height and fired a fast three times.

A hundred feet away, all three of the men cried out. Clutching different parts of their bodies, the coldhearts fell over to reveal Krysty. Her pants were undone, but still on her hips.

Moving fast, Doc lunged for the pile of their possessions as Mildred pumped the last three rounds into the farthest motorcycle. The range was impossible for a short-barrel handgun, but the gods who had stood by her side in the Olympics so very long ago were again with her this night. The wide bandolier of fat 40 mm shells for a combo rapidfire jumped, then exploded, flame and thunder filling the glen in growing fury as each detonating gren set off the next in line until it seemed like doomsday had arrived all over again.

Crouching low, Mildred dumped out the spent shells and tried to use the speed loader, but couldn't manage it in the dark with the cuffs on her wrists. Then from the very heart of the staggering fireball the battered bike unexpectedly erupted in a searing blue electrical explosion, fat sparks spraying out in every direction.

"Nuking hell, the healer's got a blaster!" a huge barrel-chested man screamed, getting back to his feet, a hand clutching his stomach. "Somebody ace that crazy bitch!"

Pocketing the useless brass, Mildred shoved the empty blaster into her belt and desperately raced for the pile of their belongings. In the dancing firelight, she scowled at the lack of blood on the outlander's clothing. Goddammit, she had forgotten about their body armor!

Already pawing through the pile, Doc grabbed his revolvers and fired from a kneeling position, the two big-bore blasters blowing hellfire in a deadly cacophony. Both were fully loaded, since Doc had never gotten off a single shot before they were captured back in Broke Neck, and now he needed every damn one of the rounds. The LeMat would be impossible to reload wearing handcuffs, and there was no sight of the pouch full of spare brass for the deadly Ruger.

Praying that his gambit would work again, Doc started boldly toward the outlanders. They didn't seem to want to harm him in any way. Well, this was the time to test the theory to its fullest. It was chilling time!

Snarling, Doc charged, acrid smoke exploding from the black-powder LeMat, while the Ruger boomed stilettos of flame.

Bypassing her med kit, Mildred grabbed an MP-5, worked the bolt and sprayed the three Rogans across the legs. Only one dropped, but from the cursing, her rounds had obviously hit flesh this time.

Pausing to grab the three gunbelts, Mildred searched for the grens, but couldn't find any. Burping the rapidfire, Mildred joined Doc in charging for the three remaining bikes. The physician tossed the old man his gunbelt and maintained cover while Doc hastily reloaded the Ruger. Loose brass tumbled through his fingers, but he got the blaster packed and closed the cylinder with a hard click.

"Ready!" Doc said, firing both blasters, desperately keeping count and trying to figure out their next move.

Meanwhile, Mildred buckled on her own gunbelt and clumsily slapped a fresh clip into the exhausted rapidfire.

"Alan?" a voice called from the shadows. "Alan?"

"I think he's chilled!" somebody answered in a twisted mockery of a human voice.

"Fragging bitch! I want her alive, ya hear!" the first voice commanded. "At least long enough for me to ace her. But don't hurt Tanner!"

Firing at the shouts, Doc felt his blood run cold at that announcement. Tanner. They knew his name. If he remembered correctly, Mildred and Krysty had only called him by the nickname of Doc while they were in the net, so how did these coldhearts know his name? Doc grimaced. Unless they were agents for Operation Chronos!

"Any bright ideas?" Mildred asked, burping the MP-5 in short, controlled bursts. The coldhearts had quickly spread out and were lying on the ground, making it much harder to target them without exposing herself. They were also starting to shoot back with their handblasters, but only at

Mildred. Wisely, she moved closer to Doc, and the incoming barrage of lead stopped instantly.

In the calm air of the glen, the smoke from the LeMat was making it difficult to see things, the cover both a blessing and a curse to the two companions. Any second now, the coldhearts would figure out that Krysty was the key and turn their blasters on her. Then it would be all over. Seconds counted. But what to do?

"How about using those bikes to charge the Visigoths?" Doc asked, breaking the Ruger to dump spent brass and hastily reload. More brass was lost, and he only managed to get in five rounds before running out. "The best defense is a good offense, Ryan always likes to say."

"Yeah, him and Sun Tzu," Mildred growled, working the bolt to clear a jam in the ejector port. Glancing at a motorcycle, she saw a blinking red light on the dashboard. That might only be a car alarm, but somehow she got the feeling these coldhearts wouldn't depend on a tooting horn to protect their possessions. There would be anti-pers boobies, or worse, without a doubt.

"I think we're on foot," Mildred retorted.

Suddenly the three coldhearts broke cover and dashed across the glen, but in different directions. Two were heading for the blockhouse, while the really big man went for the unconscious Krysty.

Dropping the inaccurate MP-5, Mildred drew

her ZKR and banged a shot at the guy. He stumbled and grunted, but still reached Krysty. Grabbing a fistful of her long hair, the coldheart hauled the unconscious woman erect. Mildred felt herself flinch from the imagined pain of having the living filaments pulled that way. If Krysty had been faking before, she certainly was knocked out now. The pain would have been unimaginable.

"Lower those blasters!" Edward bellowed, placing a knife to the woman's throat. "Or I'll cut this bitch like a—"

Dropping the knife, the man released Krysty and slumped to the ground, giving a loud moan. Revealed standing behind him was a slim young woman with long black hair, holding a bloody rock. As the big man went flat, she picked up the fallen knife and pounced upon the man, hacking and slashing like a wild thing.

"Two down," Mildred quipped, turning for the other men. But they were already scrambling inside the blockhouse as she got a bead. The physician fired again, and only hit the metal frame of the doorway, the slug musically ricocheting inside as the steel door slammed shut. Then it loudly bolted tight.

"And we have an ally, so it seems," Doc muttered, advancing toward Krysty and brandishing both blasters. "You there, girl! Come with us, if you want to live!"

Nodding eagerly, the young woman tucked the

bloody knife into her belt and grabbed Krysty under the arms to start dragging her toward the bikes.

No, the stranger was older than a teen. Doc saw the face and full figure through the thinning smoke. She was a beautiful young woman.

Slinging the rapidfire over a shoulder, Mildred rushed to assist, while Doc grabbed the boots and shirt off the ground. Modesty was a thing of the past these days, but without some sort of protection the cold desert night could ace Krysty just as fast as during the hot day. Then again, this was a wooded glen. How long had they been asleep? It had been early afternoon when the ville was attacked, and now it was dusk, going into night. Where were they?

"I'll take her," Mildred said, draping the limp Krysty across her shoulders. Thank God for her years of training. Every EMT in the world knew how to do a fireman's carry. The tall redhead was heavy, but manageable. But more importantly, still alive.

"Thanks for the help…" Mildred paused.

"Lily, I'm Lily," she replied. "Can…can I come with you please, master? I will serve you well."

"Of course you're coming with us." Mildred grunted, hauling the unconscious redhead toward the gate in the bushes. "But we don't keep slaves." She paused awkwardly, then held out a hand. "Here! Reload that, and keep me covered!"

Utterly astonished, Lily stared in wonder at the huge blaster and speed loaders she held, the

polished metal shining like a dream in the reflected light of the campfire. A wep. The strangers had given her a wep! Remembering what the
Rogans always did with a blaster, Lily carefully
opened the cylinder to look inside. All spent.
Removing the dead brass, she used the speed
loader, amazed at how easy it was. Then Lily
flipped her wrist to snap the handblaster shut with
a sharp click and thumbed back the hammer. She
didn't consider blasters tech, merely tools, like
hammers or a fry pan.

"We'll never make it on foot," Lily declared, new
resolution in her voice. "If you can drive the two-
wheelers, I know how to make them safe to touch
and not chill ya. I've watched them do it often
enough." The woman didn't want to touch the filthy
machines, but it was the only way to escape. The
dirty act would only be one more thing Lily forced
herself to do to survive.

Her heart pounding from the adrenaline in her
system, Mildred grunted at that pronouncement. So
she had been right about the lethal car alarm.
Mildred had expected no less from the slavers, or
cannies, or whoever the hell these bastards were.
Coldfire, Doc had said once before. But that was for
later. Run now, talk tomorrow.

"Deal!" Mildred snarled, changing directions.
"I'm Mildred, and that's Doc. Now move!"

In a burst of speed, Lily took off ahead of the
physician. By the time Mildred reached the remain-

ing motorcycles, Lily stepped back to reveal that all of the red warning lights were turned off and inert.

"Well done, Lily," the physician said, easing Krysty onto a cushioned seat.

Wiping her hands clean on her pants, the young woman smiled at the compliment. Then she cast a furtive glance toward the blockhouse and tightened her grip on the blaster. "They'll be coming out soon," she warned tersely. "And with grens."

"We surmised as much, dear lady. But now we are properly armed once more," Doc rumbled in his stentorian bass, opening the cargo compartment and lifting out one of the homie pipe bombs. There was no sign of the mil grens, but these would do for the nonce.

"Better and better," Mildred said, climbing onto the bike. "But this bomb will do nothing to that blockhouse. Any grens?"

"Sadly no, madam," Doc stated, pulling out a butane lighter and flicking the flame alive before applying it to the fuse. With a fast move, he sent the charge hurtling toward the barbed wire and broke glass gate in the bushes. "However, I do believe this may be more than sufficient to blow down their impromptu walls of Jericho!"

The strident blast shook the entire glen, sending birds flying from the trees and actually rattling the pots and pans around the campfire. Suddenly the door to the blockhouse swung open and the two coldhearts cut loose with the combos, the chattering rapidfires chewing a line of destruction along the ground toward Mildred and Lily.

The raven-haired woman gasped in horror, the blaster forgotten in her grip. But Mildred answered with a long burst of the MP-5, and Doc fanned the LeMat until it clicked empty, hoping the gunsmoke would aid them one last time to escape.

"There's boobies everywhere!" John shouted over the rattling rapidfire. "You'll never make it out of here alive!"

Firing once more, Doc started to reply when he caught a motion out of the corner of his vision, and turned to see something flying through the air to land in the campfire. A second later, a tremendous explosion rocked the night and the fire was obliterated, instantly casting the glen into darkness. Caught by surprise, Mildred and Doc both looked at Lily lowering an arm, another pipe bomb tucked into her belt. The rear cargo compartment of her motorcycle was open, showing ammo clips, MRE packs and what looked suspiciously like a pile of human scalps.

"Ignore what John says, it's a lie," Lily stated, shouldering the bag of brass. "There's nothing outside here, but free."

As the two men in the blockhouse started to fire again, Mildred answered with the MP-5 and Doc flipped a sizzling pipe bomb their way. It landed between the bikes and the blockhouse and violently detonated, throwing out a blinding cloud of dirt in every direction.

"Doc!" Mildred snapped, raising her arms. "Do me!"

The old man swung the Ruger, aimed and fired, the booming .44 Magnum round blowing apart the chain of the handcuffs. Mildred grunted from the impact of the round, her wrists feeling like they had been hit by a sledgehammer. But then the physician spread her hands in triumph. Holstering his blaster, Doc assumed the position, and she returned the favor with the ZKR.

"Okay, let's roll," Mildred ordered, taking hold of the grips at the end of the handlebars and twisting the throttle. Hopefully, these bikes used the same style of controls as a civilian model.

With a subdued purr, the electric engine came to life and the dashboard began to glow with hologram gauges and digital readouts. She was astonished! This would have been high-tech in her own time period of the twentieth century! For the Deathlands it was damn near magical.

"I do not know how to ride one of these," Lily whispered, her moment of bravado gone in the face of the unclean tech.

"Then come, my dear," Doc urged, grabbing her by the wrist and hauling her onto the seat behind him. "This steely Pegasus certainly has wings enough for two!"

As Lily circled her arms around his waist, Doc worked the throttle to activate the sleek machine, the powerful engine purring softly. On the glowing dashboard, he could read that the energy reserve was less than a quarter charged. That wasn't very much, especially with a double load, but it would have to suffice. Certainly more than enough to get them very far away from there. Wherever that was.

"Move it, or lose it, ya old coot," Mildred whispered, and threw another sizzling pipe bomb.

As the blast shook the glen, the two companions sent the bikes streaking toward the smoking opening in the thick wall of shrubbery. The Rogans cut loose with the combo rapidfires again, but the companions needed hands to steer, so they twisted the throttles all the way and prayed that speed would be enough to get them out alive.

Then Lily removed one arm from around Doc and started to fire her revolver backward at her brothers.

"Eat shit, ya little dick mutie fuckers!" Lily screamed above the roaring blaster. Then she pressed hard against Doc and dropped her arm. The handblaster fell away and vanished in the smoldering bushes.

"Lily?" Doc shouted anxiously over a shoulder.

The woman started to slide sideways, so Doc hurriedly reached around to grab her with a free arm. The bike nearly toppled from the movement. Doc wildly fought to stay erect and keep Lily on board. The woman was breathing but had gone limp in his grasp.

As her bike shot out of the tattered bushes, Mildred switched on the halogen headlight, wary of any pits or mantraps. The brilliant white beam illuminated the greenery ahead, and Mildred braced herself for some last barrier, but nothing barred the way and she hurtled out of the copse of trees onto a wide-open range of stubby weeds. Doc was right behind, his machine wobbling slightly as if he was having trouble with his balance. But as the bike reached the open field, Doc poured on the power and it straightened immediately.

To the left, Mildred could dimly see black mountains standing against the purple sky. Those could be the Mohawks. To the far right were the golden sand dunes of a desert. The Zone? Had to be. They hadn't been unconscious long enough to get out of the state, even on these futuristic two-wheelers. The question was, which direction to run? Without much of a choice, Mildred started for the desert. If this was the Zone, then Ryan and the others would be coming from that direction and not from the mountains.

"How's Krysty?" Doc asked through gritted teeth. The bikes were so silent that he could hear the grass and sand crunching under the weight of the people and machines.

"Alive!" Mildred replied, the handcuffs jiggling on her wrists painfully rubbing the scraped areas where she had tried to get them off.

"Excellent! But make speed, old friend," Doc observed, pulling alongside. "We need to stop, and soon."

"Were you hit?" Mildred asked, not daring to look away from the landscape. There were rocks and tree stumps and chunks of predark wreckage hidden in the weeds. That John fellow and Lily had both been right. There was nothing dangerous outside the glen, except the landscape itself. A single second's inattention could send her and Krysty flying. And Mildred had no doubt that John and his two comrades would be after them in short order. Or at least one of them would. There was only that one bike left. Unless the bastards had more.

"I was not hurt, madam, but our young rescuer was shot during our escape," Doc replied, driving with one hand. The other held a pale arm to his chest, the limb streaked with red. "I cannot see! Is she dead?"

"Can't tell in this light," Mildred answered, risking a fast glance. The others were merely blurs in the night. Great, they were free, but with two wounded, low on juice and no idea where the hell they were located.

"Ryan, where are you?" Mildred growled like a prayer in the night.

CHARGING OUT THE BUSHES, the three Rogan brothers fanned the darkness with their rapidfires, launching 40 mm grens randomly. A lot of landscape exploded, but nothing else.

Pausing to reload, John pumped a Star Shell upward. The charge streaked high into the dark sky, then billowed out a parachute before igniting into a brilliant magnesium flare that threw a swatch of bright white light down upon the landscape. There was no sign of the two stolen bikes, or the riders.

"That fragging little bitch!" Robert screamed, shaking his wep. Fresh blood was still trickling down the side of his head and along his scarred neck to soak into the handkerchief tied there. "I'll do her myself! It'll take Lily a moon to chill. A year!"

"We still got a bike," Edward said, working the bolt on the rapidfire, then resting the hot wep on a broad shoulder. "One of us could give chase."

Breathing heavily, John took a step into the weedy field, staring hatefully at the twin sets of tire tracks on the soft ground.

"Get the bike," he said in a barely human growl. "But we're all going. Bring every sleep gren we got, and this time we only bring Tanner back alive. Nobody else."

"But what about Lily…" Robert started.

"We chill 'em all!" John repeated, shouting. "Now, mount up! I know how to find them."

Chapter Twelve

The soft sounds of blasterfire drifted on the evening wind, a muted staccato that ebbed and flowed, then vanished.

"What the frag was that?" Sec chief Stirling demanded, reining in his mount.

The Two-Son ville sec men stopped their animals and listened hard to the wind. There was only the silken sigh of the bending weeds moving against one another. In the far distance a coyote howled and a stingwing announced a kill.

Then the crackles and pops came again. It sounded like explos and blasters.

The chief sec men frowned. No. Not blasters, rapidfires!

"Must be Ryan and the others," Renée stated, kicking her mount into a gallop. "Nobody else has those kind of weps!"

"We found them!" Alton cried, lurching into action. "Yee-haw!"

"Cut the drek and get razor, people!" Stirling commanded, swinging the BAR rifle off his back.

"If Ryan and the others are throwing lead, then you can be sure we're riding into a shitstorm!"

"Well, that's what Baron O'Connor sent us out here for!" Gill replied, holding the reins in one hand while drawing his sawed-off blaster with the other. "To protect their ass and get them back home, safe and alive."

"Blood for blood!" Stirling shouted, giving the ancient code of unbreakable honor between sec men as a war cry. Ryan and the others had saved countless lives during their brief stay at the ville. Could the sec men do anything less in return?

As the others repeated the call, Nathan snapped his head toward the desert to the east. The light was dim, but it had almost seemed as if there were a couple of two-wheelers powering into the shifting dunes. But when he looked again, the shapes were gone. Had to have just been a moon shadow.

Unexpectedly, a star blossomed in the sky to their right, and slowly began to float back to Earth, shining an impossibly bright light on the flatlands.

"Over there!" Alton cried, pointing the way with his Remington.

Leading the way, Stirling jumped a small ravine and gave his mount full rein. The rough ground flashed below the pounding hooves of the black stallion as he headed for the dying star. Never seen anything like that before. Had to be Ryan and his people. Who else had tech like that?

Cresting a swell in the ground, the five riders

galloped down into a depression and then exploded out of the other side onto level soil. Tightening his grip on the reins, Stirling frowned at the sight of a large copse of trees in an open field. One section of bushes was burning, and some men were shouting, but he couldn't see them. Then as the sec chief watched, three big men burst out of the copse all piled onto a single two-wheeler. A motorcycle, as his grandpa would have called the machine. Stirling had never seen one of the wags in working condition before.

"Chief! Over in the dunes!" Renée shouted. "I think that I just saw—"

"Later!" Sterling barked as the sec men galloped closer to the stand of trees.

Suddenly the barrel-chested driver of the bike squealed to a ragged halt and his two passengers tumbled to the ground. Where they hurt? But then the men stood and worked the bolts on their longblasters. No, those were the rapidfires he had heard earlier!

"Idiots," Gill said, sneering. "We're too far away for any blaster to reach!" That was when he threw back his head and blood sprayed into the sky, followed by teeth and bits of bones and hair. The aced man went slack, and the horse screamed in terror as a line of black holes appeared across its chestnut skin, each of them pumping out a river of red life.

Nuking hell! Twisting the reins, Stirling fought to bank his stallion when the rapidfires chattered again and he felt something red-hot scrap along his rib cage. Stirling cursed at the pain, but knew it was only a flesh wound and nothing life-threatening. That was a mistake on their part. Standing in the light of that wag, the gunners were perfect targets. Easy pie for the BAR.

"Spread out and take 'em!" Stirling commanded, wheeling his horse around. "That ain't Ryan's folks, so feed 'em lead! Nobody chills a Two-Son sec man and lives to tell the tale!"

"Blood for blood!" Nathan shouted, the cry taking on a whole new meaning. But as the sec men rode apart, the bright headlamp of the bike winked out.

Instantly suspicious, Stirling brought his horse to a stop, then slid off to take cover in the rustling weeds. A few seconds later there was an odd thump, closely followed by a whistling noise in the air, then a thunderous explosion. A hellish fireball lit up the field for yards, clearly exposing the three mounted sec men even as dirt rained down from the sky.

Grens! Rolling away from the detonation, Stirling caught his breath, then crawled back toward the crater, knowing that was the only safe direction. Reaching the charred earth, he went into a crouch and swept the landscape, looking for targets. But the night was much too dark and the fire in the trees was already starting to die, its meager illumination fading into a muted scarlet hue.

A black-powder longblaster boomed, then another. The rapidfires chattered: there was another

explosion; a man screamed. A horse burst into
flames. Bucking insanely, the burning animal
started to gallop into the distance, dripping fire and
endlessly screaming.

Using the beast as cover, Stirling charged into the
fray, shooting at anything not on four legs. Longblasters thundered, the rapidfires hammered away.
Something white-hot hit him in the leg and then the
arm. Mouthing obscenities, Stirling dropped the
BAR from his throbbing arm and whipped out his
handblaster. A woman cursed. There was another
loud explosion, then those mil rapidfires started
chattering nonstop, firing on and on, the terrible
noise seeming to fill the universe....

WITH A SHOUT, Krysty awoke and launched a punch
at the shadowy figure kneeling over her doing
something to her shirt. The tall man with silvery-
hair made an inarticulate noise as the fist sank into
his stomach, and he dropped to the rocky ground.

Half-dressed, Krysty threw herself at the
attacker, yanking a huge blaster from his belt. The
thing was colossal, some sort of double-barrel handblaster that was damn near identical to the one
carried by... Gaia!

"Is that you, Doc?" Krysty demanded, thumbing
back the hammer on the titanic LeMat.

A low moan answered in the affirmative.

Looking hurriedly around, Krysty saw that she
was on a stony ridge set along the base of a towering

mesa, the top of the column lost in the clouds above. Huge boulders and clumps of sagebrush dotted the landscape, giving good cover. There was just the two of them in sight, nobody else was nearby.

"Why the frag were you dressing me?" Krysty demanded, tossing her friend the blaster. "Where's Mildred? What happened?"

"Our noteworthy physician is off tendering professional care to Lily," Doc muttered, fighting for air as he slowly stood.

"Who?" Krysty asked, buttoning her shirt closed.

Rubbing his stomach, Doc briefly told her what had happened.

Finishing with the buttons, Krysty noted the shortness of the sleeves. "This isn't mine," she said.

"No, dear lady. Yours is gone, so Mildred donated a spare. She said it might be a little tight across the—" Doc faltered at the word "—across the, ahem, shoulders. I hope it is not too uncomfortable."

"It'll do," Krysty said with a smile. "How long was I out?"

"How long?" Doc repeated, glancing at the stormy sky. A few stars peeked out from behind the ever-flowing bank of tox chems as they as they moved over the mesa and out of sight. "About two hours, perhaps less."

"I see," Krysty said, zipping up her denim pants. Walking over to Doc, she wrapped her arms around the old man and hugged so hard that he thought his ribs would break. Then she planted a gentle kiss on his cheek.

"Thank you," Krysty whispered from the heart, gazing in his young but so-very-old eyes.

"A gentleman does what he can, dear lady," Doc demurred, feeling slightly embarrassed by the show of raw emotion.

"Anyway," Doc said hurriedly, "your…uh, your weapons are over here by my bike."

Sitting on a rock, Krysty began to pull on her boots. "Your bike?" she asked in amusement.

He flashed his perfect teeth. "Well, it is mine now. Finders keepers, as they say."

Standing, she stomped the boots into place. "You'll get no arguments from me," she stated. "Lead the way."

Going behind some scrub brush, Doc removed a few tumbleweeds to expose the sleek black two-wheeler.

"Mildred believes the machines are solar-powered," he said, patting the metal frame. "Which means that we are stuck here until daylight. The power reserves were low when we appropriated the machines, and by now they are totally exhausted."

Which explains why we're hidden in the bushes, she thought. "So we're stuck here for the time being," Krysty said, her hair flexing gently against the breeze.

"Indeed, yes."

"Fair enough." Krysty picked up her gunbelt and

strapped it on tight. There was no sign of the MP-5, but her S&W .38 Model 640 was in the holster, the loops full of extra brass.

"Anything to eat?" she asked hopefully, checking the load in the revolver. It was clean and undamaged.

"Surprisingly, yes, there is," Doc answered, going to the rear cargo compartment of the bike and lifting the lid. Nestled inside were spare ammo clips for the combo rapidfires, a canvas bag full of grens, a few tools, a bandolier of 40 mm rounds and dozens of bulky MRE packs.

Eagerly, Krysty ripped one open and yanked out an envelope of beef stew, using her fingers to wolf it down and licking the envelope clean afterward.

"Gaia, I needed that." She sighed in relief, crumbling the Mylar pack into a wad and tucking it into a pocket. The material reflected light better than a mirror, especially at night, and leaving it on the ground would be like marking their trail. Riffling through the rest of the MRE pack, she used a wet nap to clean her hands, and then popped a stick of gum into her mouth.

"By the way, where's my bearskin coat?" Krysty asked, chewing contentedly. Asking for a gift of strength from Gaia always left her exhausted and starving. She was still hungry, but experience had taught her the hard way that it was wise to eat in stages or else her stomach would rebel.

"The same location as my frock coat," Doc

answered lugubriously, sitting on a rock. "With our esteemed physician and her patient." He jerked a thumb. "About a hundred yards that way inside a small natural cave we found before the power ran out and the bikes died."

"A cave? Why didn't she stay here with us? There's safety in numbers."

"True, dear lady, but Mildred needed to make a fire, and it would be infinitely less noticeable inside a cave."

Mulling that over, Krysty popped the gum. A fire. That could mean Mildred was doing surgery. "How bad was this Lily hurt?"

"Unknown at present." Doc sighed, facing in that direction. Then he glanced down at a shirt-sleeve marked with red. "But she was bleeding for quite a while."

"Come on, then," Krysty said, standing. "Mebbe they could use our help."

"But, madam, we really should stay apart," Doc said in an urgent tone. "Mildred warned about a device called a low-jack, and somebody should stand guard in case those Rogan brothers return!"

"Lily took lead helping us escape," Krysty told him, going to the bike and lifting the canvas bag of grens. "I'm sure as nuking hell not going to sit here warming a rock, doing nothing." Removing a gren, she pulled the arming pin and then tucked the explos charge behind the rear wheel of the bike where the shadows were thick. Then she took some loose sand

and sprinkled it on top of the explos charge. Good enough. Anybody moving the wag would be blown to hell and give warning that the Rogans had arrived.

"Besides, my mother taught me a lot about fixing wounds," Krysty added. "I'm going."

"All for one, and one for all," Doc muttered under his breath. "If you are determined to be D'Artagnan, than I shall be your Planchet."

Traveling along the base of the mesa, the two companions kept their backs to the rocky facade of the stony column, moving almost entirely by touch. The crescent moon was behind the mesa, and the reflected light from the fiery clouds above did little to relieve the gloom. Rocks and brush were everywhere, along with the occasional cactus. Krysty tripped on some loose stones at one point, and Doc ripped his shirt on an outcropping. Grimacing at the pain, he said nothing and kept going.

Awkwardly climbing down a ridge in the ground, the companions paused when a lonely cougar snarled somewhere in the distance, the challenge answered by the cry of an eagle.

Just then, Krysty raised a clenched fist. Knowing what the hand gesture meant, Doc stopped and eased the massive LeMat from its holster. He was low on ammo for the .44 Ruger, but the .455 Civil War handblaster was fully charged and ready once more for battle. The range was short, but the LeMat could blow the head off a man at close quarters.

Tensely, the two friends listened hard to the

moaning wind, then caught the snort of a horse. Correction. There were several horses, followed by a familiar voice.

"To the left?" Ryan asked, stepping out of the wall of the mesa and into the dim moonlight. The Steyr SSG-70 was slung across his back, the SIG-Sauer in his hand.

"No, the right," Mildred answered from within the rockface.

"Hi, Charlie," Krysty called.

His blaster leading the way, Ryan spun at that. Charlie? The code was something the companions had developed over their long travels. If they meet each other after being separated, a code was used to make sure all was well. "Charlie" meant it was clear.

"Hey, yourself, Charlie," Ryan answered with a grin, holstering the blaster. "Triple glad to see you alive."

"Same back at you, lover," Krysty said.

As the two went into a clinch, Doc politely slipped past them to give the couple a moment of privacy, and walked around a large boulder that partially blocked the entrance to a small cave. The rest of the companions were inside, and relieved smiles were exchanged.

Then Doc faltered at the sight of Lily. His frock coat was folded under her head as a makeshift pillow, Krysty's bearskin coat draped over her like a blanket. Candles flickered all around the young woman, and a small alcohol lantern blazed brightly perched on top of a nearby rock.

"How did you find us?" Doc asked, looking anxiously at the unconscious woman. In the heat of battle, the old man hadn't noticed how truly lovely she was. Her hair was as black as a raven's wing, her delicate features lined from hard work and a lack of sufficient food. Thirty years old? Eighteen? It was difficult to guess her age. Besides, a child became an adult in the Deathlands on the day he or she learned to fire a blaster.

"How easy." Jak snorted in disdain. "Been ticks behind since left ville. Bikes leave trail blind man follow."

Sitting on a rock, Doc didn't doubt the statement. The albino hunter boasted that he could follow a fish under water, and he had witnessed the lad follow tracks across bare concrete. "But how did you know…"

"Four bikes go west," Jak said patiently, as if explaining to a child. "Then two go east, with double loads. What else but folks escaping?"

"Of course. How obvious. Thank you, Mr. Holmes."

"How is Lily?" Krysty asked, walking in with Ryan.

As if in reply, the young woman gave a low moan and tried to turn over, but Mildred forced her to lie back down. Lily's denim pants had been split to the crotch, exposing a bloody bandage near the big artery along the inner thigh.

Her hair flexing wildly, Krysty frowned at the sight. Jak had taught her that the inner thigh was a prime chill point for knife fighting. Stab a person there and they were aced from blood loss in only a couple minutes.

"She's not good," Mildred admitted, placing a sheet of cloth from her med kit on the sandy floor. "I have to cauterize the wound, or we're going to lose her." One at a time, she placed an assortment of crude medical instruments: longfingers found at an auto repair shop, surgical pliers from a veterinary clinic, pressure clips looted from an office supply store.

"Looks like there's enough wood," Ryan said, checking the small pile near the mouth of the cave. Several backpacks had been stacked to block the wind from the fire and to help hide the flickering light. The boulder would block most of it, the cave had been well chosen, but every little bit counted when coldhearts were out on a hunt.

"Sure. Got lots," Jak replied, gesturing at another stack deeper within the cave.

"Good." Checking the stack, Ryan saw that a lot of it was green wood, still alive and full of juicy sap. "No way a butane lighter is gonna start this going," he muttered. "Anybody got a flare?"

"I have even better," J.B. replied, lifting a hand to display a small pellet.

Taken back, Ryan raised an eyebrow at sight of

the pyro tab. J.B. had to have been hoarding this prize for months, maybe longer.

Kneeling by the stack of wood, J.B. placed the tablet on a flat rock and crushed it with a single blow from the grip of his handblaster. The smashed tablet glowed for a moment, and the Armorer quickly stepped back. Soon, the glow began a sizzling flame that grew and enlarged until it was almost a yard high, the light nearly blinding in the stony passage. As the lambent rush faded, the pile of green wood was merrily burning away, including the larger branches set to help maintain an airflow to the heart of the blaze.

Rising from his rock, Doc began to lay thick sticks on the fire in a crisscross pattern, and Ryan pulled his panga to place the blade near the crackling flames.

Removing the cap from her canteen, Mildred poured some water into a palm, then broke open a tiny cardboard envelope from an MRE pack and sprinkled a couple grains of salt into the fluid.

"Here you go," she whispered, dribbling the mixture onto the lips of the pale woman. The physician hated giving anything liquid to an unconscious person, choking to death was always a very real possibility, but Lily had lost so much blood that emergency measures had to be taken.

Mumbling something indiscernible, Lily licked the moisture from her lips. Mildred sprinkled some more, and after that was gone, she gave the woman a sip of plain water.

"Why do?" Jak asked, frowning.

"Blood is very similar in composition to salt water," Mildred explained, putting away the canteen. "Lily has lost a lot of blood, but unfortunately I don't have an IV of plasma, or isotonic saline, to give her, so this will have to do. Every little bit helps." The physician sighed. "Besides, it's all that I have."

"Salt water?" Jak asked, tilting his head.

"We come from the sea. Evolution. I told you about that."

"Right," Jak said in a noncommittal manner.

Thoughtfully stroking his chin, Doc glanced out the mouth of the cave toward the forbidding Mohawk Mountain range. They were much larger than when seen from Broke Neck ville. The range had to be a lot closer, perhaps only fifty or sixty klicks away by now, less than a day's hard ride.

"Anything like that in the local redoubt?" Doc asked hopefully.

"Doubt it highly," Mildred replied, both hands busy. "There was a full medical unit in Blaster Base One, but before that...hell, I can't remember the last time I saw blood plasma in a redoubt."

From outside, one of the horses nickered softly.

"I stand guard," Jak said, and he eased out into the chill desert night.

"Any antibots?" Krysty asked hopefully, brushing the thick ebony hair of the comatose woman. Everybody in the Deathlands could stitch a wound shut and knew how to cauterize a bad bleeder. But very few healers knew to wash the wound first, or how to stitch it closed so that a limb would still work afterward. Wherever she went, Mildred tried to pass on some of her knowledge. But a lot of people refused to listen, the ancient taboo against any form of science still strong. Baron O'Connor of Two-Son ville had been wise enough to welcome the physician and have her start to train every woman in the ville as a healer. An army of healers! What a grand thought. But then the news came of the strange chillings and the companions had had to leave long before the complex training had been finished. Hopefully, after this was over, they could go back.

"Lost all of the sulfur compounds and penicillin in the river last month," Mildred answered, pulling a plastic bottle of clear bluish fluid from the med kit. "Only this is left."

"Shine?" Krysty asked, taking a look inside the bag.

The contents of the old M*A*S*H field surgery kit were labeled in some sort of code that the physician had been working on for a long time. That way, if they were captured, Mildred could try to bargain their way free with the med supplies. But mixed among them were several doses of poison. Grim justice for any thief who jacked the irreplaceable med kit.

"Close enough," Mildred answered sadly. "Mouthwash. But the good antiseptic stuff."

Scowling, Doc muttered something in Latin.

"Best hold her down, John," Mildred directed, taking a deep breath. "This is going to hurt."

Gently, J.B. slipped a piece of soft leather between Lily's teeth, then placed his hands on the woman's shoulders. Without any further preamble, Mildred poured the antiseptic mouthwash over the bloody bandage, letting it soak down deep into the cloth to reach the wound underneath. Pale and still, Lily gave no response as purplish fluids dripped onto the rocky ground.

"Goddammit, I was hoping for a scream of pain. I'm losing her," Mildred said, her throat tight. "How is it coming?"

Turning the handle over, Ryan inspected the orange-hot blade deep in the campfire. "Almost there," he said. "Better start stitching."

Placing aside the bottle, Mildred nimbly began threading a tiny veterinary needle designed for surgery on cats with the thinnest fishing line she owned. Removing the wad of bandages from the young woman's thigh, she worked with bare hands, stitching the nicked artery closed in record speed. When Mildred leaned back, the blood was no longer squirting out of the wound, but it did continue to fill the small depression.

"Give her some more saline, John," Mildred whispered, preparing the needle line again. "Krysty, move that lantern closer!"

The redheaded woman did as requested, and

J.B. dribbled more lightly salted water onto Lily's lips. She sputtered a little at first, then started to hack and cough. J.B. stopped until she settled down, then gave her a few drops of clean water. Mildred washed the wound clean with water, then the last of the antiseptic wash, then touched up the stitching as best she could.

"Ready," Ryan said, stepping forward. The end of the panga was glowing red-hot like the eye of a demon.

"Light!" Mildred snapped, reaching for the handle of the knife.

Wordlessly, Doc pumped the handle on Mildred's survivalist flashlight, then flicked the switch. The bulb gave a weak yellow glow brighter than a couple candles, but almost immediately started to fade.

"Bulb must be dying," Doc lamented, sounding apologetic. "Just need a moment to change the bulb."

"No time," Mildred said, artfully applying the hot metal to the inside of the deep bullet wound.

There was a prolonged hiss, and this time Lily convulsed, throwing back her head to cry out. J.B. and Krysty fought to keep her limbs still and allow Mildred to do the cauterizing job properly. So many hours had been lost getting away from the cold-hearts, it might already be too late to save her. There certainly was no time for a second attempt. This was it. Win or lose. Live or die.

Ignoring the stink of roasted flesh in her nostrils,

Mildred emotionlessly flipped the blade over and touched the other small leak. There was another sizzle, but no response from Lily. She had fainted from the unbearable pain.

"Now what?" Doc asked, tucking away the flashlight. He felt useless, unable to do a thing to assist in the surgery.

"I'll sprinkle in some black powder for the sulfur, stitch the outside closed, and wrap it in clean bandages." Mildred sighed, wiping her sweaty brow with the hand still holding the hot knife. "But we better stay here for the night. Another ride on a motorcycle would only open the wound again, and kill her. This is a major artery. I was lucky to be able to fix it at all with the primitive tools I have."

"Then we make camp," Ryan declared, taking back the panga. "This is a good place to hide until dawn, and we could all use a little sleep."

"Horses, too," J.B. added pragmatically.

"Damn straight."

Casting a look at the mouth of the cave, Krysty asked, "And if the coldhearts show up?"

"Their name is Rogan," Mildred said unexpectedly. "Lily muttered it before. John, Robert, Edward and Alan Rogan. The four of them are brothers."

"There are only three remaining," Doc added with surprising anger. He glanced again at the sleeping woman, and felt his heart oddly quicken.

"Three, four, ten, don't nuking care," Ryan

growled, shoving the still warm blade into the
leather sheath. "There'll be none of the bastards
left after they meet us again."

Chapter Thirteen

There was the faint smell of burning wood on the warm wind, and the cicadas sang their eternal song among the thick plants of the weedy field.

With a start, Stirling awoke to pain; throbbing agony that seemed to fill his entire body. He had been shot several times, then fallen unconscious.

So why am I still sucking air? Stirling wondered, feeling the insect-like trickle of sweat, or perhaps blood, flowing down his face. There had come the sound of a rapidfire shooting…no, several rapid-fires, and then his sec men fell dying on every side.

Nathan had been the first; he'd tumbled from his horse without a face and hit the grassland so hard his boots came off. How remarkable that memory was. The boots coming off and his stockinged feet displayed, one toe showing as the young man trembled his way onto the last train west.

Trying to track the attackers from the angle of the wounds in the lad, Stirling had worked the bolt and trigger on the big Browning longblaster like a madman. The muzzle-flashes had lit up the night, and then he'd seen them, tiny flowers of flame shimmering in the distance. Burning flowers from the muzzles of their unseen enemies.

Snarling and spitting curses, Renée fell, shooting into the darkness. Then Alton's blaster had jammed and he'd dived through the flying lead to reclaim the sawed-off scattergun. He'd lit up the night with the twin discharge, and the three outlanders were running.

Rushing to a horse, Alton had grabbed a bag of Molotovs, and advanced to finish the job, when a bright white light banished the night. Caught in the deadly glare, Alton tried to get a Molotov ready in time, but the outlanders had ripped the man apart in a shitstorm of lead.

As the light faded, Stirling had stumbled through the weeds to grab the second BAR from Renée's bloody hand. Checking the load, he'd found it was empty, and dug in his pockets for any spare brass.

Soon voices had started coming his way, and as soon as Stirling could dimly see figures in the starry blackness, he'd opened fire with the Browning, then dropped it and did the same with the other. The range was long, damn near impossible, but Stirling had known there was no other way. That first volley had hit his people from six hundred yards away. Mebbe seven! What kind of a longblaster could hit a person that far away? Only the BAR could respond, nothing else had the range.

A cold breeze blew over the sec chief as Stirling remembered that Ryan had a longblaster that could ace that far, and so did his companions. Vehemently, the sec chief shook his head in refusal to accept the idea, only stopping when the agony in his chest grew to the point where he had trouble breathing.

"Impossible," Stirling whispered, dried blood cracking off his lips. No nuking way Ryan would jack sec men from Two-Son ville. But then, had Ryan known it was them? Mebbe the companions thought some outlanders were doing a nightcreep. Could Ryan have done this to them?

Suddenly jerking awake, Stirling realized that he had fallen asleep again and somebody was walking toward him. Feebly, his hand moved for the handblaster at his side, but the fingers were too weak to pull the heavy .40 revolver from the holster. By the blood of his fathers, was this how he was going to get aced? Lying in the weeds, unable to draw his own wep like some green sec man on his first day wearing shoes?

"And whom do we have here?" a soft voice asked from above.

The words were plainly spoken, but for some reason they sent a shudder through Stirling and he rallied once more to reach the blaster. But the weight was impossible, and he might was well have tried to lift a mountain. In defeat, the sec chief lay on the ground and concentrated on breathing as the stranger came closer.

"I asked you a question," the soft voice said, growing slightly tense. "But I suppose simple courtesy is quite impossible with a dozen machine-gun bullets in your flesh. Actually, I am rather impressed that you are yet alive." There came a laugh without merriment, a cold rattling thing as joyless as the grave of a child.

Some weeds crunched and a pair of weird shoes came into sight. The damn things were made of cloth, like a moccasin, only the material was silvery-bright, like the hair on Doc Tanner. The resemblance was striking. The shoes were the exact same color, almost as if they had been spun from the hair of the wrinklie, or other wrinklies like him. Bizarre.

"Still alive after so much blood loss," the outlander commented, sounding interested but not impressed. "Honestly, I could almost think that humanity was evolving into a tougher species if I didn't know that was genetically impossible." He gave a hard chuckle. "Oh, a mutation might crop up, they always seem to, and at the oddest times. But there could never be an overall improvement. Oh, no, that would be statistically absurd."

One of the slippers swung forward to nudge Stirling, and he cried out in racking pain.

"Please forgive my rudeness, but we have not been properly introduced," the outlander said casually. "I can see on your shirt that your name is Stirling. And from the abundance of your weaponry, I would say a sec man, perhaps a sec chief?" The metallic eyes twinkled. "Yes, of course, Sec chief Stirling. I am Delphi."

Who gave a frag care what his name was? Squinting hard, the sec chief discovered that he could dimly see the field and the black lumps of his fallen comrades dotting the ground. The horses were gone, run away...no, the realization hit him like another bullet. The coldhearts who attacked his people had taken their horses, leaving behind the blasters and black powder as if the weps were useless. Guess they were when you had rapidfires.

We weren't jacked for our blasters, Stirling understood in cold clarity. But for our horses! Everything else they threw away. Desperately, the man squinted into the darkness, and there it was, only a few yards away. The med kit, the canvas bag med kit!

Strolling among the corpses lying in the field, Delphi stopped and turned. "Did you say something?" he asked politely.

"B-blasters," Stirling managed to croak. "All ya w-want..."

Quite bemused, Delphi crouched, bringing his face into view. It was a calm face with dead-black eyes like an insect, or a predark doll. His blond hair was slicked back tight to his head, and there wasn't a single scar on his features. Not one! Stirling had never seen anybody like that before in his life. Even barons and gaudy sluts got into fights. The jaw and cheeks were smooth and unmarked, as if the man didn't even shave yet. Or never had. The hands were slim, like a young girl's, and the clothing was all white, a crisp clean white of new-fallen snow. Silver shoes and white clothing.

"Blasters you said." Delphi smiled. "Well, I can see that you still have your formidable-looking side arm, so I can only assume that this is plea for clemency, perhaps?"

"My baron...reward..." Stirling forced the words out of his aching throat, then he broke into painful coughing that seemed to last forever. He was exhausted when it finally stopped, and through his blurry eyes Stirling could see that the stranger was still crouching there, smiling just a little bit, as if entertained by his pain.

"Oh, I see," Delphi said slowly. "You were offering me a bribe to assist you? Bad choice, I'm afraid."

The man stood and started to stroll away. Stirling couldn't believe what he was seeing. Who turned down a reward of blasters? But then, there were a half dozen lying in the weeds, and the pale man was walking around them as if trying to avoid piles of fresh nightsoil.

"Now if you had asked for help under the auspices of a moral imperative, that I might have listened to," Delphi said, fading into the night. "After all, it was my employees who shot you, and your associates, so I do feel some amount of responsibility. But your attempt to purchase my efforts as if I was a mercenary is insulting! I am an artist! A creator! Those paper-pushing bureaucrats at Overproject Whisper tried to buy me, and they soon learned the error of their ways. Oh, yes, they did."

By now the man was gone from sight, even the steps of his silver moccasins disappearing into the darkness. "A reward, he said! Bah. Please die quickly, Sec chief Stirling, and lighten this world from the deadweight of one more incompetent fool." Merciless laughter filled the air, then abruptly stopped as if a door had been closed.

Listening to the wind rustle the blades of grass, Stirling could only hear his own rasping breath and thudding heart. As the itching on his skin grew worse, the sec chief felt his muscles tighten, and stiff fingers raked the soil as anger filled his body. So, I'm a feeb, eh? We'll see about that, ya motherless nuke-sucker!

Forcing himself into a lurch, Stirling painfully rolled over, then shoved a knee forward and pushed his boot backward to start stubbornly crawling toward the med kit. Every move was fire in his wounds, and the dirt rasped against his face, pebbles and sticks jabbing his skin until fresh blood flowed. But Stirling gritted his teeth and kept going. Laughed. The fragging bastard had laughed at a sec chief!

WITH A VIOLENT SHAKE, Stirling came awake again and saw some sort of small animal sniffing at Renée nearby. He cursed and spit at the thing until it scampered away. But not very far. It sat to closely study the bleeding man, and Stirling knew if he passed out again, he would never wake up. Gotta keep moving. Don't stop. Not for a tick. Concentrate! Use the pain! Keep moving, Steve, keep moving…

Something tapped his head and Stirling snarled to scare away the scavenger, but only saw the canvas bag. He'd done it! Resting for a few laboring minutes, he rolled over sideways, and went into convulsions, hot agony tightening his chest until he rolled over onto his back once more. Nuke fucking hellfire! Must have a busted rib! Well, nothing he could do about that for the moment.

Fighting for air, Stirling forced his numb hands to fumble open the canvas bag and start pulling out everything: bandages, candles and then a bottle of sterilized water. Yes!

Twisting off the cap, Stirling poured some over his sticky face, then into his mouth. It tasted like blood, but eased the soreness inside his throat and sent a delicious chill into his stomach. There was food in the med kit, too, not much but some, along with plenty of bandages, plus the needles and things needed for stitching closed big wounds. He had been hit in the back a few times. Not much he could do about those aside from washing them with shine and cover with bandages. No person could sew up his own ass, as the saying went. Mebbe with the dawn, he could pull the lead out of his legs, but that was for later. First things first. Stop the bleeding. Wash the dirt out of the wounds. Eat, drink, and find some safe place warm to rest. Warm, that was important. Damn, the ground was cold! But afterward, Stirling would track down the fragging bastard in white, and shove those fancy silver slippers so far down his fucking throat he'd nuking choke to death. Delphi had laughed at a sec chief.

Finding a roll of clean cloth, Stirling started to stuff the material into his wounds. Laughed! The bastard was going to pay dearly for that insult. Even if it took the rest of his life, Stirling would find the motherless son of a bitch and make him pay in long bloody screams.

"Run, Delphi," Stirling muttered, using the hate as fuel for his exhausted muscles. "Run far and fast, mutie-fucker, 'cause I'm coming…."

STIRRING THE FIRE with a green stick, Doc watched the red-hot embers rise on the warm currents and float away. Drifting on the currents, the dying sparks sailed over the large boulder and out of the cave to ascend into the desert night until they seemed to become twinkling stars.

"Star light, star bright." Doc sighed, then tossed the green stick into the fire, causing an eruption of sparks.

Perched uncomfortably on a rock, Doc listened to the horses softly snoring outside, and knew there was nobody near the cave. Their hearing was much more acute than a human, so there was no sense sitting out in the cold when the horses could stand guard for him, and do a better job of it, too.

A few yards away in the cave, the rest of the companions lay huddled together, sharing their body warmth, horse blankets on the ground and jackets bundled as crude pillows.

There was a horse blanket set aside for Doc to use, but he had decided against that. If he got too comfortable, it could lead to sleep, and that was an express train to death with so many enemies after them these days.

No, they're all after me, Doc corrected, frowning deeply as he took another sip of cold coffee in the plastic cup. Overproject Whisper, Operation Chronos, Department Coldfire—the names may change, but the goal was always the same. Me. I was the key to time travel. They didn't know why, and the good Lord knows that I certainly don't have the answer, or else I would be back home with Emily. My dear, sweet Emily.

Feeling embarrassed, Doc sneaked a glance at Lily. The young woman was sleeping peacefully under some spare blankets, her pale face turned his way. Feeling an ache of longing in his throat, Doc studied her delicate features, then vehemently shook his head and clawed for his wallet. Yanking it free, Doc withdrew the fifty-dollar bill hidden inside the fold. He had found the antiquarian greenback in Zero City when he was going through a rare coin store for kindling to start a fire. But when he'd seen it in the display case, he'd known at once he had to possess the fifty. Paper money was without any value nowadays, except as a lavatory aid, but it had amused the old man to take the bill. The greenback came from his time, so it was a sort of souvenir from home. Besides, fifty dollars was a year's income to a teacher. Having that much cash in his wallet made Doc feel rich. It was silly, he knew, but true nonetheless. Then he'd turned the bill over.

There were words written on it in bright blue ink, faded over time, but still discernable if the light was just right. Words written in a handwriting that he knew by heart. His throat seemed to close as Doc focused on the words, the impossible words, written on the ancient piece of script. "Theo, you will find a way back. I'm waiting. Emily."

What happened next, the scholar really didn't remember, but Mildred had found him curled into a ball under a desk and weeping uncontrollably. His wife was dust in the grave, but still very much alive in the past. She was dead and alive at the same time. Time. It was all a matter of time. And of timing.

As if sensing Doc's troubled thoughts, Krysty shifted in her sleep, murmuring something too soft to hear. A branch in the fire gave a pop as a drop of resin oozed out from the fresh wood, and J.B. snorted in response, which set off Jak into a soft snore.

There was a tin pot from a U.S. Army mess kit sitting near the small fire. Doc tossed aside the cold coffee. Pouring some of the warm water into a plastic cup, Doc added a packet of instant coffee from a MRE pack, then stirred in powdered milk and sugar. Sipping the tepid brew, Doc watched over his sleeping friends, knowing that this would be the last time he ever saw them.

Time again, Doc thought sadly, savoring the dark flavor. It seems that I have finally run out.

Just then, something moved in the darkness outside the firelight. Spinning in a crouch, Doc pulled both of his blasters and thumbed back the hammers in unison. At the metallic clicks, a fat rodentlike creature scampered into view, then darted back into the shadows again, moving, Doc thought, as if it knew what a blaster meant.

"Perhaps it does." Doc chuckled softly, easing down the hammers on the LeMat and Ruger before sliding the blasters back into their holsters. "After all, two heads are better than one." Or did it have three? He wasn't really sure, and cared even less. There were so many aberrations in the world, what did a two-headed rabbit matter? None at all. By the Three Kennedys, he had even seen one of those back in his day. Mutations happened constantly. Humans were a mutation, just a mighty good one. So were ducks, dogs and dinosaurs. There was nothing new in the world, just old ideas constantly recycled.

"Hey," a voice said.

Moving fast, Doc brought up the Ruger, then lowered it as Ryan walked around the crackling campfire, buckling on his gunbelt.

"You could not sleep?" Doc asked, holstering the blaster.

Ryan shook his head. "No, I've come to spell you," he replied, running stiff fingers through his wild mane of black hair. "You need to get some rest. Coffee isn't sleep, old friend, and tomorrow we go after those coldhearts and get this matter settled. Permanently."

Impulsively, Doc started to quote the old saying that violence never settled anything, but then stopped himself. Violence settled more matters than anything else he had ever seen. It was the war hammer, not a gavel, that brought justice to the world. Sad, but true.

"How is Lily doing?" Ryan asked, casting a glance her way.

"Still asleep," Doc replied. "Which I would guess is a good thing. Aside from being shot, Mildred said she was also suffering from mild starvation."

"She was starving, but the bikes were stuffed with MRE packs," Ryan said, his expression growing hard.

Studying the fire, Doc shrugged. "Apparently, the Rogan brothers were not firm believers in sharing their prosperity."

Sitting on a rock, Ryan grunted at that. The Rogans had enough food to feed a small army, and they starved their slave. That was just stupe. Sounded more like revenge than casual cruelty. Lily had to have offended the brothers in some way. Stolen one of their blasters, or something.

Pouring himself a cup of black coffee, Ryan
admitted that the presence of the bikes and MRE
packs raised the important question of where the frag
the Rogans had gotten the mil tech. The M-16/M-203
combo rapidfires worked better than anything the
companions owned, as did the grens. Plus, those
black two-wheelers were in perfect condition, as if
they had just come out of the factory yesterday. Or
out of a deep storage locker inside a redoubt?

Politely, Doc offered the powdered milk and
sugar, but Ryan passed and took a sip of the black
brew. Had somebody found a redoubt? That was a
disturbing notion. The villagers at Broke Neck
knew the legend of the redoubts, mebbe somebody
had discovered the secret of the underground bases.
Then again, there could be a second Anthill, a
thriving enclave of the predark world still alive and
functioning, making machines, weps, war wags,
and whitecoats laying plans written in human
misery for world conquest. Blind norad, what world
was there for folks to conquer anymore?

Glancing outside, Ryan hadn't wanted to leave
the two bikes where they might be discovered. On
top of which, even though the companions couldn't
use the brass of the M-16 rapidfires in their own
blasters, all of those grens had to stay out of the
hands of the Rogans. Mildred assured him that the
lowjack was turned off, and all of the ammo clips
for the rapidfires had been tossed down a crevice
and covered with dirt. Only the 40 mm shells for the

gren launcher had been saved for J.B. to disassemble and extract the wad of C-4 plas from the warheads. He'd molded the deadly material like a block of clay, and stuffed it into one of the homie pipe bombs. That one he'd marked with a strip of gray duct tape. The other bombs were all packed with fulminating guncotton made back in Two-Son ville. Powerful stuff. But the C-4 bomb would be an earthshaker. That would be a nasty surprise to the Rogans.

"Remember anything else about the brothers?" Ryan asked, leaning the Steyr against the granite wall, and settling into place.

"Aside from their names, not much," Doc admitted, sliding on his own coat. "John, Alan, Robert, Edward. But there is no way of knowing which one is gone."

"If any."

"Oh, one of them is absolutely deceased, my dear Ryan," Doc said in a hard voice, his hand tightening on the lionhead of his ebony stick. "Of that there is no doubt, whatsoever."

Fair enough. "Speaking of which," Ryan said, taking the other man by the shoulder. "I owe you for saving Krysty from the bastards." Then the Deathlands warrior paused, unsure if he should say more, but the feelings welled from within and there was no stopping them.

"She's my Emily," Ryan said softly.

Nodding in comprehension, Doc exchanged

looks with the man, then rose to walk away. There were some things just too difficult to openly speak about, even to a good friend in the middle of the night.

"I'll go check the horses," Doc said, heading into the darkness.

"Use my bedroll when you come back," Ryan offered, taking another drink of the coffee.

"Thank you," Doc said, a sob almost catching in his throat.

Lowering the cup, Ryan looked puzzled at that, and Doc hurried away, afraid that one more word might break his resolve.

Walking around the front of the mesa, Doc found nothing out of the ordinary. Satisfied for the moment, he went to the horses. Their reins were tied to a tall cactus. A stallion was diligently chewing on a leather strap, but stopped when Doc approached.

"I know exactly how you feel," the scholar whispered sadly, scratching the animal behind the ears.

The horse chuffed in pleasure at the treatment, then settled down. It was just nerves, Doc realized. The horses could tell the people were tense, and that made them think a predator was close. How right they were.

Choosing Jak's mare, Doc started untying the reins. The animal looked suspiciously at him, but didn't make a sound. Doc had been counting on that. Trained by sec men to hunt stickies, the noble beast knew when to be quiet. And the slightest sound could ruin everything.

Standing guard alone, Doc could have left at any time. But that would have left the others unprotected, which was not acceptable. So he had been forced to stay and bide his time until somebody else took his place. Now he could finally depart without endangering the other companions. His pockets were full of spare ammo, and he carried enough MRE packs for a week. That would have to do. Whoever was supplying the Rogans with predark technology wanted Doc alive. But he knew from bitter experience the others would not be under that blanket of protection. Anybody who stood between the Rogans and Doc would be chilled. Or worse, they might be captured alive for the unknown master of the Rogans to use in his experiments.

Doc climbed onto the horse and rubbed its muscular neck. Shifting its hooves on the loose sand, the horse gave a little whinny, and Doc quickly fed it some sugar he had been saving as a bribe. Readiness was all, as Ryan liked to say.

"Goodbye, my friends," Doc whispered, shaking the reins to guide the mare away from the other animals. His heart was heavy, but his mind was made up. To protect the others from the brutal administrations of the whitecoats, he would have to leave the companions forever.

Doc would lead the Rogans on a desperate chase

across the shattered continent. His travels with the others had taught him a thousand places to hide, and a hundred tricks to use against being tracked. It would take them years to capture him, perhaps never. But Doc would buy the others a slim chance at life. No matter the price. Somehow, he felt sure that Emily would approve.

Keeping the mare to an easy walk away from the mesa, Doc stayed alert for any of the companions to check on the horses. But the night was quiet, and he proceeded along until a cresting dune took the mesa from sight. It was done.

Breaking the horse into a gallop, Doc set off toward the north. With luck he could lure the Rogans away from the companions and the redoubt in the western mountains. After that...well, Doc had escaped from a hundred deathtraps before. Maybe he could do it one more time.

Time. It really was all just a matter of time.

Chapter Fourteen

The crescent moon rose high behind the thickening clouds, the flashing sheet lightning and rumbling thunder of the angry heavens not harbingers of a coming maelstrom, but merely reminders of the long-past apocalypse. Nature it seemed, had a very long memory, and never forgave a transgression.

Galloping through the night, Doc leaned low over the horse, moving to the rhythm of the powerful animal, its unshod hooves throwing back a contrail of sand and dust. He tried to keep his mind blank, to concentrate on the future. But the past kept intruding into his troubled thoughts. Had he done the right thing? What if the Rogans attacked the companions when they were down one blaster? What if...what if...

Slowly, the long hours passed and the land changed from flat desert to hilly terrain. Doc was still waging his internal conflict when he heard the chuffing noise of the horse hooves on sand abruptly change into ringing clangs. Eh? Shaking the dreams from his eyes, Doc realized that the horse was galloping at breakneck speed and was thundering across the remains of a predark bridge. Flooded with cold adrenaline, Doc urged the horse on to greater speed. The structure was shaking from the pounding hooves, bits and pieces falling away to disappear into the darkness below. Lost in his private reverie, Doc had failed to stop the animal from entering the crumbling ruin, now it was too late. Speed was his only hope, to outrace the spreading destruction caused by their very presence.

Then Doc saw the end of the world. Only fifty feet ahead, the bridge ended in fused girders and loose cables dangling to sway in the wind. Unexpectedly, the horse started to gallop even faster. The beast was going to try to jump across the valley!

"Whoa, girl! Whoa!" Doc shouted, frantically tightening the reins, but it was already too late.

Straight over the edge of the bridge they went, rider and mount, sailing through the air to gracefully descend until slamming into the sloped embankment. In stunned horror, Doc heard the legs of the horse snap as he went flying out of the saddle. The mare screamed as he hit the dirt hard and went tumbling into chaos.

Rocks, trees and cactus flashed by as Doc helplessly careened down the side of the hill. Totally out of control, the horse and rider tumbled wildly along for what seemed like miles until suddenly hitting flatland in a jarring crash.

Long minutes passed as the dust cloud of their journey settled onto the two bedraggled figures, the noise of their descent echoing off the canyon walls into the distance. It was quite a while until the loose rocks stopped rolling down the slope, and even longer before either Doc or the horse moved.

Groaning into life, Doc painfully sat upright, gingerly checking himself for damage. He was astonished to find only bruises and scrapes. His ebony swordstick was gone, as was the LeMat, along with numerous small items from his pockets. Forcing himself to stand, Doc pulled out a butane lighter and flicked it alive to check the ground nearby. A MRE pack was only a few feet away, his stick lying on a cactus at just the limit of the weak light. Shuffling over, Doc groaned as he bent to retrieve the MRE pack, and stuffed it into a pocket. Moving in an outward spiral, he located a pipe bomb, and then more items, painfully gathering the ones not smashed.

Finally, he located the LeMat. The Civil War blaster seemed completely undamaged from the fall. The cylinder rotated freely, and the big hammer clicked back into the firing position without any hindrance. Whether any of the charges were still loaded in chambers was another matter entirely. But Doc had plenty of reloads for the wep, and the Ruger was fully loaded, so he was still armed for the moment. Thankfully, his wallet was still safe and secure inside his frock coat.

Sitting on a rock to catch his breath, Doc flexed his shoulders and moaned. He hadn't felt this bad since the last time he had been whipped at a post. Then anger flared, and Doc muttered a bitter curse. Idiot! He had fallen asleep at the wheel, and paid a terrible price for his foolishness.

Then an anguished whinny caught his attention, Doc quickly limped over to find the horse lying against a small juniper tree. The berry-filled branches covered the mare like a protective shroud, but blood dripped from the pointy leaves.

As Doc approached, the horse struggled to stand, and began to scream at the effort, crying hysterically from the incalculable pain of its broken legs. Kneeling, he tried to calm the animal and ascertain the level of damage it had suffered. In the dappled light from the clouds above, Doc could see that all four of the legs were bent at impossible angles, sharp white bone sticking out of the hide in spots. No blood was spurting, but that hardly mattered. Four broken legs. Sadly, the old man knew that there was only one cure for a horse with that sort of injury.

"There, there, old girl," Doc whispered gently to the writhing animal as he pulled out the Ruger and thumbed back the hammer. "Hush now. Settle down, it will all be over soon. I promise. Hush now, old girl, easy does it."

Listening to the calming voice, the mare stopped trying to stand on its shattered limbs and lay there gulping air. There was moisture in Doc's eyes as he placed the cold barrel of the .44 Magnum revolver against the forehead of the injured animal and fired.

The muzzle-flash illuminated the beast as its whole body shook, and then the mare went limp forever.

A coyote howled at the sound of the blaster shot, and Doc wearily stood to holster the wep. There was no way for him to bury the animal. He would have to leave it for the scavengers of the night.

"Sorry," Doc whispered to the dead horse for no logical reason. "I am so very sorry."

Tugging the saddlebags free from under the body, the old man checked the supplies, then draped them over a shoulder. Brushing back his hair, Doc hitched his gunbelt tighter and started to walk away quickly. The noise of the shot, mixed with the well of fresh blood, would attract all sorts of things that he really didn't wish to encounter.

Glancing around, Doc saw only darkness along the sloping side of the valley, chasm, whatever the hell he was at the bottom of, and knew there was no way to reach the top from here. Moving downslope, Doc reached flat ground once more and looked around, trying to decide on a direction. There was only utter blackness around him, the storm clouds moving in to completely cover the crescent moon and steal away even that weak illumination.

Vaguely, Doc thought that he could see the opposite side of the cliff he had gone over so unexpectedly. It seemed to be just as impassable. So traveling north or south was no longer a viable option. The man was left with east and west, and west would send him toward the Mohawk Mountains and the Rogans. No, not that way. With the decision made, Doc shifted the saddlebags on his shoulder and started due east along the floor of the valley into the black unknown.

After a few miles, the valley opened onto a darkling plain as inhospitable as the far side of the moon. Trying to continue in the same direction, Doc slowed when something loomed in front of him in the night. Pulling a blaster, Doc advanced slowly until he saw it was merely some ruins. But whether the destruction was recent, or from predark days, he couldn't really tell. The walls were adobe, but lots of folks used that abundant material nowadays.

Circling warily around the structure, Doc saw that it was a military installation of some kind. The ramshackle fortress was in total disrepair. The walls were crumbling apart, with loose bricks scattered across the ground. Explosion damage? Perhaps. The roof of the outbuilding had collapsed inward, with the windows only gaping holes, the glass long gone. There was a stable that didn't look in bad condition, and a stone well surrounded by a nest of tumbleweeds. However, Doc had a full canteen and saw no reason to rest this soon in his travels.

Leaving the ruins behind, the man trundled onward, the saddlebags becoming constantly heavier and starting to chafe his back until the old man was forced to call a brief halt. As he rested, Doc unhappily started to sort the supplies into items that could be safely abandoned and the ones deemed vital to survival.

He was still shifting through the saddlebag when the softly moaning wind carried a faint smell of wood smoke. Doc jerked up his head at that, then froze at the delicious aroma of roasting meat. That meant people. Was he near a ville? Possibly. But of course, it could also just be some pilgrims, or travelers, making camp for the night. Such as the Rogans.

Briefly, Doc debated the wisdom of trying the other direction across the valley when a soft chanting came to his attention. The words weren't in English, but a singsong tongue of flowing syllables that resembled Apache. Doc knew that there had once been Indian reservations in New Mex, but he didn't think that this was Apache land. Then again, the Indian nations had been at war with one another long before the Europeans arrived, so it was eminently possible that the Indians who survived skydark built new nations amid the technology debris of their former conquerors.

Deciding that discretion was the better part of valor, Doc started back toward the perdition valley when there came a motion in the air and something stabbed down into the ground directly in front of the scholar. He recoiled at the sight of a wooden spear sticking out of the dirt, a tuft of eagle feathers on the long shaft fluttering in the breeze.

Spinning fast, Doc drew both of his handblasters and waited for the next move. The Indians of old valued courage and honor above everything else, as did some of the Deathlands barbarians. A warrior was often welcomed with open arms, while a frightened outlander would be slain on the spot. The slightest sign of weakness now could mean his immediate death. That spear hadn't missed him. It had gone exactly where the caster had wanted it to land. This was a calling card to announce the arrival of the owners. However, the big question was whether this nuke generation of Indians would have the same social ethics as their long-gone ancestors.

Softly, there came a patting noise like distant rain, and a dozen people on horseback rode into view.

They were big men and women, all of them dressed in loose leather vests and pants laced together with rawhide cord. Everybody had a headband supporting an assortment of feathers in the rear, although the number and color of the feathers was different for each, and all of the riders had delicate scars on their faces in elaborate designs.

A couple of the Indians carried a quiver of arrows and a bow on their backs. The rest held bolt-action longblasters with bandoliers of brass across their chests, and every horse had a scabbard attached at the saddle carrying a wooden spear. Only one man had a handblaster in a beaded holster at his side, the grip turned backward for a crosshand draw. His scabbard was empty.

Not knowing what else to do, Doc holstered the LeMat, and then touched his heart, lips and forehead in the greeting. It was a very nonthreatening gesture and hopefully would be interpreted as a sign of friendship. Try as he might, the old man couldn't think of any other nonverbal greeting, aside from wiggling his fingers hello, which would just look ridiculous.

The riders seemed puzzled at the gesture, but not offended. An older warrior with gray in his hair talked in the flowing tongue to a young woman, and she replied with a guttural snort.

That didn't sound good, so Doc walked backward to the spear and yanked it from the ground. The Indians became instantly alert. They openly placed hands on weps as the old man approached them again, then halted.

After a few moments the leader of the Indians walked his horse close and stopped a few feet away. Silently, Doc flipped the spear over and offered it to the rider, shaft first. The elder accepted the wep, and held it for a few seconds with the wicked barbed head pointed at Doc's heart. The old man stood still, not moving a muscle. Then the rider flipped the spear over and tucked it into the scabbard.

Trying not to show relief, Doc had the strong feeling he had just passed a very important test.

No longer scowling, the leader of the Indians asked something in a language unknown to the old man. Doc shook his head in reply. The other warriors muttered among themselves, and the leader tried again, in a different tongue. It seemed vaguely familiar to Doc, but still he had to shrug to show his inability to comprehend.

"English?" Doc asked hopefully.

The Indian leader frowned. Shaking his head in annoyance, the chief rider pointed a finger at Doc, then over his shoulder. Doc nodded in agreement, and the dozen riders reined around their mounts to start walking back from where they came. Holstering the Ruger, Doc followed alongside, knowing that to fall behind them would be taken as a sign of submission.

The mixed group moved in silence, pausing for a moment as a howler moved on the horizon, the mutie thrashing the air with its tentacles. As it disappeared, the Indians continued up a sloping rill and around a large sand dune. Straight ahead there were twinkling lights, dancing pinpoints that grew into the campfires of a small settlement as they trudged closer. A tall barricade of thorn bushes tied together made a formidable barrier around the encampment, the only opening guarded by Indian women carrying scatterguns, with large mastiff-like dogs standing obediently by their sides.

Walking through the gate of the ville, Doc studied the area carefully in case he had to leave at a run. There was a knotted-rope corral full of horses off to the side, and numerous tents dotted the camp. The fabric was brightly decorated with highly stylized figures of people, horses, bears, eagles and other animals, none of them muties. Four tents were clustered around each campfire, the burning wood lying in a pit that was several feet deep. Doc knew that trick. The pit helped hide the light of the fire, and made food cook faster. The companions had used the same thing themselves several times.

A crowd of people wrapped in crude blankets watched with marked interest as the horseback riders led Doc directly to a large geodesic dome in the center of the settlement. Just for a moment, Doc thought it was a colossal beaver mound, as crazy as that sounded. Then he could see the dome was a wigwam, a wooden Indian lodge. He knew the process well. Young sapling trees were buried deep into the soil, their tops bent over and lashed together firmly. Then small branches were laced through the supports, and everything was covered with reinforced mud. Actually, it was a form of adobe concrete that Doc knew from experience was extremely strong. The wigwam could stop most blasterfire, and even hold back the acid rains.

At an incomprehensible command from the chief rider, the other Indians reined in their mounts and slid off the horses on the wrong side. Doc gave no reaction to that. But he knew Ryan and J.B. often did the same thing. It was a combat move to use the horse as protection in a battle. The sight wasn't encouraging.

The chief rider talked to his sec men for a few minutes, and they spread out on different errands.

Walking over to the wigwam, the chief rider waved at Doc, then knelt to crawl inside the dome.

Knowing that to refuse would be seen as extremely impolite, and quite possibly fatal, Doc dropped his saddlebags at the entrance and started inside. Soft leather mats decorated with unknown symbols covered the ground, and Doc could see flickering lights at the end of the long tunnel.

Reaching the interior, Doc slowly stood. Tin oil lamps hung from the wooden struts, the yellowish light brightly illuminating the domed enclosure. The floor was an elaborate sand painting of a spiral that centered on a small fire pit filled with glowing red coals, the smoke rising upward to exit the dome through an elaborate vent.

Primitive did not mean stupid, Doc reminded himself strongly. This civilization was much older than his own.

Sitting around the smoky fire pit was a collection of somber elders dressed in loose buckskins covered with more of the cryptic symbols. They formed a solid line around the fire pit, except for a location where there was a gap, as if a person was missing.

Walking with extreme care to not disturb the sand painting, the chief rider approached an old woman sitting on the far side of the circle. Her skin was as wrinkled and dark as a dried riverbed after a hard rain, but her eyes sparkled and her long ebony hair shone with the vigor of youth. A single eagle feather stuck out of her long tresses, the tip dyed an electric-blue.

Doc didn't need to be told this was the leader of the tribe. Or at least, their shaman. Either way, there was no doubt that she was the ruler of the settlement.

Touching his heart, the chief rider spoke to the woman for a few minutes. She nodded in reply, then dismissed him with a curt wave. Walking past Doc as if the old man were invisible, the chief rider entered the tunnel and crawled away.

Left alone with the tribal elders, Doc approached the empty spot in the ring, paused to wait for a rebuke, and when none was forthcoming he carefully sat. The temperature of the coals felt good after the chill night wind, and Doc luxuriated in the soothing heat, feeling his tense muscles slowly relax.

"Greetings, venerable elders," Doc offered, unsure of what to do next. "I come in peace."

"Yet violence stalks your path, time walker," the old shaman intoned, tossing a handful of dried leaves onto the coals. Thick fumes rose to fill the dome. "But the whole world is filled with violence now, so we bid you welcome."

"Long have we waited for your arrival," another woman added, almost too softly to be heard.

But Doc nearly didn't hear the second greeting, his mind was still whirling from the first. What did she call me—"time walker"? The dome seemed to start spinning, and Doc began to feel madness well. But with a concerted effort, he forced himself to stay focused. Trying to choose his next words carefully, Doc just sat for a while breathing in the pungent fumes. Then his thoughts became crystal-clear, and for the first time in recent memory, there were no ghostly images filling the back of his mind. The kaleidoscope of scenes and information vanishing like graffiti washed off a blackboard.

Grunting at the reaction of the outlander, the older woman tossed in another handful of leaves and the smoky fumes intensified. The air was becoming thick, but to Doc it seemed as if his eyes had never been sharper, or seen in greater detail. Everything was in such bright colors, and the sounds of the settlement were as rich as a philharmonic orchestra.

In a soft chorus, the elders began to chant, the words rising and falling like the pulse of a heart. Outside the wigwam, a drum began to beat.

"How do you..." Doc stopped and tried again. "What do you know of me?"

"Only a little," an old woman answered hesitantly.

"When we walk in the dream time," the shaman moaned, "we can see your life stretching from the past, into the future and back again, weaving throughout the history of this land like a single red thread in a huge tapestry of colors."

"You do not belong here," another woman added, turning the dead-white orbs of her blind eyes directly at him. "Nature has been violated by your passage. The balance is disturbed, all things tremble."

"They took me," Doc stated firmly, clenching a

fist. "This is not of my doing. I only want to go back home!"

"To your family," they said in unison.

"Yes!"

The drums beat faster, and the fumes from the coals rose darker, thicker, sweeter, until the air in the lodge was murky with the swirling fog. Doc blinked hard. No, the air was clear. His mind was filled with a mist. Was he being drugged? Or was he finally going insane?

"Would you leave your friends?" a withered old man asked, leaning heavily on a short stick covered with indecipherable markings. "The one-eyed man?"

"Yes!"

"No," the shaman said softly, the word cutting through the music and mists like a blaster shot. "No, you must stay with the one-eyed man. He seeks a lost battle, and that is your way home."

That really got Doc's attention. Home? Could it be?

"A doorway will be opened," she continued, running her hands through a bowl filled with tiny engraved beads. "But it will only be open for a moment, a heartbeat. A double moment of time."

"Do not hesitate," the wrinklie next to Doc whispered, resting a frail hand on his shoulder. "Do not pause, time walker, or you will be lost forever."

"Forever," they chorused as the drums beat louder.

Another old man added, "When you see the gateway—"

"Jump!" the tribal elders all shouted together.

Jump. Was that a clue? Why did they use that word? Doc felt dizzy, and it seemed that his sanity was cracking. Oh, God, was any of this actually happening? Or had he hit his head on a rock when the horse fell off the cliff, and he was lying unconscious in the desert ground, moaning and twitching like some demented thing?

"We are not doomies," the shaman stated, touching the symbols on her clothing in an unknown litany. "But we walk the spirit path and can see without mortal eyes." Reaching into the bowl, she tossed a handful of beads into the fire. Instantly the flame rose from the coals and a blue-tinted smoke rose to swirl about the domed lodge.

"Your mind is broken, but this we will fix," another elder said, adding a handful of sticks tied into the shape of tall man, a tuft of silvery threads at the top for hair.

"Why would you help me?" Doc whispered, watching his tiny effigy turn dark and burn.

"You are a blessed one," somebody answered. "You have been tested and found worthy."

"You are the time walker."

"One of many."

What? Impossible! There were other survivors of Operation Chronos? With that thought, lost doors opened in Doc's mind, and suddenly he saw the cells again as he was dragged into the laboratory for testing. Needles came from every direction, piecing him countless times to check his blood, his heart, his brain. They probed him inside and out, then seemingly sent him through time again, the racking pain reaching unimaginable levels.

Then clarity filled his mind with the grim memory of a smug whitecoat scientist who had foolishly turned his back on the test subject. Moving fast, Doc grabbed an instrument from a nearby tray and slashed the man across the spine. With a shrieking scream, the bloody scientist fell, and Doc cut through his bindings just as sec men poured into the room, burly guards carrying crystal rods that sparked with electricity at the tips. Stun guns, cattle prods, different names for the same thing. Givers of pain.

Remembering his college fencing lessons, Doc killed two of the guards with the stolen scalpel before making his escape from the room. Stark naked, the Vermont school teacher pelted down a shiny white corridor that he could now recognize as the inside of a redoubt. The mat-trans. Were they the key? Could they send people through time, as well as across space? Then all he needed was the formula, the right code sequence to tap into the keypad and he would go back. Home to Emily!

Suddenly doors slammed open in the redoubt, and more guards appeared, leveling stubby rifles. Twin beams of light stabbed out from the muzzle of the weps, and when they both touched him, there was an electric crackle that made Doc's arm go numb. He dropped the scalpel, then charged the guards, screaming like a wild man.

Stepping out from behind a recessed doorway, a pale man in white fired a gun at the advancing guards, a silenced weapon. The guards fell, red blood on their chests, the rifles falling to the hard floor. Doc grabbed one and turned to face his rescuer. But the man was gone, just a fleeting shadow…always in the background…always hidden…somebody who helped Doc during one of his many failed escapes from the whitecoats of Operation Chronos.

Unable to hold any more knowledge, Doc cut loose with a raw scream as additional memories poured into his beleaguered mind like burning waters. No, the stranger wasn't a friend. Doc had escaped, and the stranger sent him back! Only it wasn't one of the guards, or technicians from Chronos, it was somebody else…no, something else…a man? A machine? Marked with a blue ring with a red star on his forehead…the symbol unseen, but always there…a norm who was cold, as cold as dead fire…Coldfire…

"He remembers!" the shaman cried, rattling a rainstick. "Time is healing!"

Then the drums outside stopped, and there was a loud explosion.

"Spirits protect us!" a wrinkled woman yelled, raising both hands as to ward off a blow. "He's here! Delphi, the dark walker!"

The side of the wigwam exploded as a flaming object punched through the adobe shell to streak across the ring of cringing elders and blow out the other side, closely followed by a violent detonation. The blast shook the dome so hard that bits of adobe sprinkled down in a dirty rain. The glowing coals in the fire pit instantly darkened, the fumes dissipated, the images vanishing completely.

By the Three Kennedys, that had been a military rocket! Doc sluggishly realized. But even as he weakly stood and drew his blasters, people began to scream across the settlement as the hard chattering of large-caliber rapidfires filled the night.

Chapter Fifteen

"Get out of the way!" Doc yelled in warning as hot lead began to pour through the gaping hole in the adobe dome.

Torn apart by the incoming fusillade, several of the old Indians in the ring fell over, clutching their faces, crimson fluids gushing from between their fingers. A man tried to stand, but instead fell into the fire pit, causing a whirlwind explosion of red embers. His screams stopped almost immediately.

A piercing horn sounded from outside, followed by the sound of black-powder blasters. Turning toward the shaman, Doc felt an icy stab to see her sprawled on the ground. There was a dark hole between her sightless eyes, and the back of her skull was missing, pinkish brains splattered on the curved wall behind. Damn, she had almost told him the way home! *Ryan was the way, but so were the redoubts, and Coldfire, and a symbol of a blue circle with a red star...*

The rapidfire spoke again, and more people shrieked into death.

Shaking the omens and portents from his mind,

Doc concentrated on the present and charged for the exit tunnel. He got only halfway when it collapsed. Trapped! But the fresh air coming through the gaping rents in the dome cleared the last tendrils of herbal mist from his mind, and Doc scrambled outside with both of his blasters at the ready.

Everywhere was chaos and confusion. Horses were screaming, people yelling, and the entire thorny barricade around the encampment was on fire, filling the night with hellish light. The dull staccato of big-bore rapidfire filled the darkness, and bloody bodies were toppling everywhere.

A second missile streaked past the flaming bushes to slam into the cook fire in the middle of the ville. The detonation was deafening, and a fireball lifted skyward to form a mushroom cloud of smoke.

Staggering backward, Doc raised an arm to protect himself from the flying debris. Mother of God, who was attacking them? Was it the Rogans, or that Delphi the old shaman had spoke of just before getting aced?

Horses were running wild. A warrior with a broken arm was using her other hand to fire a blaster into the darkness. A shrieking child was kneeling by a lifeless corpse. Somewhere, the mastiffs were barking and howling, and a flurry of arrows arched high into the sky to curve back down and hit something in a metallic patter. Metal? That meant a war wag!

Sprinting that way, Doc went around the burning

wigwam and recoiled at the sight of a huge machine dominating the desert settlement.

The vehicle was smooth and egg-shaped, the chassis shiny. Multiple sets of armored treads lined the bottom in flexing sections and, as Doc watched, the top lifted to display a honeycomb of launch tubes. A rocket lanced outward into the billowing smoke, and a tremendous explosion boiled upward from the strike.

Leveling his two blasters, Doc unleashed hot lead at the deadly machine, but the rounds only bounced off the smooth side of the armored war wag as if he was throwing gravel. Holstering the LeMat, Doc pulled out a pipe bomb, paused, then stuffed it back into a pocket of his frock coat. Instead, he withdrew a gren, pulled the pin, flipped off the arming handle and expertly rolled the deadly sphere directly under the lumbering death machine.

The thermite blast rocked the wag, chem flames engulfing the armored treads. But as the searing thermal charge dissipated, the strange war wag wasn't even scratched!

Just then the front of the transport started to fade in color, and Doc ducked behind a canvas tent that was, miraculously, still standing. Sneaking a fast peek, Doc saw the front of the chassis became transparent, and the scowling operator of the wag came into view. Seated in a small cockpit was a pale man with slicked-back blond hair, the flashing lights from the control boards covering his stern features with a twinkling rainbow.

It was him, the man from his vision! That had to be Delphi. Doc's enemy and benefactor. Leveling the Ruger, Doc fired twice, the booming predark slugs smacking onto the clear material. But they only flattened and stayed where they hit, like squashed bugs on a windshield.

"Impossible," Doc whispered, lowering the piece. Not even bulletproof glass did that! This was something else, some material as strong as steel but clear as glass.

Armaglass. The word came unbidden to his mind. Clear armaglass. Doc didn't know how he could be so certain, but the answer felt right. This machine had something to do with the makers of the redoubts and the mat-trans chambers.

Doc could see Delphi reach out a finger to scratch at the lead sticking to the outside of the machine. Delphi frowned and moved a joystick. The top of the globular wag lifted once more and a strident machine gun chattered from the complex weapons pod, the muzzle-flashes strobing the night, but no spent brass fell from the wag.

Doc wasn't impressed. He had seen a Heckler & Koch G-11 caseless rapidfire before; this was just a really big version, nothing more. As Doc grimly prepared another gren, the driver of the war wag looked his way and the two men locked eyes for a long moment. Then Delphi smiled and jerked the joystick. The treads of the wag dug into the loose soil and sent the massive machine surging across the settlement, crushing people and dogs under the armored treads.

Pulling the pin on the gren, Doc dropped the handle and lobbed the bomb at the wag. Delphi kept going. As the willie peter charge detonated, blinding flame covered the wag. Instantly, Doc sprang into the charred pit of the dead cooking fire.

Shadows engulfed Doc as he stepped on soft things he tried not to look at too closely. Reaching the other side, he scrambled out as a net fell on the crater, just missing him by inches.

His long legs pumping, Doc dived frantically over a collapsed tent, and a net descended to entangle a warrior trying to reload a double-barrel scattergun.

Charging past some trotting horses, Doc dashed toward the opening of the burning thicket. Another net fell, catching a woman and child just as they climbed onto a horse. Wrapped in the strands, the woman hugged the child tight and kicked the terrified animal into motion. Acting purely on instinct, Doc followed in their wake. There were no details in his mind, no clever escape plans, only the primordial urge to flee for his life.

As the woman and child galloped through the thorny barrier, Doc was close behind. The flames reached out for the escapees, but they were out and away into the cool night.

Something fluttered in the smoky air above Doc, and yet another net landed on the crackling bushes. The black strands lay immutable in the dancing flames, neither melting nor catching fire.

Redoubling his speed, Doc charged into the darkness. This explained why Delphi hadn't simply blown the wigwam apart on the first volley. The whitecoat wanted Doc alive. Delphi had to be the source of all of the mil tech used by the Rogans! Dear God, did this mean that the Rogans were here, too? What should he do? What could he do? *Run. Hide. Escape.*

The ancient mantra of his days in captivity came back with galvanizing force, and Doc charged to the left. Most people were right-handed, and always veered that way in a chase. Ryan had taught him that. If you went to the left, it bought you precious seconds of freedom.

Crashing through the thicket, the polished war wag headed straight for Doc as if it could see in the dark.

Damnation, it could! Doc realized. The blasted thing had to have infrared scanners. Running from the burning settlement only made Doc that much easier to locate as the only moving heat source in the desert.

Looking around in desperation, Doc saw some horses galloping across the desert and took off after them. He was about halfway there when something moved in the sky. Doc wildly dived to the right. A net smacked onto the ground, a strand brushing the hem of his coat and clinging for a long moment

before coming loose. The sight filled his stomach
with dread. Okay, running wasn't working. Time to
change tactics.

Reaching into a pocket, Doc pulled out a gren.
Yanking the pin, he dropped the spoon and counted
to five before throwing the explosive charge at the
war wag. J.B. said all of their grens were set to
detonate after eight seconds, so holding it for that
long was cutting things dangerously close, but there
was no other choice.

A grinning Delphi waved at Doc as the gren
exploded three seconds later and a lambent blanket
of hellfire flooded the open top of the war wag to
engulf the exposed honeycomb. Set ablaze, the
warheads of the missiles began to detonate, then the
solid stage fuel ignited and the entire wag shook
violently as it disappeared inside a deafening
fireball of colossal proportions.

Not waiting to see the results, Doc changed direction and pelted furiously for the old ruins. The
predark brick walls might hide him from the
thermal sensors of the machine, or they might not.
But it was his best chance. Only chance. Go! Move!

Putting his every ounce of strength into running,
Doc dashed across the open expanse that led to the
crumbling base. With every heartbeat he expected
another net to fall from above or a laser to stab into
his back and bring the horribly electric shock of defeat.

The sounds of the burning ville became distant,
and there was only the noise of his pounding boots.

The battered gate of the dilapidated fort was hanging from sagging hinges, the wood eaten by insects and partially softened by the relentless acid rains. Throwing up an arm, Doc braced himself and hit it at a full run. He smashed through without slowing. Ducking into a pool of shadows, Doc desperately looked around for a suitable hiding place and found it at once. The well. The stone well. The solid rock would shield his body heat from the sensors of the war wag. Perfect!

Scrambling to the side, Doc felt sick as he once again heard the chatter of rapidfires and the screams of dying people. The fact that there was nothing he could do to help the Indians didn't ease the sadness in his heart. Doc prayed for their forgiveness as he grabbed the rope attached to the crank set above the dark well and swung himself over the side. At first the wooden crank creaked to turn incredibly slowly, gradually lowering him into the well with the speed of winter molasses. Snarling a curse, Doc tugged on the rope hard, and it came loose to spin freely, dropping him quickly down the well, only to snag on something and jerk to a hard stop. Tugging once more, Doc cursed as the ancient rope snapped.

Plummeting out of control, Doc clawed at the rough stone wall for any purchase as the yawning blackness swallowed him whole.

ROLLING THE MODIFIED LAV over the sandy plain, Delphi looked about at the landscape and scowled at the sight of the smashed fortress. He dimly remembered when it was brand-new, but that was so long ago...

Checking the infrared scanner, Delphi saw no sign of anything that resembled Tanner. Switching to a sonic scanner, he filtered out the cries of the Indians, the crackling of the fire and the whispery wind. But there was nothing else. How could that be? The man couldn't simply disappear into thin air. Where was Tanner? Holding his breath in some alcove?

Shoving the joystick forward, Delphi listened as the engine smoothly engaged and the APC rolled forward. Then he scowled at the harshly blinking section of the control board that showed that the net cannon and missile pod were totally destroyed. Who knew the old fool had a thermite gren? Had to have gotten it from the Rogan brothers. Delphi grimaced. The fools would pay dearly for that mistake.

Flipping toggles, Delphi pressed a palm to a flat screen to activate a new weapon system. With a whine, a stubby barrel extended from the front of the transport. Pressing the arming switch with a thumb, Delphi pulled the trigger on the joystick and a scintillating ruby-red beam of cohesive light stabbed out to sweep across the ancient buildings, slicing through stone and steel as if they were warm butter. As the half-melted material fell aside, Delphi listened carefully to the sonic sensors for any cursing or sharp intakes of breath. But there was only the assorted noise of the destruction.

Anxiously, Delphi glanced at a rear monitor showing the annihilated Indian settlement. Had the time traveler somehow gotten behind him, and was hiding among the Indians? He shuddered at the horrible thought that Tanner might be dead. With a wave, Delphi banished the very notion and sent the LAV rumbling straight at the fort. Tanner was intelligent, there was no denying that. The scholar had tried to escape numerous times from Operation Chronos without the help of Coldfire. He survived in the Deathlands for some time with only his addled wits, yet wherever he traveled, the agents of Coldfire died: Dr. Tardy, Silas, Overton, Lord Kinnison...

Smashing through the adobe wall, Delphi braked the tank in an open area and flicked on powerful searchlights. In the stark white glow of the sourceless laser field, he saw the answer to the riddle at once. A stone well! Clever, but not clever enough.

His hands started to move across the control panel, but Delphi forced himself to stop. There was nothing the tank could do down there. If the massive machine even came close, the weak sides of the vertical shaft might collapse and crush Tanner to death. If the man was hiding at the bottom.

Muttering obscene curses under his breath, Delphi flicked a row of switches and set the tank on autopilot. Rising from the chair, he stomped out of the cockpit, the door automatically opening at his approach, then closing again in his wake.

Going to a ferruled box made of ceramic armor, Delphi pressed a hand to a glowing plate. The subelectronic locks disengaged and the cabinet sighed open to display a small arsenal of weapons. Making fast choices, Delphi slammed the cabinet closed and headed for the exit. The side of the tank irised open as he approached it, and a metallic ramp extended to the ground like a silver tongue. Striding to the well, Delphi dilated his pupils to gather in more light, and the darkness brightened to a pale gloom. But he could still see nothing important.

Listening closely, Delphi heard an echo fading away down below. Fading? What did that mean? Sticking his head over the side, Delphi strained at the Stygian depths, but even his augmented vision couldn't see in total blackness. Then he spied the ragged end of the swinging rope, the threads showing brown on the outside, but pale tan on the inside. A fresh break! Could it be a trick? Of course, but he didn't think so. Tanner had to be below. Probably wounded and just waiting to be captured. Yes, this was child's play now.

Turning to glance at the egg-shaped tank, Delphi touched his throat. "Defend," he subvocalized. The lights in the cockpit instantly changed as more weapon systems activated, and the hull became lethally charged.

Nimbly going over the side of the well, Delphi started to climb down, his fingers easily finding purchase. But then a rock came free, and he slipped a little. Snatching another handhold, more rocks come free and Delphi found himself falling. Bracing for the impact, the cyborg activated his forcefield and landed on top of something soft and yielding. Horrified that he might have just crushed Tanner, Delphi turned off the forcefield and scrambled along the wet rocks to finger the sodden material. It felt cold, not warm, and there was no coppery smell of fresh blood. His eyes opening to their fullest, Delphi still couldn't see anything, so he flexed his hand and the palm monitor began to softly glow, the blue radiation oddly resembling moonlight. Now Delphi could discern that he was merely standing on top of the rest of the rope.

Glancing around, Delphi saw that the bottom of the shaft was inches deep in water, which explained the odd echo. Fluids distorted sound waves in the strangest ways. Inspecting the rough stone walls at the bottom of the ancient well, Delphi thankfully saw no sign of blood anywhere. Nor of Tanner. Which meant the time traveler was still alive. Somewhere. Then Delphi noticed the wide crack in the stone wall. There were a few loose threads sticking to the rough stonework, along with a tuft of silvery hair.

Tossing away the rope, Delphi started eagerly forward. So the well opened onto an underground river or stream. Well, that wouldn't avail Tanner now! The old man was fast running out of places to go, and his capture was imminent.

The fit was tight, but Delphi managed to squeeze through the crack by shoving a few of the loose stones out of his way. As one of the stones fell away, a small metallic sphere was revealed, sticking to the wall with a wad of chewing gum. Delphi barely had enough time to register that it was a military grenade when the charge detonated.

The strident chemical blast filled the well, smashing it apart, causing an avalanche of stones and timbers from above. But even as the flames, shrapnel and debris raged impotently against Delphi's personal forcefield, the dirty water in the shaft flowed across his silvery slippers and the im-material winked out as if it had never existed.

Caught in the last vestige of the detonation, Delphi was brutally slammed against the shattering walls, the ricocheting shrapnel hitting him in a score of locations. Red blood gushed from wounds as a large timber crashed down from above and smashed Delphi across the left knee with trip-hammer force. White-hot agony filled his leg as Delphi dropped, crying out in pain.

Long minutes passed before the reverberations of the boobie faded away. Weeping openly, Delphi was still cursing when he raised a glowing hand to inspect the damage. There were countless small holes in his clothing, the ragged openings edged with crimson, but the bleeding had already stopped.

Unexpectedly, there came a whiff of smoke, and Delphi opened his shirt to see a deep gash across his hairless chest. But the circuitry woven into his muscles and organs was already extruding mono-filaments to suture the wound closed. The cyborg watched emotionlessly as the flesh and plastic joined together again, and a shiny ball bearing was pushed to the surface of his skin to drop away and hit the water with a splash.

Picking up the piece of shrapnel from the grenade, Delphi scowled at it angrily, then tucked it into a pocket. A grim souvenir to remind him never to be so complacent again. Tanner had set a trap, in the dark, and on the run. Most impressive. It was just blind luck that Delphi had stumbled into water and grounded out his forcefield, or else the blast would have done nothing. The time traveler was simply lucky, nothing more.

Stepping forward again, Delphi stopped when he found the damaged leg didn't properly respond. Mentally, he screamed at the autorepair mechanism implanted into his body, but there was only a garbled reply from his internal minicomputer. Glancing upward, the cyborg tried to contact the tank with the same lack of response. Damn it! The very stones that hid Tanner from the thermal sensors also kept Delphi from accessing the emergency computer. He could climb to the surface, but by then Tanner would be long gone and the hunt would begin again from the start. That was unacceptable.

Pulling a stubby crystal wand from inside his
sleeve, Delphi limped forward through the jagged
crack in the earth, the glow of his palm shining like
a beacon in the subterranean gloom.

Chapter Sixteen

As Delphi splashed into the deepening water, he discovered it was a shallow stream. The thermal sensors in his clothing registered an average temperature of 50 degrees Fahrenheit. Clearly, this had to be made of the melted snow running off the Mohawk Mountains.

Looking around for any more traps, Delphi heard a shot ring out from the darkness and the rocks exploded just to the left of his glowing hand. Contemptuously, he sneered at Tanner's bad marksmanship. Then the old blaster fired again, this time an equal distance to the right of the hand, and Delphi was slammed in the chest by a white-hot sledgehammer.

Crumpling to his knees, Delphi blindly stabbed back with the crystal wand, the sizzling crimson beam lancing along the waterway to angle down and touch the surface. The fluid erupted into steam, creating a cloud that soon filled the subterranean passageway. The black-powder blaster fired twice more, but the shots went wild and only hit the walls and ceiling.

Gritting his teeth, Delphi waited for his body to

effect repairs from the wound in his primary heart, his secondary one pumping wildly to compensate. In short order, the bleeding stopped. But the wound remained open, the raw muscles and wiring in plain sight, and the pain merely lessened to a dull ache. Damn! He'd been afraid of that. He had received too much damage, too fast. His resources were waning, and the microfilaments were unable to perform a full repair on the spot. With the forcefield canceled by the river, this meant the time traveler's primitive weapons could now reach Delphi, do real damage, even endanger his life.

Swallowing hard, Delphi turned to glance at the vertical passage of the well and seriously considered a retreat. Then he turned with a grim expression and boldly stood. No agent of Coldfire was going to run from an old man with a popgun! Ridiculous! Unthinkable!

Setting the charge on the crystal rod to maximum, the grim cyborg started sloshing through the water in search of his elusive prey.

FOLLOWING THE FLOW of the water, Doc paused to glance behind again at the thinning cloud of steam rising from the boiling stream. Thankfully, just like the sewer tunnel near Blaster Base One, the walls of this underground river were covered with luminescent green moss. Were the two tunnels connected? It was possible, even though the redoubt was more than a hundred miles away. Arizona was

famous for its underground rivers and caverns. The
Nuke War had to have simply opened new fissures
to honeycomb the whole state into a subterranean
warren. For one horrible moment, it occurred to
Doc that the water could be deadly radioactive, but
without a rad counter like those worn by Ryan and
J.B., he had no way of knowing. Resolute, he
marched onward.

Just for a brief instant he saw the glowing hand,
and fired both handblasters twice. The gamble was
rewarded by a startled cry and the soft white light
winking out. Quickly ducking to the side, Doc saw
the returning energy beam cut through the green
darkness, the heat of its passing feeling like the
breath of some great animal. Where the ray hit the
walls, the rocks turned red and softened to flow like
warm candle wax. A large patch of the glowing
moss shriveled from the radiated heat and slowly
turned a lifeless gray.

Reaching under the cold water, Doc found a rock
and threw it down the passage toward Delphi. In
response, the crimson beam stabbed into the water,
creating another steam cloud. Taking advantage of
the cover, Doc dashed forward trying to find an exit
to the surface. The air was sweet and clean down
here, not dank in the slightest, so there had to be a
direct route to the desert. All he had to do was to
find it, then use a gren to block the path after he was
through. Past that idea, Doc wasn't really sure what
he would do then, so he just concentrated on getting

out. And he'd have to move fast; the stream was icy-cold. Already his feet were feeling numb, his steps becoming a bit clumsy. If Doc stayed down here too long, he would soon be unable to walk and Delphi would catch him for sure.

Setting his jaw, Doc took out one of his last grens and pulled the pin. Kneeling in the freezing water, he found a large flat rock and placed the sphere carefully underneath. Withdrawing his dripping fingers, Doc eased away from the crude boobie until a curve in the passage took it out of sight.

Just then a shimmering beam of intense red stabbed along the river and hit the distant wall. Instantly there was an explosion of rock, and another section of the moss died.

But that gave Doc an idea. As the booming concussion of the blast echoed along the waterway, Doc charged to the opposite side and got as far away from the energy weapon as he could. The companions had encountered laser beams before. Nasty weapons. Mirrors didn't reflect the beam unless the surface was flawless, which few mirrors were even back in predark days. Mildred said lasers were used in surgery to cure all sorts of ills, but he had never encountered any of those. Doc only knew the mil lasers, energy beams that were powerful enough to stab through armor plate. People boiled inside their skin when the beams touched them, and death was a blessing when it finally arrived.

And that's my edge, Doc raged internally, going

over a mound of loose rocks. He still wants me alive. These shots are all high in an effort to make me scared and do something foolish. But the moment Delphi decides that I'm getting away...

The laser stabbed out again and Doc spun to level the LeMat. But he withheld triggering the blaster and waited, trying to hold his breath and listen past the choppy water. Doc knew that moving too fast, or too slow, would mean being targeted. Then the beam could come again and end his tribulations.

"Come on, Thor," the scholar whispered, thumbing back the big hammer. "Throw your lighting, and I shall eagerly play Loki."

As if in response, the beam came again, silhouetting the turn in the passageway. Then it returned a moment later in a flurry of short bursts. In the strobing red light, Delphi was momentarily visible, his white clothing soaked in fluids, black wires sticking out of his flesh like the antennae of an insect.

Then as Doc watched, the gashes in Delphi closed all by themselves and the bleeding ceased. At the sight, Doc felt his heart lurch. Dear God Almighty, Delphi was a cyborg! Part man and part machine. Just like the Wizard, or the Magus, only a much more advanced model, version, whatever the right damn word was for the abominations.

Desperately, Doc patted the pockets of his frock coat and felt for the two remaining grens. Both were antipers and useless against the man-machine.

Without another thermite gren like he used on the war wag, or an implo gren, Doc didn't stand a chance in hell against a cyborg equipped with energy weapons. Escape was his only option.

Sliding behind a lumpy rock, Doc held down the trigger of the LeMat and fanned the hammer, his other hand firing the single-shot revolver a fast three times. A cry answered the deafening gunshots, followed by a watery splash. Then the passageway was lit by fiery light, and an echoing detonation told that the boobie had been found.

Turning, Doc frantically ran away as the laser stabbed along the waterway in a mad barrage. Everywhere it touched, rocks shattered from the intense heat of the energy beam and more of the moss perished, leaving gaping patches in the smooth green carpeting of unearthly luminescence. Good.

Thanking J.B. for insisting that he carry some of the new weaponry, Doc holstered the empty LeMat and eased out the Ruger to risk a shot on the run. The muzzle-flash seemed unnaturally bright in the splotchy darkness, and with every shot Doc stepped to the side. There was no shout of pain, and this time Delphi laughed as the crimson laser stabbed back in reply, rock splinters exploding from every fleeting contact from the energy beam.

Reaching a section of dead moss, Doc crouched in the dirty water and quickly began to reload the Ruger. The LeMat was wet, utterly useless for the time being, aside from shotgun charge. Doc would save that for an emergency. The shotgun charge of double-aught stainless-steel buckshot could cut a person in two. What it would do to a cyborg, he had no idea, and wasn't really eager to find out.

The laser stabbed again, sizzling the water into a blast of steam. Then, touching the wall, it swept along low.

Biting back a curse, Doc crouched lower as the beam swept overhead, shivering from the combination of the icy water and the hot wind of the mauling power ray.

By the Three Kennedys, that was close! Okay, Delphi had the superior weaponry, Doc admitted gruffly, closing the blaster and easing back the hammer. But Delphi was no combat soldier. If all of Doc's travels with Ryan and the others had taught him anything, it was how to fight. Delphi was judging a book by its cover, which was always a foolish thing. But that gave Doc another idea...

WADING THROUGH THE COLD water, Delphi paused as the sparking wires in his crippled hand slowly withdrew into his skin and the fingers were able to move once more.

That grenade under the water had been a good trick, Delphi admitted grimly, flexing his palm as the last few traces of damage faded away. Tanner was clever. No wonder the fellow escaped from Whisper and Chronos. But he was facing Coldfire now, and that division never failed. Half of the work of Coldfire was repairing the damage done by the other two bureaucratic agencies.

Delphi closed his eyes for a moment, then opened them again, and the darkness of the tunnel was gone, replaced by an eerie black-and-white view. Glancing at the rippling surface of the shallow river, he saw his eyes as silvered mirrors, expanding and contracting as the need for light fluctuated.

Standing still, the cyborg waited for the moving water to quiet. The cold water was making his broken knee throb, but he banished the pain from his mind and listened for the labored breathing of the elusive scholar. Somewhere in the dark sections, a rock slipped and splashed into the stream, but Delphi did nothing. That could have happened naturally, or been a diversion. The cyborg needed to wait until he knew for sure where Tanner was located. Only then would he strike with the stunner and take the damn fool alive.

Suddenly, a wild hooting sounded from farther down the tunnel and Doc screamed, his blaster firing. But not toward Delphi. The shots were angled off to the side.

Nuking hellfire, were there stickies down here? Delphi raged furiously. The idiot muties were going to ruin everything!

Charging along the waterway, Delphi boosted the light from his hand until he was a nimbus of illumination filling the craggy passageway for a dozen yards.

"Get away from the norm!" Delphi commanded, his voice echoing oddly off the bare rock and moss-coated walls. "Do not harm that norm, my children!"

Reaching a bend in the tunnel, Delphi now knew why Tanner had disappeared off his instruments. Stalactites festooned the roof like the fangs of a prehistoric beast, the cold stone interfering with the readings of his sensors. Beyond the stalactites, the stream stretched into the distance, but there was no sign of Tanner or the stickies. Had it been a trick of some kind?

Something moved behind him, and Delphi glanced over a shoulder to see a loose section of the glowing moss fall away to expose Doc holding two blasters. Ambush!

Spinning, Delphi tried to bring up his crystal rod when Doc fired the LeMat, the shotgun charge blowing off the cyborg's hand at the wrist. The wand went flying as a shrieking Delphi staggered backward clutching the mutilated limb, blood spurting from the severed arteries.

Tripping on a submerged rock, Delphi went over backward to land on top of a granite outcropping just as the second blaster discharged, the flame reaching out to be deflected only inches away from his face. Oddly, the noise of the gun was muffled, and the chill in the air was gone. Only then did Delphi realized that his moccasins were out of the water, and the forcefield was back, the immaterial barrier shimmering a soft rainbow effect around the wounded cyborg.

Blood was still pumping from the end of the shattered wrist as Doc savagely swung the blaster to try to pistol-whip Delphi, but the wep bounced off the forcefield with no effect whatsoever. Fighting to stay conscious, the panting cyborg watched as black wires erupted from the end of his arm to start making hasty repairs.

"Looks like a stalemate, Tanner," the cyborg said with a sneer. "I can't hurt you, and you can't harm me."

Holstering his blasters, Doc muttered a phrase in Latin that Delphi recognized. *The only thing without limit is foolishness.*

Now, what did that mean? Delphi wondered, reaching behind his back for the miniature 1 mm HK needler hidden there. But he found only an empty holster. The gun had to have fallen out when the well exploded. Damn the luck!

Kneeling in the muddy water, Doc came up with the crystal rod and the hand, the fingers madly twitching in the manner of some ghastly spider. Removing the hand, Doc leveled the rod at Delphi, but nothing happened. He tried changing his grip, but the result was the same.

"The beamer only works for me, fool." Delphi smirked, cradling his tattered arm. The bleeding had already stopped and the pain was fading quickly.

"Let us see, shall we?" Doc growled. Retrieving

the hand, he wrapped it around the rod, then squeezed the disembodied flesh with strong fingers. Instantly the rod emitted a searing power ray tuned to its last setting. The beam cut through the gloom and stabbed into the stream, creating another geyser of steam. Temporarily blinded, Doc grimly held on, trying to point the laser at Delphi. However, the hand seemed reluctant to aim at its owner, and the beam went wide, cutting a white-hot slice through the roof to the sound of shattering stone.

"What are you doing?" Delphi screamed, starting to slide off the outcropping. But he paused at the sight of the swirling water below. One step into that and he was helpless as any person.

As the beam cut in deeper, the hand holding the rod began to sizzle softly, the flesh cooking from the excess heat.

"Wait!" Delphi cried in anguish, cradling his crippled arm. "We can make a deal! I'll…I'll send you home!"

Amid the mounting destruction, Doc paused, the fleeting dream of hope quickening his heartbeat. The scholar looked hard into the face of the cringing cyborg, and the truth lay there for all to see. Betrayal.

"Liar!" Doc snarled, widening the circle of annihilation above them, cutting away the supporting stones. "If I must die, then I shall take you to Hades with me!"

Delphi's reply was lost as the whole passageway

gave a low groan and the ceiling thunderously cracked apart. An avalanche of loose dirt and rocks began pouring into the stream and covered Delphi completely. The stalactites broke loose and stabbed into the mud, shattering as they hit the granite bottom and sending out halos of splinters.

The whole tunnel was shaking, rocks crashing down everywhere around Doc as he waved the energy beam madly around, extending the damage as far as he could. Then the beam winked out, drained of power, or deactivated by the death of its master. Flipping the grisly trophy away into the murky green darkness, Doc took off at a run, desperately splashing downstream in an effort to outrace the spreading destruction.

Chapter Seventeen

"It is done." Baron Harmond stated, raising his weary head.

Gratefully, the boy leaned back in his chair, sighing as if a barbed dagger had been removed from his flesh. There was still disharmony in his mind, but it was becoming less with every passing second.

Just then, a loud explosion sounded from outside the window of the throne room. The doomie baron glanced sideways to see debris flying into the air, only to fall back down upon the burning ville. The sec men were using the last of the gunpowder to blow up key buildings and make a firebreak to try to hold back the raging inferno before it destroyed everything. At the moment, the sec men had no leader; they were working together out of sheer necessity. Bateman had died when the gunpowder mill detonated. The sec chief had been riding his horse when the concussion wave hit, sending him flying from the saddle to crash into the gallows and break his neck. Now the sec men and villagers all understood why Harmond had changed the name of the ville on the first day he became baron.

Another blast shook the night, and the baron turned his vision inward. Yes…yes…the future was murky in some spots and crystal-clear in others. The fate of Ryan and the others was unknown, as was his own destiny. No doomie could see his or her own life. It was a blessed blind spot in the mind's eye that kept them somewhat sane. But already Harmond could see the new sec chief for the ville coming this way. He would arrive under a cloak of lies, a sworn foe of Break Neck, but he would serve the ville faithfully until his own future dictated a certain course of action.

Thick smoke drifted in through the window, driven by the winds of the conflagration, and the boy started to cough. It was gone, the fleeting glimpse carried away by the distraction of an acrid breeze. The future was unknowable once more, a matrix of ever-flowing chaos that flowed like a waterfall cascading from the mouth of the moon.

WITH A DEAFENING ROAR, the ceiling of the riverway collapsed, and Doc threw himself forward in a frantic burst of speed. Rocks and boulders were rolling everywhere, and the man tripped more than once, but grimly forced himself to keep going.

As the dusty exhalation moved down the passageway, the old man braced for death, but the noise of the falling rocks soon lessened. Then the stream rushing past his knees slowed and began to lower until it was a mere trickle snaking between his soggy shoes.

Could it be? Was it possible? There was still live moss on this length of the passageway, and Doc took a fast glance backward. The passage was blocked solid now, several of the larger stalactites acting as a crude bulwark to hold back the rest of the rubble.

"Finito," Doc whispered, allowing himself a small grin. Then he lurched into action once more, wisely determined to keep his cold feet moving. That final avalanche should have done the job. The tons of rock had buried that damn cyborg alive, and then the blocked river would drown him. So much for Department Coldfire. Delphi was well-protected, but still just a man inside his protective shell of advanced tech and machinery.

Sloshing through the trickling water, Doc hastily reloaded the Ruger and cursed softly at the discovery that he was now out of ammo for the revolver. The realization only made the scholar more resolute to escape the underground warren. The passage was getting wider, and in the dim glow of the moss he could see numerous side channels going off in random directions. The implications were unnerving. If he got lost, Doc knew that he could end up spending the rest of his life walking in circles trying to get out again. He had to stay on a singular course and trust that the source of the fresh air would eventually be discovered. He sniffed hard. Yes, the breeze was still with him, not blocked by the avalanche behind. But it seemed altered now, changed somehow, and the scholar really could not tell what was subtly different.

Pulling the ebony stick from his belt, Doc withdrew the Spanish sword and slashed the wall moss to mark his way. Counting to a hundred paces, he did it again, and then again at the same distance. But the glow of the moss was getting dimmer, and Doc felt a touch of fear at the thought of being trapped underground in the pitch black. Entombed. Buried alive. The very death he had bestowed upon Delphi might now be his own ultimate fate. It would seem that life was not without a sense of irony.

Wrapped in the dire thoughts, Doc didn't catch the noise at first, then went motionless as the sound came again. Was another cave-in starting? Was some great subterranean beast rising from its lair to feast upon the hapless traveler? Holding his breath, Doc listened for all he was worth and clearly caught the noise this time. A bird. There was a twittering bird somewhere to his right.

Heading that way, Doc saw that the trickle of water was going in the same direction, and his heart lightened at the positive omen. Suddenly a warm breeze caressed his face, and Doc broke into a grin as he dimly saw a patch of stars twinkling directly ahead. He had found the exit!

Proceeding with care, Doc sheathed the sword and used the swordstick to test the ground ahead as he walked toward the stars. Minutes later, he bumped his head on the mouth of an irregular opening. Bending slightly, he stepped through the mouth of the river and found himself standing on the precipice of a waterfall. The riverbed was glistening with moisture, the footing treacherous with slime. Squinting hard, Doc could only see a vast open space below, a yawning chasm that reached to unknown depths. Looking up, Doc saw the starry sky, the fiery clouds far off to his left while the crescent moon shone a cool silvery-blue light on the surface world. He had made it!

Moving carefully over the slippery stones, Doc stumbled to the nearby bank of the river and crawled onto dry land. Lying there, he hugged the earth, savoring the smell. There were sharp rocks in the loose soil, but never had dirt felt so good between his fingers.

The bird called again, and Doc slowly stood to see it winging away on an unknown quest. It wasn't a screamwing, or any form of mutie, just an ordinary bird. He tried to make out the species, but it was already gone, racing away from his unwanted presence.

Advancing to the edge of the cliff, Doc turned to look down at the abyss below and tried to imagine what it would have been like with the stream flowing at full force. He would have been washed right over and sent plummeting to whatever there was in the Stygian dark. The explosion that chilled Delphi had also opened the door for his escape.

"Timing." Doc chuckled out loud. "It was always a matter of timing."

Savoring the warmth of the desert air, Doc glanced around and easily found the burning wreckage of the Indian settlement a mile or so in the distance. Had he really gone that far through the river? Amazing.

Shaking the dust from his hair, Doc briefly checked his soaked belongings, then started away from the cliff. He was exhausted, half frozen and sore all over from countless bruises, but this wasn't the place to rest. His horse was gone, but with any luck, he might be able to find Delphi's war wag and figure out a way inside. J.B. had taught him a lot about locks, and there was always brute force. The sleek transport would certainly have stores of food and weapons for the cyborg. But even more importantly, there could be data files containing information about Coldfire: notebooks, a journal, perhaps a computer file. Mildred had taught him about accessing those.

Using the burning settlement as a landmark, Doc started inland, angling away from the waterfall. However, the ground sloped toward the dead stream, and the loose pebbles kept slipping and sliding under his damp boots. More than once he started a small landslide and began heading sideways toward the edge of the cliff. Dropping to his hands and knees, Doc let the disturbance settle, then began to crawl up the slope. The going was tough, but he was determined and he was nearly at the crest when he heard a familiar voice.

"Theo?" a woman called out softly.

Going motionless, Doc felt the hairs rise on the back of his neck. No. Impossible.

"Theo, my love?" the woman said again.

Slowly, ever so slowly, a terrified Doc turned to look over his shoulder. There she was, standing at the edge of the cliff, her clothing wet from the spray, her hands clenched tight as if in prayer. But there was no doubt about the identity of the woman. It was Emily Tanner, his wife.

"How…" Doc croaked, feeling his sanity reel. Tears flooded his eyes and his stomach hurt. For a split tick the old man thought he might be sick, but the queasy feeling passed. "Is…is that you, my dear sweet love?"

"Theo?" Emily asked in reply, taking a step forward, then hesitantly pulling it back. "Where are you, Theo?"

Awkwardly standing, Doc started toward the woman with a glad cry. But then she turned away and called out his name once more in another direction.

That made him stop. Couldn't Emily see him? He was only fifty feet away! That was when Doc felt a rush of suspicion. Emily was doing the same things over and over again. Saying the exact same words, in the exact precise order. Then Doc inhaled sharply as he saw that the figure of Emily was not standing near the edge of the cliff, but past it, a good yard out in thin air.

"A hologram," Doc growled, touching the blaster in his gunbelt. That wasn't his wife, just some sort of three-dimensional recording of someone who looked like her. If he had rushed blindly into her arms, he would have gone over the cliff to his death.

With that thought, Doc turned to charge up the slope once more. By the Three Kennedys, she was a trap! How this was accomplished, he had no idea, but if time travel was involved, then he wanted no part of it. Fighting his way up the slope, Doc slipped and fell, only to throw himself forward again and keep going. To Hades with the war wag, he needed to get away from here as fast as possible. Perhaps he could buy a horse from the surviving Indians. Hopefully, he wouldn't be forced to steal one. But either way, he was leaving New Mex, and right now!

As Doc scrambled to the top of the slope there was a motion in the air above, and a net dropped over him, the heavy weight driving him flat to the ground. Frantically, Doc fought against the entangling lengths, but the sticky strands seemed to tighten at every effort until the scholar was forced to lie still to keep breathing. Shaking with rage, Doc could do nothing as a dark shape rose from behind the crest and slowly walked closer, the combat boots crunching on the loose gravel.

"Welcome back, Tanner," Edward Rogan said with a grin, swinging his leg forward.

The steel-toed combat boot slammed into his side, and Doc cried out as a rib broke. The thick nylon strands around him absorbed some of the impact, but a few more of those and the old man would buy the farm for sure.

Good. "H-he squealed, you know," Doc gasped, talking through the pain.

Leaning in close, the scarred features of Edward came sharply into view. "What the fuck was that you said?" he demanded, spittle flying from his mouth.

Defiantly, Doc glared back. The net was blocking most of his view of the big man, but there now seemed to be two more shapes nearby. "I said, sir, that your yellow-belly brother wept like a little girl as I cut out his heart!" Doc braced himself for death. Long ago, he had made a vow that Coldfire would never capture him alive again. If this was the only way, so be it.

"Nobody talks to a Rogan that way!" Edward roared, pulling a huge blaster from his gunbelt. Kicking Doc over, the barrel-chested man shoved the cold barrel into Doc's mouth. "You're gonna pay for that..."

"Don't touch the wrinklie," John ordered brusquely, slapping the blaster aside. "Fuck with him and Delphi will skin us alive."

"But he chilled Alan!" Edward yelled in unsuppressed fury, brandishing the blaster while his left hand reached for the bound scholar. To Doc, the hand looked large enough to crush his skull like an egg.

"And shot me, and jacked our bikes, and took Lily," Robert answered in his twisted voice, massaging his bandaged arm. "I agree with what you're saying, brother. But remember this."

"Yeah?" Edward asked, still staring at Doc in open hatred.

"There's not a fragging thing we can do to Tanner that will be half as bad as what Delphi has planned for him," Robert snarled in sneering contempt.

Grinding his teeth, Edward merely breathed for a few minutes. "Yeah, that's true." The big man relented, holstering the blaster. "Tanner will get his soon enough." Then he scowled. "Hey! Do ya think the wrinklie was trying to play us? Make us chill him so Delphi never has his fun?"

"Yeah, mebbe," Robert muttered, rubbing the handkerchief tied around his neck. "It's what I would have done, that's for nuking sure."

"Bastard is smart," John said thoughtfully, walking around the helpless man. "You gotta give him that. Nobody ever got away from us before." The elder Rogan could see the ebony stick and revolvers of the prisoner through the black netting. He seriously disliked leaving any captive armed, but it was safer to keep the net in place until Delphi took possession. Tanner had escaped once before. That wasn't going to happen again.

Cracking his oversize knuckles, Edward gave a sound that might have been a laugh. "Any chance of Delphi letting us watch?"

"Who knows? Mebbe we can even help. Delphi doesn't know everything."

A lone eagle winged by the cliff, its cry echoing along the rocky expanse. In the talons of the bird was the limp corpse of a small songbird.

"That's for damn sure," Edward added so softly the words were nearly lost in the gentle breeze.

Even through his pain, Doc caught the comment and wondered exactly what it meant. These cold-hearts worked for Delphi, but apparently not willingly? Interesting. If so, that might leave a little room for negotiations. Or even better, he might be able to make them turn against one another.

"Listen, I know—" That was as far as Doc got before John kicked him in the ribs again, the impact blossoming into white fire that stole the very breath from his lungs.

"Speak again, and we start cutting," John stated. "Delphi wants you alive, but he didn't say untouched. Get me?"

Doc weakly nodded, waiting for the pain to subside.

"Smart boy." John chuckled, sliding the combo rapidfire off his shoulder. "Okay, you two, haul his ass away from the cliff. I'm not going to risk him rolling off the edge."

Rough hands grabbed the old man and flipped

him over. Staring upward, Doc could only see the outline of the coldhearts against the starry sky. Their faces were blank masks in the darkness.

Sliding on plastic gloves, two of the Rogans grabbed the sticky netting and roughly hauled Doc along the ground, over the crest and onto the hard-packed sand of the desert. Sand poured over his collar and down his shirt, but Doc said nothing, knowing that speech wasn't an option right then. He was helpless, unable to reach any of his weapons.

Releasing the net, the Rogans dropped Doc onto the ground. He hit his head on a rock and everything went hazy for a while. When he could see again, Doc noted that the Rogans had a campfire going and were making coffee. The smell was a tantalizing agony. Behind them was a single black bike and a couple horses munching on feedbags tied around their necks. Doc blinked at the unexpected sight. How strange. The animals carried the brand of Two-Son ville. What did that mean? Had Baron O'Connor turned against the companions?

"So where is he?" Edward exhorted, brushing his ponytail off a shoulder. "The message on the radio said we were supposed to get here triple-fast. Been an hour already."

The fact that an hour had passed while he was unconscious meant little to Doc compared to the casual comment that the Rogans had been contacted over a radio.

"We answer his call," Robert muttered hatefully, taking a sip of hot coffee from a tin cup. "Not the other way around, bro."

"Fragging bastard. I don't like playing the slut for any man."

"He isn't a man," John said, holding a cup, letting the steam rise around his tight face. "He isn't a mutie or a predark machine...nuking hell, I don't know what the frag he is aside from dangerous."

"Chilled," Doc muttered, his lips in the dirt. "He's chilled."

"Did you just speak?" John demanded, lowering cup. The elder Rogan reached for the sheath on his belt and pulled out a handle without a knife attached. Then he pressed a button on the side and with a hard click, a steel blade snapped into sight.

A switchblade knife! Doc hadn't seen one of those in years.

"Do him, bro," Edward encouraged.

"I told you to stay quiet," John said, standing slowly. "Now, you're gonna pay."

"Delphi is dead," Doc said quickly, the words rushing out. His eyes searched the faces of the three brothers around the crackling flames. Their disbelief was obvious. "It is true. I chilled him this very night."

Reaching for the bubbling iron pot, Edward poured himself more coffee. "Shut the fuck up," he snorted.

Without speaking, John came closer.

"Your master is dead," Doc said, fighting a ragged cough. His chest felt as if it were full of water, and every breath only made it worse. "I have accomplished what you could not."

"That so?" Robert mocked, placing down his cup to wipe his mouth on a sleeve. "And how'd you do it?"

"We were in an underground stream. I used a gren," Doc said honestly. "The roof collapsed, and he was buried under tons of rock."

Less than a yard away, John paused to shift his grip on the predark switchblade. He had heard a lot of people beg for their lives over the years, making wild promises, telling crazy stories about redoubts and other mutie drek. Usually the coldheart could tell when somebody was shooting from the hip or throwing pure horseshit. It bothered the elder Rogan that the wrinklie thought he was speaking the truth. Was it possible? Could Delphi have been chilled?

Uneasily, the three brothers exchanged puzzled looks, then cast worried glances into the darkness outside the dancing nimbus of the campfire.

"What do you think?" Edward asked, worrying his scarred jaw.

Moving slowly, John folded the knife closed. "I think we should go see this stream," he answered, tucking the knife into a pocket. "Robert, you stay here with the wrinklie."

"What if he's lying?" Robert demanded, picking up his rapidfire and opening the breech for the gren launcher. Taking a 40 mm shell from the bandolier across his chest, he slid the fat brass into the launcher and closed it with a satisfying click. "There might be a boobie waiting there."

"Mebbe. But what if it's true?" Edward countered, dropping the clip from his rapidfire to check the load. Slapping the clip back into the longblaster, he worked the bolt, chambering a round.

"It is true!" Doc said from the ground.

"Yeah, right," John said in a measured tone of voice. "So where is this stream?"

"Just past the cliff, where you showed the hologram of Emily," Doc said quickly. "How did you do that, anyway? Did Delphi give you that recording?" That had been preying on his mind ever since he'd seen the image. Was it a picture taken through time? Or did Chronos, or Coldfire, have his wife captive in one of their cursed labs? Oh dear God no, please, anything but that!

"What the frag are you yammering about, wrinklie?" John Rogan grabbed Doc by the silver hair and forcibly hauled his face upward. "What's a hollow-grim, and who the fuck is Emily?"

They didn't know. But then, who could have created the hologram? Delphi was chilled. Did that mean there were more agents of Coldfire in the area? Suddenly in a blind panic to escape, Doc tried to concoct a believable lie when Robert cried out and dropped his rapidfire.

Stumbling backward, the bald coldheart clutched his chest and collapsed just as the powerful report of a large-bore longblaster echoed across the rocky slope.

"Ambush!" John snarled, swinging up his rapidfire and sending a stuttering stream of lead into the chilly air.

Chapter Eighteen

Even as the M-16 rapidfires filled the night with hot lead, Edward kicked over the coffee pot to drown the campfire, and Robert crawled to his feet and grabbed a wep to join his brothers.

"Rogans!" John shouted as a battle cry, the muzzle-flash from his rapidfire strobing in the darkness.

From along a low ridge came a fusillade of return fire, the lead slapping into the sand throwing up tiny geysers, or humming past the three brothers.

Doc couldn't believe that Robert was still alive, until he spotted the large rent in the bald coldheart's vest exposing the angular body armor underneath. Payment in advance from Delphi, eh? Gathering air, Doc tried to shout a warning, but his cry was lost in the yammering fury of the assorted weaponry. The terrified horses whinnied loudly, ricochets zinged off stones in the ground. Brass and lead flew everywhere, the firefight sounding louder than skydark.

"Stupe bastards can't hit drek." Edward laughed, spraying the ridge. The hardball mil rounds smacked into the soft sandstone, chewing a line of chips and dust.

"You idiot, they're trying not to hit the wrinklie!" Robert bellowed, inserting a fresh clip into his weapon. "Must be Ryan and his boys come for a rescue!"

"Good!" John snarled, backing away while still shooting.

Carefully keeping Doc between him and the ridge, the elder Rogan reached the frightened horses and kept firing while he fumbled in a saddlebag with one hand. Pulling a gren, he crouched to prime the canister and then threw it high.

The sleep gas gren was still airborne when J.B. popped up behind the sandstone ridge and triggered his scattergun. The canister exploded in midair, spreading a thick cloud high above the combatants, the desert breeze slowly pushing it toward the dead waterfall.

Then from among the companions firing along the ridge, a pretty face surrounded by wild ebony hair appeared, a slim hand triggering a huge handblaster.

"That was Lily!" Robert snarled, sounding shocked. "The fragging slut must have told them how to track us through the radios!"

"If she's not with us, then she gets aced with them!" Edward yelled, pulling out a mil gren. But the barrel-chested coldheart jerked as he caught a flurry of rounds across the stomach. Grunting in pain, he staggered. The sphere dropped from his hand and rolled aimlessly along the sand.

As the gren stopped near Doc, he tried to kick the

explos away, but his bound legs were unable to reach that far. Unable to do anything but watch, Doc suddenly burst into laughter when he saw that the pin and arming handle were still attached. Edward had never gotten a chance to arm the charge!

Exhaling in relief, Doc concentrated on trying to reach the butane lighter in his pocket. With luck, he might be able to burn through enough of the nylon strands to get one hand free, then toss the gren back to the Rogans to end this conflict in a single stroke.

Leveling his combo rapidfire, John worked the gren launcher and thumped a 40 mm shell at the ridge. A hellstorm of double-aught buckshot peppered the sandstone, and Mildred cried out to grab the side of her neck. Then Jak stroked his .357 Magnum Colt Python, and the booming handblaster slammed the elder Rogan off his feet, the M-16 rolling into the soggy ashes of the campfire.

Several pipe bombs went skyward from behind the ridge, the fuses sizzling and emitting bright sparks. Robert tried to shoot them out of the air but missed, and the pipes landed behind the Rogans. As the brothers dived for cover, the homie bombs detonated, blowing the horses into bloody gobbets. Caught by the shrapnel, the last bike erupted into an electrical blast that illuminated the entire landscape for one long searing heartbeat. It was a prolonged lightning strike that seared the sand into glass and sent off a reeking cloud of bitter ozone.

As the incandescent glare faded, Doc arched an eyebrow at the sliver of black metal quivering in the ground only a hair away from the gren. Muttering a quick prayer to whoever was watching out for him, Doc continued playing the butane flame along the nylon strands, slowly melting his way through the stubborn netting. The fumes mixing with the ozone were making it difficult for him to breathe, but Doc doggedly continued, stealing tiny sips of air where he could.

Retreating behind the smoking corpses of the aced horses, the Rogan brothers tore open the tattered saddlebags to stuff their pockets with grens and every spare ammo clip still intact.

Another pipe bomb sailed high. Spinning, John shot it out of the air with his revolver. The resulting roar echoed across the landscape, the noise seeming to roll to the distant mountains. A few moments later, a soft hooting sound carried on the wind. The companions and the Rogans slowed their battle at the terrible noise, and then ceased firing at one another as more hoots came, louder and closer.

Fumbling with his rapidfire, Robert loaded an illuminating shell into the gren launcher and pumped the brass into the sky. The 40 mm Star Shell detonated high and drifted slowly downward, the shiny parachute reflecting the brilliant light of the magnesium charge to spread out a cone of illumination.

Moving like ghosts in a dream, tiny humanoid figures were loping across the flatlands, lumpy misshapen things that only vaguely resembled norms with their tattered clothing.

"Stickies!" Krysty cried, dumping the spent brass from her revolver and frantically thumbing in fresh rounds. "Dozens of them!"

"There's a lot more than that," Ryan reported, inserting a fresh clip into the SIG-Sauer's grip.

Quickly, the Deathlands warrior glanced around and weighed the options. This was a bastard poor location for a stand-up fight with stickies. There was only flat ground ahead of the companions, and behind was the cliff with a drop that ended far out of sight. The companions still had their horses, but that would mean leaving Doc behind. It would be kinder to put lead in the old man than abandon him to the muties and the Rogans.

"This is the work of Delphi!" Robert cursed in his broken voice. "When the wrinklie buried him alive, the whitecoat had to have summoned his nuking pets to get revenge!"

Ryan and J.B. shared a fast glance. Delphi was aced? Good news, if it was true.

"Mebbe we could dig him free..." Lily whispered, hesitantly lowering her blaster. Then she screamed at the sight of a stickie running along the ground, its sucker-covered arms splayed wide.

"No time!" J.B. snarled, spraying the mutie with his 9 mm Uzi. The stickie crumpled to the ground, oozing fluid from its head. But more muties appeared behind it, and even more from the sides.

There seemed to be an endless supply of the shambling monstrosities.

"Looks like we all buy the farm, or stand together!" Ryan shouted, pulling a pipe bomb from his pocket. "Your call, Rogans! But make it fast!"

Growling in barely controlled fury, John turned his head away as if unable to face the truth, then turned toward the one-eyed man across the drifting sands.

"Agreed!" the elder Rogan huffed, as if expelling a piece of rotten offal from his mouth. "But we settle our biz after we ace these things!"

"Done!" Ryan shouted, lighting the pipe bomb and heaving it out toward the dunes. The bomb landed with a thump, and all of the nearby stickies turned at the noise, then converged to fight over the sizzling length of fuse. A moment later the pipe bomb detonated, blowing the muties into a grisly spray of organs and watery blood.

"What the fragging...these aren't smart!" Robert cried, shooting from the hip. A big stickie rocked back from the violent impact of the handload round and fell flat, its arms and legs shaking. But the other muties seemed to become excited by the sound of gunfire, their cries increasing in volume.

"Eat this, nuke-suckers!" Edward shouted, his gren launcher thumping. The 40 mm gren hit like a thunderbolt among the creatures, broken mutie bodies flying everywhere.

Chewing on a cigar butt, J.B. unleashed the Uzi,

while Mildred emptied her MP-5 in one long burst.
A dozen stickies fell and the rest tumbled over the
corpses, their arms and legs becoming wildly entangled. But the last two arched around their comrades
and threw themselves at the entrenched people.

Steadily firing his Webley handblaster, John
dashed forward to retrieve the fallen M-16 from the
warm ashes. Ejecting the warm ammo clip as too
dangerous to use, the elder Rogan slapped in a fresh
clip and worked the bolt to clear the ejector port,
then burped the blaster to stitch a couple stickies
dangerously close to Doc. While John yearned to
crucify the wrinklie, common sense dictated that the
old man had to be kept safe until he knew for sure
whether Delphi was feeding the worms.

With the Colt Python blazing away, Jak blew the
head off a female stickie. Pumping out a horrible
spray of blood from the ragged neck stump, the
body kept going past the group of entrenched
people and straight over the cliff.

"Dark night, it's like the nest in Two-Son all over
again!" J.B. muttered, burping the Uzi in short controlled bursts.

"Don't let them get behind us!" Krysty warned,
her hair a wild corona as she triggered death into the
infested dunes.

Concentrating on their brother, Edward and
Robert gave cover fire as John raced back to the
meager protection of the dead horses. But from out
of nowhere, a stickie rose into view from behind the

shattered juniper tree and reached for the man with
its deadly hands.

Dodging out of the way, John cut loose with the
rapidfire at point-blank range, the muzzle-flash engulfing the face of the inhuman creature. The 5.56
mm hardball ammo blew out the back of the
stickie's head in a frothy mix of bones, brains and
blood. The mutie went limp, but stayed erect, its
suckered hands clinging to the bark of the tree. But
more stickies came into view. There had to have
been a dozen of the creatures, waving their deadly
hands in the air and hooting loudly.

In a deadly cross fire, Ryan and Edward both
took out a stickie, while Lily fired and missed.
Mildred blew up a group with a pipe bomb, while
John did the same with his last 40 mm shell. J.B.
used the S&W M-4000 to blast the leg off a mutie
trying to scramble up the sandstone ridge.

As the limb fell away, the stickie grabbed the
scattergun and made a swipe for the Armorer's face.
Releasing the blaster, J.B. ducked and his glasses
came off. Dropping the scattergun, the wounded
stickie awkwardly lunged for the man just as Jak
flicked his wrist. A knife slammed into the throat
of the stickie, and the mutie made gurgling noises
as it swatted at the painful obstruction.

Pivoting at the noise, Krysty leveled her blaster
at the creature, but Lily was blocking her view.
Snarling in rage, the Armorer racked the scattergun
and blew off the stickie's head. Stumbling back-

ward, the one-legged mutie went over the ridge and rolled lifelessly along the ground.

Two stickies started toward Doc, trapped in the netting, and the old man instantly stopped using the butane lighter on the resilient nylon. The flame was doing little damage to the material, and was beginning to attract the unwanted attention of the lethal muties.

"Lily, go free Doc!" Ryan ordered, working the bolt on his Steyr to yank out a clip and shove in one of his last spares. Ignoring the ache in his right arm, Ryan triggered the longblaster and chilled the two muties near his friend. But more took their place.

Pausing for only a second, the young woman hobbled over the ridge and slid down the sandstone on the seat of her pants to shuffle toward the trapped man. Her left leg was swaddled with bandages, and after a few steps the cloth started to seep with crimson.

Ignoring the throbbing pain, Lily hurriedly crossed the flatland, while trying to reload her blaster. Stickies headed her way, and the companions blew them away. Realizing that she was being used as bait, Lily frowned, but kept going, firing her wep at the inhuman horde until flopping down next to Doc, his face barely visible through the black nylon strands.

"Warn me if one gets close," Lily ordered, breaking open her revolver to dump the spent brass and hastily start to reload.

"On your nine!" Doc barked through the net.

The confused woman paused for a moment, then spun to her left and fired, catching a stickie in the belly. It staggered away, holding in its ropy guts and hooting plaintively.

Placing the blaster on the sand, Lily pulled out a knife and started cutting the mil netting. "Stickies," she whispered, putting a wealth of emotion into the single word.

"I agree wholeheartedly," Doc whispered from the ground. "Well done, lass. Good shot."

"Thanks." She grunted, leaning over more to put her weight onto the blade. "Next time, just say left or right, okay?"

"My mistake."

Already softened from the flame of the butane lighter, the strands began to part with musical twangs and a layer peeled way. Brushing back her long hair, Lily concentrated on the job of melting the net without setting the man trapped inside ablaze.

From his prone position, Doc was startled to discover that he could see straight down her loose shirt at a pair of firm young breasts unfettered by a predark bra. Blushing mightily, Doc quickly averted his gaze.

"Look all you want to," Lily told him, noticing the direction of his gaze. "You saved my life yesterday, Tanner...I mean, Doc. Iffen we get out of this alive, I'll thank you."

Only able to sputter in reply, Doc fought for

words when something exploded a few yards away, showering both of them with acrid smoke and stinging sand. A stickie raced back, covered with flames, and blasters chattered nonstop.

"I—I also got you shot, dear child," Doc mumbled in apology, flexing his arms against the confines of the netting. There was some give, but not much.

"Ain't no child, wrinklie," Lily shot back, then softened the harsh words with a weary grin. "A gaudy slut ages fast lying on her back all day." Moving the flame to another nylon strand, she snorted rudely. "Or do you prefer boys, old-timer?"

"Good heavens, no!"

"Fair enough then. I'll do you proper, and that's a promise."

More explosions shook the desert. Bullets were everywhere.

"Cut faster," Doc urged, struggling to get loose. "Or your generous offer will be moot!"

Unsure of exactly what the frag that meant, Lily bit her tongue to not sound like a feeb, and redoubled her efforts.

As a group of hooting stickies charged along the ridge, Jak pulled out a pipe bomb. Fumbling for his butane lighter, the albino teen went cold as something moved in the flickering light of the burning motorcycle. Instinctively, he dodged to the left.

A sucker-covered hand grazed his jacket, and the stickie hooted in agony as it withdrew a hand minus several fingers. Blood flowed into the camou fabric from the severed digits still attached to the razor blades hidden along the collar.

Coming up in a crouch, Jak shot the mutie in the chest, then Krysty and Mildred both put a round into the wounded creature, and it limply toppled over.

Unexpectedly, Robert screamed in his guttural voice, and a stickie stood behind the big man holding a large chunk of bleeding flesh. Shuddering all over, the bald Rogan fell to the desert sand, blood pouring from the ghastly wound in his neck.

"No!" John screamed, emptying an entire clip to shoot the mutie's head apart. But more of them converged on the elder Rogan and he disappeared within the hooting crowd of stickies waving the exhausted rapidfire. The muzzle-flashes of his handblaster could be seen between the wiggling bodies, then he began to shriek and the wep went silent.

His face a mask of feral anger, Edward started that way, firing at every step. But then he stopped as his M-16 jammed and he hastily worked the bolt to try to clear the brass caught in the ejector port.

"Fragging piece of drek!" Edward snarled, dropping the half-spent clip to insert a full one.

As the creatures began to noisily feed on the aced Rogan, Jak lit the fuse on the pipe bomb and started to throw it at them. Then he bent forward slightly so that his snowy hair tumbled back into his scarred face.

Levering single rounds into the Steyr to shoot at the hooting throng, Ryan recognized that posture as the teenager's combat stance, and wondered what he had planned. It better be good because the companions were dangerously low on ammo and almost out of bombs.

Angling around, Jak heaved the bomb past the crowd of feeding stickies and threw it toward the cliff. It landed amid the loose gravel and loudly detonated, the rumbling echo from below making it sound like a thousand grens. That immediately caught the attention of every stickie. Hooting wildly, the muties swarmed past the norms and headed for the smoking blast crater.

"It worked!" Mildred shouted in delight.

Ryan pulled out a pipe bomb. "Okay, drive 'em in!"

Hurriedly, fuses were lit and bombs were hurled to rain destruction upon the stickies on the cliff. With every blast a dozen perished and more rushed over in blind, mindless need.

Cornered on the cliff, trapped by their own lust for fiery destruction, the muties coalesced into a group target, and the norms ruthlessly mowed them down. A few tried to escape and only plummeted out of sight into the darkness below. Ruthlessly, the companions maintained the assault, and in only a few minutes, the hooting stopped and there was only the multiple, overlapping echoes of the detonating charges thundering along the rock walls of the vast chasm.

Quickly reloading, Krysty and Mildred went over to assist Lily in setting Doc free from the net, while Ryan, J.B. and Jak joined Edward in a slow walk among the twitching bodies, firing rounds into the head of any mutie that didn't quite look chilled enough. They hated wasting live brass on the creatures, but there was no other option.

The slaughter continued in a steady procession until the group reached the edge of the cliff. Staying sharp, the norms double checked the bodies on the bloody ground, but there weren't any stickies left intact.

"Well, that seems to be all of the bastards," Ryan declared, inserting his last clip.

"Looks like," J.B. agreed, titling back his fedora. "Which only leaves one Rogan to deal with."

Covered in entrails and blood, Edward checked his rapidfire blaster and watched the other people through narrowed eyelids. There was only half a clip of brass left in his blaster, but if the outlanders wanted to dance, he would put at least one of them on the last train west.

Stepping over a blast crater, J.B. stopped a yard away from the last Rogan brother, deliberately just out of reach. The gorilla-like man looked more than capable of chilling with his bare hands.

"Blood for blood," the Armorer said as the wind blew a cloud of loose dust along the cliff. "That means it's okay with us if you walk out of here."

"Yeah?" Edward demanded suspiciously. Somewhere in the fight, his ponytail had come loose, and the long hair hung down around his wide shoulders, giving the barrel-chested man the appearance of a wild barbarian from out of a predark vid.

"You can load it into your blaster," Ryan stated honestly, resting the wooden stock of the Steyr on a hip. "Bury your kin, and leave in peace. Or come at us right now. It's aces or eights with me either way. Your choice."

"Just go far," Jak said in a low growl, thumbing back the hammer on his Colt Python. "If see again, chill. Savvy?"

Shifting his grip on the rapidfire, Edward hawked and spit. The dust was so thick in his throat it was like trying to breathe underground, and the dirt carried the taste of the grave.

"Sounds good," Edward stated, resting the M-16 combo on a broad shoulder. "Just give me Lily, and I'm gone."

"No, not the girl," Ryan countered sternly. "We don't barter with people as if they were jack. All the blasters and brass you can carry, and a bag full of self-heats, but nothing else."

Frowning deeply, Edward used stiff fingers to brush back his loose hair. "Don't have much of a choice, do I?" He sighed in resignation. "Fair enough, then. No deal."

The words were said so simply they caught the companions by surprise. Shooting from the hip, Edward dived to the side. A line of impact geysers formed where Ryan had just been a split moment before, and the one-eyed man was already in motion, the SIG-Sauer chugging death. The rounds ricocheted off the angular body armor under Edward's gore-streaked shirt, and the big man staggered from the impact but triggered another short burst from the predark rapidfire. Ducking low, Jak fired the Colt Python, the impact making the big coldheart step backward and trip over a chilled stickie. Dropping to his belly, J.B. unleashed the scattergun just as Edward pulled a gren from his pocket.

Crying out, Edward clutched his bloody face and went over backward, losing the gren. The mil sphere rolled along the ground and dropped in a blast crater still misty with smoke.

"Down!" Ryan shouted, and the companions dived for cover.

The fiery detonation illuminated the entire cliff in stark relief. Then Edward screamed, but it sounded more like surprise than pain. As the harsh glare of the explos dissipated, there was no sight of the last Rogan. But his scream could still be heard fading away into the darkness below. The noise seemed to last a long time, but the cry abruptly stopped, and there was only the sound of the sighing wind.

Chapter Nineteen

With a loaded blaster in hand, Jak stood guard on a rill, while Ryan and Jak went through the battlefield checking on the scattered belongings of the Rogans.

Most of the debris was burned, crushed or riddled with bullet holes. But a few of the 40 mm shells seemed undamaged. Plus, there was an entire nylon bag full of MRE packs. The Mylar envelopes were sprinkled with stickie ooze and human blood, but could be washed off with no problem. Sadly, the horses were aced, the exploded bike reduced to flaming wreckage. A thick plume of black smoke rose high into the stormy night sky.

"Wherever we go, it's going to be on foot," J.B. declared, slinging a gunbelt over a shoulder. The blaster seemed okay, and there were even a few live brass left in the loops.

"Yeah, the only real question is where," Ryan stated, stuffing a knife into a pocket. "Those horses came from Two-Son ville, which means they were either stolen or Baron O'Connor sent sec men after us."

"That doesn't mean they were dispatched to chill us," J.B. retorted, adjusting his glasses.

"Also doesn't mean they were sent to protect us," Ryan said in a somber tone, flexing his sore arm. "The only way to be sure is to go ask, and by then it's too late."

"Yeah, I know." J.B. sighed in agreement. After so many betrayals, lies, ambushes, even friends becoming enemies, it was difficult to believe that anybody was on their side.

Suddenly, Jak's blaster rang out and the men pivoted with weps in hand. As they watched, the albino teen gave the all-clear signal. A moment later an aced stingwing fell from the sky to land with a meaty thump near the burning motorcycle.

Startled by the crashing arrival, Lily paused in shock, then went back to looting the bodies, stuffing items into a saddlebag recovered from a chilled horse.

Wordlessly, J.B. indicated the looting with the barrel of his Uzi. Grimacing in acknowledgment, Ryan noted the things she was appropriating and approved. The young woman had fought by their side, and even tried to free Doc, when running would have been a logical choice. Fair enough. Blood for blood. That was a code of honor any warrior could understand down in his bones. Lily could keep anything she found. Except grens, of course.

Scooping loose sand in both hands, Krysty poured it over the sticky filaments of the net, the particles adhering until the strands were no longer shiny but a dull brown. She had seen the Rogans handle the net with gloves, but those were nowhere to be seen among the tattered corpses and spent brass. However, the sand coated the material just fine, making it possible to touch the netting without also becoming ensnared.

"Okay, this should do it," Mildred said, pouring shine on the blade of a knife and hacking once more at the resilient material.

With a loud snap, the last strand parted. Stiffly, Doc rose from the prone position, groaning like a corpse escaping from the grave.

"Easy now," Krysty said, slipping an arm around the wounded man and helping him to a nearby rock. "Keep your weight on me."

Keeping a hand on his aching left side, Doc made it to the rock and sat heavily. "Thank you, dear lady," he whispered, his dirty face sweaty.

Splashing more shine on the blade, Mildred wiped the knife clean and sheathed it at her side. "Okay, where does it hurt?" the physician asked, kneeling on the ground.

"Indeed, where does it not hurt, madam?" Doc retorted with a subdued groan. "I have had fun before, and this is not it."

"Aw, shut up, ya old coot," Mildred admonished, peeling back the man's shirt to expose a badly bruised chest.

Gently as possible, she probed his skin with fingertip pressure. Every touch evoked a grunt, but there was no fresh blood welling or white bone showing through his skin. All of the crimson streaks seemed to be from the Rogan brothers or the horses. Excellent. A wound contaminated with a stickie's blood got an infection that was difficult to cure.

Flicking a butane lighter alive, Krysty lit the wick on a lantern and lifted it high for the physician to see clearly. In her other hand, Krysty kept her S&W revolver in a loose grip.

In the yellowish glow, Mildred examined the old man's wounds and sighed gratefully when none proved to be life-threatening. Just as uncomfortable as hell.

"How did you find me?" Doc asked, trying to keep his mind off the medical examination.

"An Indian showed up," Krysty said.

"Okay, you have two cracked ribs, and one that's broken," Mildred stated, turning for her med kit. "But your lungs are unharmed, thank goodness for that. I'll wrap you tight in some bandages, and try not to lift anything heavy for a month."

"A month?"

"That's what I said," Mildred retorted hotly, looking directly into his face. "Good God, Doc, you're lucky to be alive after a pounding like that!"

"Not that you don't deserve a good ass-whipping," Krysty added unexpectedly. "Leaving us in the middle of the night like that."

Trying not to move, Doc blinked in confusion. Had he really seen his wife, or was that only another hallucination? Exhaustion and pain were blurring his world until nothing seemed real anymore. His tumbled into the valley, the warning of the shamans, the underground fight with Delphi…

"Probably trying to save us from the Rogans," Mildred chided, pulling out rolls of cloth. "Damn fool. Three against one isn't a fight, that's suicide."

"Four against one," Doc corrected through clenched teeth. "However…I survived, while… Delphi most certainly…did not."

"Yeah, we heard. Buried in an avalanche," Mildred said, starting to wrap the cloth around his thin chest. "Now stop squirming, sit upright and raise your arms more."

"As you command, Torquemada," Doc demurred, gingerly doing as instructed. "And he was not buried, my dear Krysty, the cyborg was crushed to a pulp. His forcefield was down, short-circuited by contact with the river." Then he told them the entire story, leaving nothing out. Including the mysterious hologram.

"Just a trick," Krysty snorted in disdain. "Probably some automatic system in the wag to defend Delphi."

Noticeably, Doc brightened at the possibility. Yes, of course, how simple. There was no other answer that made any sense. If there were other agents of Coldfire in the area, they would surely have made their presence known by now.

Tying off the bandage, Mildred inspected her work. "Okay, you'll live," she declared, then added, "Did Delphi really have a working forcefield?"

"Most assuredly, madam."

"So who was he?" Krysty demanded frowning. "A friend of Silas, or somebody from the Anthill?"

"Much more dangerous than that," Doc wheezed, carefully easing his stance somewhat. Amazingly, the pain was considerably less. It seemed that he would live, after all. "Delphi was an operative for—" The man stopped talking.

Just then, Lily started coming their way. She had changed her clothes and now wore a black duster that reached to her ankles, denim pants, a dirty T-shirt with a leather vest, and a pair of green leather boots that looked a little big. There was also a gunbelt around her trim waist, the loops full of brass, and a .44 Webley revolver in the holster. A sheathed knife was on her other hip, and a switchblade jutted from her boot. The young woman was carrying a lumpy saddlebag and limping slightly, but there was a fresh bandage on her bad leg.

Lowering the lantern, Krysty silently asked Mildred a question, but the physician shook her head.

"I took care of Doc first thing," Mildred replied. "Must have put on the bandages all by herself."

"Beautiful and resourceful," Doc stated, unable to keep a tone of pride from his words.

"You almost sound smitten." Mildred chuckled and saw the tall man blush. Good Lord, was the old coot falling for the girl? In a rush of relief, a great weight seemed to be lifted off her shoulders. Well, it was about time he found another partner! He'd been alone for far too long. The physician was firmly convinced the isolation only served to augment his irregular bouts of memory loss. Doc Tanner needed to be firmly grounded in the present, instead of trying to live in the past. That hologram of Emily had clearly hit the man hard. Maybe Lily was the solution to that problem.

Impulsively, Mildred could not stop herself from adding, "Oh, yes, one more thing."

"Yes, madam?" Doc asked, bracing himself for bad news. Had stickie blood gotten into his cuts? Was he already a dead man?

"Absolutely no sex for at least a week."

"I beg your pardon?" Doc asked in a small voice, the words almost lost in the desert breeze.

"You heard her," Krysty said, laughing.

"Madam, I am a married man," Doc replied.

"Was married. A couple centuries ago."

"That didn't stop you from having a bed partner before," Mildred reminded sharply, tugging on the bandages. "Several of them, if I recall correctly."

Fully aware of the unspoken admonishment, Doc could only sigh, his feelings in total conflict. His love for Emily was not diminished, yet there was this growing attraction to Lily. Could he actually care for her as a person, or was it just lust, raw sexual desire? That brief view down her blouse had been wildly intoxicating. Although he appeared to be in his sixties, Doc was only thirty-eight years old. Traveling through time did that to a person. And it had been a very long time since he'd last walked with any woman through Cupid's secret groove....

"Here, I found your weps," Lily said, dropping one of the saddlebags on the ground. "Your blasters are pretty foul. Want me to clean them for you?"

"No, thank you, dear child," Doc acknowledged coolly, stressing the last word. "I can do that perfectly well by myself."

At the gruff rebuke, Lily's smile melted. She began to speak, then shifted the other saddlebag on her shoulder to a more comfortable position and turned to angrily stomp away, her bad leg dragging slightly in the loose sand.

"You really need to have that bandage changed!" Doc shouted after her.

"Go frag yourself!" Lily retorted, walking faster.

"I was only trying to help," Doc muttered, tugging on the wrappings around his chest. I'm a married man, and old enough to be her father, and a gentleman, and a good Christian, and...a total fool.

"Gaia teaches us that life is for the living," Krysty said softly, resting a hand on his shoulder. "You might want to try that sometime."

"Amen!" Mildred added with feeling.

Unable to conjure a reply, Doc said nothing, lost in a personal whirlwind of emotions.

Furiously shuffling across the sandy field of still bodies, Lily headed for the cliff. She saw that Jak was still on the rill watching for any danger. The other men, J.B. and Ryan, were studying the impenetrable blackness of the canyon below. That took some of the starch out her back. But unless her brother Edward had grown wings on the way down, he was just a smear on a rock now. Food for the scorpions and dung beetles.

"Hey," Lily said in greeting. "I just wanted to say thanks and…" She paused in the goodbye, then spoke quickly, the words rushing out in a torrent. "I can cook. Better than anybody. I know some healing, and…and I have other skills." She added the last part almost too low to hear.

The two men said nothing for a moment, pretending to consider the offer. But Ryan and J.B. had seen her bring Doc the blasters, and his blunt rebuff. They could guess at the reasoning behind both actions, and had already made a joint decision.

"Dark night, we sure could use a decent cook," J.B. lied, scratching his unshaven cheek. In harmony, his stomach rumbled, sounding like a distant storm.

"Could you?" Lily asked, her eyes alive with hope.

She'd stayed to fight, when running was the wisest course. "Bet your ass," Ryan stated gently. "Find a bedroll. A bedroll for one, mind you. We need a cook, so if you want the job, then we'll be happy to have you ride with us for a while."

Standing taller, Lily nodded in thanks and turned to limp away.

"Hope she's a better cook than she is a shot," J.B. stated, tilting back his hat.

"Doc can teach her to shoot," Ryan answered, giving a rare smile. "You know that Trader always said it's the ability to pull a trigger that has to come natural. The rest you can learn."

"You can load that into a blaster and fire it." J.B. chuckled. "But Doc is really going to have his hands full with her."

"Once he pulls his head out of his ass," Ryan said, looking around the desert valley. About a mile away, he saw the burning remains of the Indian settlement. He had noticed it when they'd arrived on horseback from the north. The dome and thorn fence were still burning out of control, and there was no sign of any survivors. But clearly visible in the reddish light, Ryan could see the strange egg-shaped wag of Delphi.

"Might be some good scav there," Ryan suggested warily. "And we do need transport to reach the Mohawks Mountains."

"Yeah, but there's also gonna be a lot of boobies," J.B. replied grimly, then paused as the big wag flickered. How odd. Just for a moment, the Armorer could have sworn that…

Delphi came walking out of the night, a blaster in each hand.

"Fireblast, light him up!" Ryan bellowed, diving to the side and firing the SIG-Sauer.

But the rounds seemed to have no effect on

Delphi as he ran among the companions, darting here and there, moving incredibly fast.

"He's trying for Doc!" J.B. cursed, triggering short bursts from the Uzi. He tried to track after the cyborg, but it was like grabbing for shadows. How could anybody move that fast? he wondered.

As Delphi darted between Krysty and Ryan, the two almost shot each other attempting to zero in on the sprinting whitecoat. In ragged formation, Mildred, Doc and Krysty cut loose from their position, and their rounds hummed past Lily, one of the miniballs grazing her cheek so closely that she felt the breeze.

Fanning the SIG-Sauer, Ryan could have sworn he hit Delphi several times. But there weren't any ricochets off his forcefield or body armor. What was going on here? Then he saw Delphi move through the body of an aced stickie. What the... A hologram!

"He's a fake!" Ryan shouted, lowering his wep.

Suddenly, a brilliant crimson beam cut through the air, missing Jak by an inch, and the rill alongside the albino youth violently exploded. The concussion threw the teenager aside and he landed sprawling in the sand, his Colt Python dropping from a limp hand.

"Laser!" Mildred cried, snapping off shots at the blurry Delphi. "From the wag!"

Moving fast, everybody went for cover, taking

refuge behind some of the boulders dotting the battlefield.

His frock coat flapping behind, Doc charged into view, moving through the illusion of Delphi and brazenly standing in front of Jak's still form.

"Get down!" Lily shouted from behind a large rock. She was trembling in terror from the predark tech. "They can see you!"

"Yes, I know," Doc rumbled in his stentorian voice. Waiting in horrible tension, the man gripped his weps with fierce determination. If he could clearly see the cyborg's war wag, then he was in range of the laser. The machine probably hadn't attacked earlier because the on-board comp wasn't sure which of the distant figures was Doc. But if the war wag was creating the holograms, then why had it tried to make him go off the cliff before?

The answer hit Doc like a fist in the stomach, stealing the air from his lungs. Because going over the edge wouldn't have killed him. There had to be a mesa below, and he would only have broken his legs. Or mayhap there was a large body of water. That could mean that Edward was still alive! That wasn't good news.

By now the rest of the companions had stopped shooting at Delphi, realizing the hologram was trying to get them to gun down one another in deadly cross fire. Or better yet, get them away from Doc and into a clear view of the laser.

Stopping to kneel by a headless stickie, Delphi

flickered and a roaring stickie charged at the companions, waving its hands and hooting madly. It took everything Ryan possessed not to shoot at the mutie as the illusion darted among the companions.

Spinning with a snarl, John Rogan appeared holding a rocket launcher.

"Is that the best you can do?" Ryan taunted.

Instantly the laser beam came again, bracketing Doc on either side, the ground erupting into lambent steam and red lava from each strident hit. Buffeted by the thermal concussions, Doc refused to budge, covering the unconscious friend behind him.

"Incompetent poltroons!" Doc roared defiantly, red fluids starting to tint the bandages around his middle. "I shave closer than that!"

As if in reply, a flurry of laser probed among the boulders dotting the battlefield. The big rocks shook at the touch of the energy beam, white-glowing holes appearing in the material, some of them a foot deep. But penetration wasn't achieved. The ancient handiwork of Nature standing indomitable to the advanced weapons technology.

Starting forward at a run, Doc holstered the LeMat and pulled a pipe bomb into view. The globular war wag was a long distance away, maybe a full klick, but if he could just get close enough without endangering his friends...

For a moment, it seemed as if the vehicle had been hit by lighting from above, then Doc realized it was gone. The huge egg-shaped wag had just vanished into thin air.

Chapter Twenty

Staying low and moving fast, the companions charged through the pearlescent dawn of the desert valley, every weapon at the ready. A reddish dawn was coming, the stars slowly disappearing as the blazing sun struggled to shine through the ever-thickening dark clouds of rad and chems.

While the horses and bike of the Rogan brothers had been destroyed in the fight with the stickies, their own mounts had been safely ensconced behind the defensive lava rill, unreachable by either the slavering muties or the sizzling laser.

Arching around to the east, the companions hid their mounts in an arroyo behind the smoldering Indian ville. Then they proceeded on foot, darting from boulder to boulder, tree to sand dune, using the natural formation of the land to mask their swift approach. Even if the enemy war wag had infrared, it would be impossible to find them among the smoky destruction of the nomadic ville, especially mixing with the growing heat of the coming dawn.

Or at least, that had been the plan, Ryan noted

dourly, his long hair sailing in the wind of the galloping stallion.

Holding tightly on to the reins with his weak right
hand, the one-eyed man held a primed gren in the
other, the pin already pulled and stuffed into a
pocket. He didn't think the AP explos could harm the
armored war wag, but it would throw a lot of sand
into the air, giving them vital cover from that big
laser until J.B. could get closer with the C-4 pipe
bomb.

During the frantic ride, Doc had quickly
recapped his previous tangle with Delphi. By taking
out that missile pod, the scholar had to have done
significant damage to the war machine. Which
meant the armor would be thin on top. If they could
just get close enough, J.B. could flip in the bomb
and open that military wag like a self-heat. Hopefully.

Following a dried rain gully, the companions
peeked out from a collection of tumbleweeds to
recce the crumbling predark fortress. The front gate
had been smashed into splinters, the brick buildings
inside dotted with molten patches from hits by the
energy wep.

Listening to the whispering wind, Ryan tried
to detect any sound of machinery. The chem-laser
of the lady Trader needed a good minute to
recharge between shots and made quite a racket.
True, this wep was a lot more sophisticated,
smaller, faster, hotter, but Ryan guessed that the

basic principles would be the same. Generate power, accumulate, condense, then focus and release. It was sort of like firing a bolt-action rifle. You had to reload completely with every shot. Deadly, but slow.

Long minutes passed with nothing happening. Then J.B. gave a fake sneeze. Everybody ducked low in the gully, Krysty pulling a puzzled Lily down with them. Then the Armorer popped up fast, fanning the Uzi across the desert. The 9 mm Parabellum rounds hit only air and sand dunes.

"Not invisible," Jak declared, rising into view, the Colt Python still in his grip. The relief of not having to fight an invisible enemy was clear on his pale face.

"Didn't think it was," J.B. told him, dropping the empty clip and slapping in a fresh one to work the arming lever. "But it never hurts to double check."

Warily, the companions crawled from the gully and started walking toward the ruins in a loose formation. They soon found the tracks of the globular war wag, and began to follow them, grimly alert for land mines or some other type of predark boobie.

"Stay razor, people. It's possible Delphi isn't chilled, after all, and is watching us from somewhere in the desert," Ryan growled, watching the shifting sands for any suspicious movements. But he felt the risk was low, and returned the pin to the gren to tuck the explos charge into his coat.

"Smoke from ville give cover," Jak declared confidently, as an acrid breeze wafted over the group.

He flinched at the fleeting smell of cooked flesh, and forced the distraction from his mind. He had to stay razor. Cyborgs were tricky.

"Besides, shooting through this smoke would massively reduce the power of the laser," Mildred declared, resting an M-16 combo on a shoulder. "The beams work on color absorption."

Easing around a cactus, Ryan only grunted in reply. A long time ago, the Trader had taught him that a green laser was pretty much useless against a green target. That's why predark mil lasers seemed to shimmer. They were rippling through the entire visible spectrum every few seconds. No matter what camou you wore, or the color of your armor, the predark lasers chilled every time. If they managed to hit you. Experience had taught Ryan that a smart person could outmaneuver a droid, or a comp, every time. As with everything else, it was the person behind the blaster that made a wep deadly.

"Rainbows that chill," Krysty said angrily. The bastard concept seemed unnatural and made her uneasy.

Her hair radiating outward against the reeking breeze, the woman changed her grip on the M-16 combo. There was only one ammo clip left for the rapidfire, and no more 40 mm shells, but it was still a deadly wep, and the neckered-down 5.56 mm mil rounds had a lot more punch than the loads in her .38 revolver.

Askance at this tech talk, Lily nervously shied away from the other people. How did they know such things? Had she escaped from her crazy brothers only to become surrounded by more stinking tech lovers?

Passing by the destroyed front gate of the adobe fort, Doc glowered at the stone well in repressed fury and fingered a pipe bomb. If the scholar had learned anything from his short fight with the Coldfire agent, it was that there was no such thing as too much firepower.

Had his fight with Delphi really only happened a few hours earlier? Doc wondered. It seemed incredible. Just for a moment, the tall man fought the urge to toss the pipe bomb down the well just to make sure the hated cyborg was indeed chilled. Then he thought better of the action and shoved the explosive bit of plumbing into his frock coat. There was no sense wasting precious munitions merely to soothe his jangled nerves. Doc was covered with cuts and bruises, his ribs busted. He knew that Delphi was dead. That ended the matter.

As the strange tracks abruptly ended, the others took guard positions while Jak knelt in the loose sand. He studied the tracks of the war wag. The deep impressions ended in the middle of a flat plain, as if the machine had simply ceased to exist.

"Not see anything like," Jak muttered, taking a handful of sand and letting it trickle through his fingers to test the composition.

"Did it fly away?" Ryan asked, scanning the sky overhead. The roiling storm clouds rumbled in dark harmony.

"Mebbe," the teen said, rubbing the old bandage on his hand. On impulse, he yanked off the cloth and saw with some satisfaction that the wound was healed. "But didn't roll anywhere, that's for sure. Not even backward over old tracks."

"You already thought of that, too, eh?" J.B. said, pushing back his fedora.

The teenager shrugged. "Sure. Old trick."

"But not done this time," Ryan stated. "It's just bastard gone."

"Mebbe it flew away, like one of the Harrier jumping jets Mildred told us about," Krysty suggested.

"Not possible," the physician countered. "A jump jet kicks out a tremendous backwash, makes a real mess of everything nearby. None of this sand has been disturbed in any way."

"The wag flew into the sky…like a stingwing?" Lily asked softly, holding on to her new Webley blaster with both hands as if it were a protective talisman.

"We'll explain later," J.B. answered brusquely, then his tone softened at the raw terror in her face. "It's just a trick," he added, smiling. "Nothing dangerous or special. Don't worry about it."

"If you say so, sir," Lily replied in a hoarse whisper. But the young woman shuffled her new boots nervously in the sand, clearly dismayed by all of this casual talk about forbidden things. Machines that flew?

"Mebbe wag not go, still here," Jak said softly. "Delphi using predark weps, have pix…" He left the sentence hanging ominously.

"Time travel?" Ryan asked, narrowing his good eye in concern. Studying the tracks, he fought back the urge to wave an arm through the air above them. "Doc, is that possible?"

"I have no idea whatsoever," the old man conceded in a strained voice. He licked dry lips. "Because, if I did know how to effect a time jump, I would no longer be here, my friend." Then there flashed in his mind the image of the Indian shaman, warning Doc to stay near Ryan. The one-eyed man was the key home. And the doorway will only be open for a single moment. When the chance presented itself, Doc would have to move fast. Only by risking everything, could he gain back everything. The wallet on his hip suddenly seemed to be hot, and weigh a million pounds. Emily…

"How sure are you that Delphi is aced?" Mildred asked, easing the rapidfire off her shoulder to point it at the crumbling fortress. A dustdevil twirled and danced madly along the front of the ruins, the morning breeze making a hollow moan as it blew through the slagged holes in the adobe walls.

"Most assuredly, madam," Doc replied, coming out of the somber reverie. "Crushed to a pulp."

"Fair enough."

"I don't really care how the wag vanished," Krysty said, her hair tightening in reflection of her dark thoughts.

"Yeah, it's where the damn thing went that concerns me," Ryan noted, warily glancing toward the western sky.

The snowy Mohawk Mountains stood imposing against the receding night, the thin sunshine dappling the eastern facade making it appear that the range was moving. Resting the stock of the Steyr on a hip, Ryan stared at the colossal range, distant and forbidding. Here and there flicked the yellow light of volcanoes, and a thick fog moved among the rock formations between the ground and the polluted clouds.

Somewhere up there was another redoubt. The problem was that their last jump through the mat-trans units had been controlled, rigged to bring them here to the Zone for a confrontation with the Rogans. Or the intelligent stickies, or mebbe even Delphi himself. The deathtrap had failed, the cyborg chilled. But if the robotic war wag got back to the home base of Coldfire, more agents would be sent after Doc. Straight-on, or nightcreeps, either way, the companions were going to be embroiled in never-ending combat, with their supplies of predark ammo dwindling fast.

"We could go back to Two-Son ville," Mildred suggested hesitantly.

Adjusting his glasses, J.B. frowned. "Don't like that fragging idea," he stated gruffly.

After a moment Ryan unfortunately agreed. On the surface it sounded like a good plan. Get behind a big thick wall, and have an army of armed sec men ready to help defend them. But if the companions went back to the ville, the Coldfire agents, Overproject Whisper, Chronos, TITAN, whatever these bastards called themselves, could strike whenever they wished. The odds would all be in their favor. But if the companions started doing blind jumps once more, the odds would be even. Aces and eights. A fair fight.

"How far away are those?" Krysty asked thoughtfully.

Pulling out his sextant, J.B. ran a few calculations. "Roughly a hundred miles. Give or take a rad pit or two."

Frowning deeply, Ryan stared at the mountains without seeing them. If they decided to jump, that would mean telling Lily about the redoubts, the greatest secret in the world, and the lifeline of the companions. And while it was true that Lily had helped fight against the Rogans, the woman was still an outsider. Blood for blood? Yeah, but that only went so far.

"Don't worry about it, lover," Krysty said, resting a warm hand on his bandaged arm. "She's gone."

Suddenly alert, the companions looked around fast, but there was no sign of the young woman.

"By the Three Kennedys!" Doc exclaimed loudly. "Did she also vanish into thin air?"

"No, girl run into dunes," Jak said, pointing at the featureless ground.

Everybody stared hard at the sand, but aside from the undisturbed tracks of the predark war wag they couldn't detect any footprints.

"You sure?" Ryan demanded curtly.

"Yeah. Left when we not looking."

"Three o'clock," Krysty said, squinting slightly.

Just then a familiar shape appeared in the distance, then vanished into the smoky dawn, moving at a frantic run.

"She ran away?" Doc rumbled, holstering the blaster. The man started to say something more, but stopped himself. The dichotomy of past and present had been solved for him.

"Lily was getting rather twitchy hearing us talk about technology," Mildred said, rubbing her jaw. "And she really didn't like the motorcycle."

"So you think she might be from a ville that still has a taboo about science?" Krysty asked.

"Makes sense."

"A technophobe? Sadly, that does indeed make sense, madam," Doc stated, a strange expression in his eyes. Taking in a deep breath, he exhaled, shaking himself like a dog coming out of the rain. "Then so be it. It is much better that Lily took her leave of us now than after we had visited a redoubt."

"I have to agree," J.B. added succinctly. Mildred and Doc used the word technophobe, but the Trader had always just called them simps. Damn fools who'd rather die than learn how to repair a wag or to can food. The Armorer had no time for such stupes.

"Okay, let's get the horses and the bike, and get out of here," Ryan commanded, slinging the Steyr over a shoulder. "The sooner we're out of the Zone, the better."

"It's going to be a long trip," J.B. said, glancing at the mountains. "We'll need to find some rope and hammers to use as climbing gear."

"Fuck that," Ryan stated roughly, heading around for the decimated Indian ville. "Delphi was smart, and that redoubt is far too obvious a bastard goal for us not to be a trap. I'm willing to bet live brass it's been rigged somehow to chill us as soon as we enter."

"If we got that far," Krysty agreed. "We're heading east?"

"Damn right we are." Ryan declared. "We'll travel cross-country, get out of the Zone. Then find another redoubt and jump."

"Moving target hard to hit," Jak said with a grin.

"And if Delphi or some other cyborg is waiting for us in the next redoubt?" Mildred asked pointedly, hitching up her med kit.

"Then too bad for them," Ryan said confidently, patting the gren in his pocket. "But we won't try for the redoubts at Shay Canyon, or in Dulce. We'll circle south and try for the one on the Grande."

"Sounds good."

"Pity that we can't take the bike," J.B. noted

pragmatically. "It's too bastard fancy. Anybody who sees the thing will tell everybody they can. And that kind of news spreads triple fast."

Ryan nodded. "Yeah, I know. And we can't leave it for Lily to use. That would only place her in the crosshairs of Coldfire."

Reaching the arroyo, the companions mounted their horses, with the two smallest people, Jak and Mildred, sharing a mount. Ryan took the bike. The electric engine was sluggish, but the two-wheeler still moved, at least for the moment.

However, if Ryan knew anything about the Deathlands, they only needed to squeeze a few miles out of the machine before reaching someplace they could safely dump the bike. If it was left intact at the rill, eventually someone would discover the predark machine and ride away, utterly delighted at the incredible find. Then Coldfire would track the moving vehicle, and probably jack the rider to torture the poor soul for info about the companions that he didn't have. Ryan had done a lot of dirty tricks to throw enemies off his trail, but sacrificing innocent lives wasn't one of them.

Riding the horses alongside the ever-slowing machine, the companions reached a glassy area that made both J.B. and Ryan's rad counters start clicking. Getting off the predark motorcycle, Ryan emptied the storage compartments, then sent the machine rolling across the fused earth to tumble into the blast crater and smash apart on the glowing rocks at the bottom.

"Nobody will try for it now," J.B. stated confidently, patting the neck of his mount.

"And the radioactivity should scramble the GPS unit just fine," Mildred added with a nod.

"Hopefully," Ryan said, stuffing MRE packs into the saddlebags of Jak's mare. "But I'll feel better when we're a hundred klicks from here."

Distributing the rest of the supplies to the other horses, Ryan finally mounted up behind Krysty astride the roan stallion. Making a crude sling with a handkerchief, the one-eyed man rested his aching arm while his companion pressed her knees against the animal, urging it into an easy canter. It was still early in the day and they had a long way to travel.

As the sun rose behind the rumbling clouds, the heat of the desert steadily increased. Stingwings and vultures appeared, the creatures attacking one another when food could be found rotting on the sands. A flash of light made the companions dive for cover, but it proved only to be a reflection off the fused glass of another rad pit.

It was noon when they passed a group of Indians trudging through the sand dunes, carrying their belonging on their backs.

Slowing his mount, Doc gave a wave, but the friendly gesture wasn't returned. The children shied away nervously from the silver-haired man.

Lowering his arm, Doc sighed at the cold

response. Obviously his welcome had been worn thin with the arrival of Delphi and the slaughter of their tribal council. Which was hardly surprising. He wanted to tell them the cyborg was chilled, but it seemed unwise to push the matter. Fair enough.

Kicking the horse into a gallop, Doc rejoined his friends, and the companions rode into the rising sun, leaving Perdition Valley behind forever.

Epilogue

The humid air was still along the nameless river, the surface of the water smooth and undisturbed from submerged rocks.

A few birds flew high above the peaceful valley stretching between the opposing cliffs, and occasionally a fish would jump from the river to snatch an insect darting among the flowering plants growing along the riverbank. There were no muties in sight, and not a single rusting scrap of evidence that humanity had ever existed. The quiet river chasm was a sylvan paradise, lost somewhere deep in the heart of the savage Deathlands.

With his boots crunching on the loose dirt, a filthy Sec chief Stirling slowly moved among the large rocks dotting the moist landscape, and listened to the trickling murmur of the nearby river. The damnable river that had saved his life.

For the past few days the sec chief had been living like an animal in the wild, sleeping under bushes and eating whatever he could chill with a thrown knife. The grasslands were full of fat gophers. But unwilling to risk a fire at night, Stirling had to consume the damn things uncooked, and raw gopher was no can of beans in his opinion. Mostly, Stirling slept. He was simply too weak to travel very far before collapsing again.

The sec chief had been carefully tending his wounds, washing off the dried blood in a small creek of icy-cold water, when the stickies arrived. A whole nuking swarm of them. The bastards had to have caught the scent of his blood on the wind and rushed over to feed. Alone, wounded and low on ammo, Stirling had no choice but to run. Taking shots when he could dare to pause for a moment, Stirling tossed away the heavy longblaster when there was no more black powder, and was about to drop the med kit when the ground disappeared from under his boots. Tumbling through the air, the cursing man hit the river hard. The impact had to have knocked him out, but the cold water shocked him awake again, and a disoriented Stirling fought for an unknown length of time to simply not drown in the swift currents. Eventually, he made it to the shore and dragged himself out of the mud utterly exhausted. Sleep took him, and the battered man didn't care if he ever woke again he was so tired.

When the sec chief came to, it was morning instead of afternoon, and a bright sun was shining down warmly. His clothes were streaked with mud, but there was little blood, and he didn't smell like the ville shitter anymore.

That was when he noticed that a fat bullfrog sat

on his chest. As Stirling watched, the frog lashed out its long tongue to snare one of the flies buzzing around the man, and swallowed it whole. With a rumbling stomach, Stirling ignored the whole cycle of life and grabbed the frog to twist its slimy neck and wolf it down. After a while, he felt nauseated, then better, more alert, and he rose to start his lone trudging along the foot of the imposing cliffs.

Hugging the med kit, Stirling swatted at the flies and shuffled along with no idea where he was heading. An unclimbable cliff rose sharply to his right, and the lazy river flowed a dozen yards away, just past the buzzing weeds. Fish swam in abundance in the quiet river, and the sec chief was looking for a long stick to make into a spear.

As he traveled, a rock broke off the face of the cliff and plummeted to wetly smack onto the ground. Obviously this was a recent fissure and the ground was still setting into place. It would be safer near the river, but the soft ground made walking difficult, so Stirling chose speed and stayed on dry ground. If a rock aced him, so be it. The hungry man was in a foul mood. He was stiff, itchy, tired, filthy, unshaved, and couldn't take his mind off the faceless bastards who had gunned down his troops. But more than life itself, the sec chief wanted Delphi in blaster range. One clean shot was all Stirling needed. Just one shot and the grinning whitecoat with the silver slippers would have a new definition of hell.

Walking along the riverbank, Stirling instantly paused when he heard a low moan coming from the reeds. Clumsily drawing his handblaster, Stirling proceeded closer until hearing the moan again. Somebody was in the weeds. He thumbed back the hammer, wondering if it was one of the stickies from the previous day.

Unwilling to leave a live enemy behind him, the wounded sec chief shuffled closer and parted the flowering reeds with the barrel of his blaster.

A buzzing cloud of flies crawled over something in the muck. It looked like a pile of rags. But then the pile moved, and a huge barrel-chested man with long hair gave a moan and tried to crawl out of the slippery mud, only to collapse after a few inches. The man's clothing was in tatters, and one boot was missing. There was a holster at his hip, but no blaster or anything else that looked usable.

Tucking away his own wep, Stirling silently wished the outlander good luck, then started to leave. The brutal fact was that the sec chief could barely take care of himself, so there was no reason in the world to help a stranger.

But the sec chief had only gotten a few feet when the man in the weeds began to sputter curses.

"Curse you…Delphi…" Edward Rogan groaned in delirium. "Gonna ace ya…bastard…."

Snapping his head around at the sound of the name, Stirling went back to the reeds. His boots sank deep into the soft mud, but he grabbed the big man under the arms and dragged him onto dry land. The effort took everything he had, and Stirling passed out from the exertion.

Some time later, the aching sec chief awakened. The sun was behind the cliff, which meant late afternoon. Forcing himself to stand, Stirling gathered some broken pieces of wood and built a small fire near the unconscious man. Then he used the canteen to rinse off the stranger's face. The flies stayed nearby, but became less interested.

The man's face was covered with tiny cuts, slashed in a hundred places, the wounds dirty and only partially healed. Using his canteen, Stirling washed the face clean, then poured some raw shine over the cuts. He was no healer, but the sec man knew that the mud in those cuts would form scars. Lots of them. This poor bastard would have a face like a quilt. But he guessed it was better than being aced. He had to have fallen off the cliff and hit some rocks while in the river. Either that, or he just missed getting chilled by a gren. Lord knew, he couldn't have done both. Nobody was that tough.

Time passed and as the campfire diminished, Stirling went on the hunt again, this time finding a nice long piece of wood suitable for fishing. Wonder of wonders! After tending the campfire, he waded into the shallows and got busy. In short order, there were several gutted trout dangling above the small blaze. The moment the fish were cooked, Stirling ate, stuffing himself like a ville pig. Sleep was all he wanted now, but the sec man got to his feet and waded out into the shallows of the cold river to get more supplies.

Evening was approaching when there came a sniff from the big man, then another, and finally his eyelids fluttered to open wide.

"Hungry?" Stirling asked, looking up from cleaning his blaster. "There's plenty. Fish are dumber than gophers, and that's saying something."

His muscular neck trembling from the effort, Edward painfully lifted his head from the dry dirt. "Where...the frag...am I?" he whispered, raising a trembling arm.

"The Zone, I think." Stirling shrugged. "Don't know for sure. Could be anywhere."

Scowling at the response, Edward suddenly noticed the clean bandages on his wrist, then blinked in surprise when he found more on his bare chest. Where was his body armor? Oh, yes, he remembered ripping it off when he was drowning under the water.

The smell of the fish was delicious, but Edward didn't think he could eat without being sick. His guts ached something awful. "Who the hell are you?" he demanded.

Finished cleaning the piece, the sec chief started reloading the blaster. "Steve Stirling, sec chief for Two-Son ville."

"Never heard of place," Edward muttered, brushing back his damp hair. The river was yards away, the tracks of his boot heels in the mud telling a clear story. The stranger had saved his life. But why?

"It doesn't matter, friend," Stirling replied, holstering the handblaster. "My ville is a long distance from here. We are on our own."

"Friend?" Edward said suspiciously, a hand going to the empty holster at his side.

Stirling noticed the gesture and looked the man in the eye. "Delphi," he said, the name dripping hate.

Edward snarled, then nodded in understanding.

"The enemy of my enemy," the last Rogan brother growled, and weakly held out a massive hand.

"Blood for blood," Stirling agreed, and they shook to seal the bond.

"Any water?" Edward asked, wiping his mouth on a sleeve.

Stirling gestured. "Over by the fire, near the fish. Help yourself. I've already eaten."

"Th-thanks."

As the giant man started to devour the fried trout, Stirling smiled in grim contentment. It looked like he had a formidable ally in the hunt for Delphi. Good. Two blasters were certainly better than one. Yet the sec chief had a feeling that they might need a fragging army to take down the whitecoat. Fortunately, he knew just the place to get one of those.

A HUNDRED KLICKS AWAY, a warm desert wind blew along Perdition Valley, the breeze creating tiny dust devils that whirled and danced along the loose sand. Popping into view, a tarantula snapped at the whirlwinds, then went totally motionless as a rattlesnake bit it from behind. The tarantula chittered fiercely in blind rage, then shuddered violently and died. Biting and swallowing, the rattlesnake consumed it whole, uncaring if it was either alive or dead.

Walking along the dusty road, Lily paused at the sound of rattling wood and looked up in time to see a wooden cart roll into view. The man and woman driving the buckboard wag seemed surprised to see her, then grinned in unabashed delight as they both pulled crossbows.

"Hold it right there!" the man commanded, tightening his grip on the wep.

It took Lily only a split second to recognize the cage behind the armed couple as a slave cage. Then she sprang into action. Exactly as she had seen the companions do in the fight with the Rogans, Lily dropped into a crouch to stabilize her stance, pulled the Webley and fired. The big-bore blaster sounded louder than thunder as flame extended from the muzzle. With a strangled cry, David flew backward off the wag, spraying out his life from a ruined throat.

"Nuking bitch!" Sharon screamed, firing the bow. The arrow went wide and she scrambled to reload.

Staying calm, Lily moved to a new position and fired again, the .445 predark round exploding the woman's head.

Waiting for the echo of the blaster to die away,

Lily judiciously approached the wooden cart. Inside the iron cage, a smelly pile of starving slaves trembled in fright.

Saying nothing, Lily went to the front of the wag and easily found a ring of metal keys. Tossing it, the keys clanged off the rusty metal bars and hit the floor of the filthy cage with a dull thud.

At the incredible act, the slaves were stunned, then frantically grabbed at the keys. They formed a human pyramid and tried to work the lock on the top hatch. It was stubborn, but they persisted, cursing and hammering with their scrawny fists. With a prolonged screech, the lock disengaged and hatch came loose. Shouting in delight, the slaves scrambled out of the cage like ants boiling out of the ground.

"Oh, thank you!" a man gushed, tears of gratitude on his sunken cheeks.

"Don't come any closer," Lily warned, thumbing back the hammer on the blaster. "Keep your distance, and take what you want from the supplies. Loot the dead, then get moving. The wag is mine."

Unexpectedly, a baby started to cry.

"What about the little one?" a skinny woman asked nervously, glancing back and forth between the sec woman and the swaddled infant. "Should we ace it for ya?"

"Harm that baby and you'll beg to get aced," Lily replied.

Trembling with fear, the freed slaves did as they

were ordered. The women pulled the boots of the warm corpses, the men took the crossbows and quivers, along with most of the clothing that wasn't soaked in fresh blood.

"Ah, there's a handblaster here…" a man said hesitantly, proffering the wep on an open palm. He clearly lusted for the tiny blaster, but wouldn't dare take it until the raven-haired woman with the big revolver gave permission.

"Keep it, got better," Lily stated.

"Bless you!" The blaster was tucked away into a pocket.

"And if you want to keep pulling air," Lily growled, reveling in her new sense of power, "then don't point it at me. Savvy?"

Nodding, the skinny man wholeheartedly agreed.

Moving away from the cart, Lily kept the others under careful watch as they raided the buckboard for food and then hastily scampered away into the shifting desert.

Holstering her piece, the young woman climbed into the buckboard and lifted the baby to cradle it in her arms, rocking slightly until the little one stopped crying.

"Hush, now," Lily whispered. "Guess I'm your new Ma. I'm Lily Ro—" She paused, torn between conflicting emotions. Then a decision was made.

"My name is Emily," she said, a strange tone creeping into the gentle words. "Emily Tanner, and you be called Lily. Best remember that when we reach Two-Son ville."

Gurgling happily, the infant wiggled to get comfortable, then went happily back to sleep, tenderly cradled by the grinning madwoman.